Cover design by Brendan Ternus

ISBN: 978-1-61927-828-8

Some elements in the chapter on Partnering were previously published in *Chapters of the Heart: Jewish Women Sharing the Torah of Our Lives*, edited by Rabbis Nancy Fuchs Kreimer and Sue Levi Elwell (Wipf & Stock, 2013) and are used here with permission.

Some of my reflections previously appeared in the article "Felice Yeskel: A Remembrance," *Bridges: A Jewish Feminist Journal*, Volume 16, Number 1, Spring 2011

Rosi Greenberg shares some of her story in the anthology *And Baby Makes More: Known Donors, Queer Parents and Our Unexpected Families*, edited by Chloe Brushwood Rose, Susan Goldberg & Susan Goldberg (Insomniac Press, 2009)

If you like this book, tell your friends! See our photo gallery and more information about consultations, workshops and writing by Julie Greenberg, at

www.JulieGreenberg.net

JUST PARENTING

Building the World One Family at a Time

BY

JULIE GREENBERG

Acknowledgments

Thank you to all the people who make a life possible. Thank you to my family of origin: Polly Greenberg, Daniel Greenberg, Wanda Reif, Miggie, Katie, Liza and Gwen.

Thank you to my beloved children: Rosi, Raffi, Zoe, Joey, Mozi, and now Richard; and to my also-children Nava and Yonah.

Thank you to Congregation Leyv Ha-Ir~Heart of the City for being such a special community.

Thank you to my village: Susan, Moon, Merle, Rebecca, Marcia, Jack, Sarah, Billy, Sara, Tamara, Arthur, Phyllis, Debbie, Noah and many more.

Thank you to the people of B'not Eysh, who championed this work from its earliest stages.

Special thanks to Bobbi for her generosity and friendship.

Thank you to farther-flung beloveds: Joanna, who has been such a steadfast friend going way back to before we started parenting and Felicia who is a pillar of love and support.

Great gratitude goes to Nancy Fuchs-Kreimer for multiple kindnesses and good counsel, and to Dayle Friedman for our weekly writing sessions at her sunny dining room table (and thank you for all the cappuccinos).

Laura Markowitz was a valued guide in bringing this book to completion as was Gail Leondar-Wright.

I was lucky to have a talented and dedicated editor, the best there could be: thank you, my dear Zoe Greenberg. Thanks to Mozi Greenberg for technical assistance with the computer and to Joey Greenberg for all the ways he looks out for his family. Abundant thanks to Rosi for her magical creative touch and to Raffi for long distance support.

My gratitude also goes to Brendan Ternus, who will be a wonderful father some day.

Finally, thank you to the donors who helped make this family and to the parenting partner who walked some of this journey with me.

For my mother Polly Hoben Greenberg, who taught me that each generation builds a foundation for the next one.

Contents

Welcome

"Why don't you have a father?" asked Rosi's pre-school friend.

"Why don't you have a brother?" she replied.

This book is for all people who are creating and raising intentional families with hopes of raising good kids for a good world. In this book, blending the genres of memoir and self-help, I take big issues of the day and look at them in the most micro circumstances of family life. There are reflections on parenting from the most magnificent—"How can I guide this young person into a life of love and goodness?" to the most mundane—"How can I handle bedtime tonight? What to do about squabbles in the soccer carpool?" This book links big concerns such as Race, Peace, Justice, with daily parenting choices.

I have spent 25 years being a parent who believes raising children is the most important thing I do. Moreover, I believe it is inextricably linked to the spiritual and activist work I do in the world. For many years my friends and family have been saying, "You should write a book about parenting!" This book is an effort to capture some of what I've learned, in the moments of quick decisions and longer ponderings, about what it means to raise kids in the world that exists while actively working to create a better one.

As we parents traverse the daily course of diapers, carpools, homework, dinners and sports, it can be hard to hold the bigger picture, which is that we are engaged in a miraculous project! The future of humanity quite literally depends on our work. Raising kids to have confidence and compassion in the fast-paced flow of family life calls on our deepest capacities and highest ideals. One of the most important legacies we leave behind will be the result of this work. In the amazing crucible of family life, we parents are shepherding a miracle of transformation by parenting a helpless human infant into an independent, caring, productive human being.

When my oldest son, Raffi, was a senior in college, he discovered the key to great literature and film. "They all come down to one thing," he told me. "They're all about the human struggle." The human struggle is the attempt to live a life of loving and being loved; to contribute to the world, and to feel a sense of meaning and belonging. A big question for parents in this day and age—with so many choices and pressures— is, "How in the world do I raise a human being to live a rich and full life of meaning?" I wrote this book in the hopes that it will be a companion for people raising human beings. This is a book of reflections and ideas about how to raise children to survive and thrive in the face of the human struggle to live a good life.

My own family is what mainstream society calls "non-normative"— a family that includes sperm donors, adoption, single parenthood, beloved former lovers, a gay male parenting partner and me. Rather than being a nuclear family, we are a web of connection that grows through relationship. In our society at this particular time we have more choices than ever before in human history about how to create families. I know first-hand about living as a free human being building this web of long-term intimacy with others, not in traditional fashion, but in deep, interconnected, committed alternative patterns. I explored the options that were available to me to have a family with children and made choices each step of the way in creating that family.

I hope this book will reflect my deep respect for many forms and configurations of family; for the different stages of family life; and for the joyful, the overwhelming and the confusing aspects of growing and changing together as a family. My family may look marginal or radical to some but from within there has been great reward and fulfillment.

Parenting is not something human beings can do alone. We are deeply situated in society which both shapes our parenting choices and is shaped by our parenting choices as we literally raise up the human beings who will carry forward the human species. Not only does parenting have significance for human continuity, it most likely is the project you care most about. Your hopes and dreams for your own life are probably intricately interwoven with the young person or people you are raising. Your hopes and dreams, and labor and love, are what builds the world, one family at a time.

This writing has given me a chance to step back and gain some perspective on this holy work, allowing me time to come up for air and remember why I am a parent and why it matters. I hope reading *Just Parenting* will serve the same purpose for you. We all need respite from the rush of interaction in family life so we can have time to reflect, restore and regroup. From my own intimate experience of the joy, grief, struggle and triumph of family life, and from years of professional work supporting other families, comes this blend of memoir and recommendation.

In pondering my own parenting, I note the dynamic of radical *chutzpah* and radical humility that are constantly at play. I need to be a strong leader for my family while at the same time I need to surrender to the realities of life. The dance of nature and nurture swirls through every situation in our family lives. There are ways I can have an impact as a parent, and there are things I can never change. I must have a vision that supports a child's inner development and at the same time a complete acceptance of this child exactly as he or she is. I must somehow find awe and joy and total acceptance of the world as it is and also remain totally committed to transforming it into a better place.

You might say, "Well she doesn't understand my situation. She isn't the mother of twins," or, "She isn't married to an alcoholic," or "She didn't start parenting when she was 55." Each parenting situation is completely unique and yet there are huge commonalities in all families. We all face the challenges of learning to relate to and grow with specific young human beings; of facing different developmental stages; of wanting our daily interactions to reflect our highest ideals.

This book, ideally, is a collaboration between us. Even though I don't know your individual circumstances—you might be partnered or single, have one child or multiple children, be in a blended or adoptive or multi-racial family, have a lot of money or a little money, deal with chronic illness or special needs or unusual talents—I invite you to ponder, adapt, tweak, reject, alter and develop the ideas in this book and continue to evolve your own ideas about how to raise your human being. All of us have a lot of stories to tell and we can only enrich one another's lives by sharing them with commentary.

I've been a parent since 1987; I've been a rabbi since 1989; and I've been a family therapist since 2005. As in any form of dedicated work, I've learned on the job. I've learned from mentors and trainings, from friends and from therapy, from congregants and counselees, and most of all from hands-on practice and reflection. I was raised by a wonderful mother and had a close, close relationship with a wonderful grandmother. My own children—their personalities, needs, talents— have been the driving force behind much of my learning.

But I've been shy about sharing these experiences and reflections in book form, wondering what value they will have to people I have not even met. I know I've found sustenance in reading the all-too-few parenting books written with wide-open understanding of the varieties of family situations and needs. I know from my own experience as a parent that we need many more books that embrace and accept and inspire. Based on the numerous families that I have helped and on my own experience with lively family life, I decided to write this book to help fill this need. I trust you will take what is helpful and leave the rest behind.

You are a parent too, or someone who cares a lot about young people, so you will understand that I have occasionally been vague about which of my children I am discussing, and I've occasionally changed details of stories to protect privacy. I've also tried to use gender-inclusive language, at least some of the time, even when it isn't traditionally grammatical, such as saying "a child takes their shoes off," instead of the more limiting and awkward, "his or her." And I intentionally switch between first and second person.

This book is my offering to you of what I have learned and am still learning as a not-so-conventional Mom in the United States of America in the late 20th and early 21st century. As the relationship guide Harville Hendrix reminds us, "There are no experts in parenting—only children and parents who are works in progress." I hope my work in progress will be a fruitful contribution to your journey, as a parent or friend-of-parents, through the human struggle, or better yet, adventure, of life.

BEGINNINGS

Where Babies Come From

In fairy tales, the quest always seems to be over which prince and which princess will end up together. In my feminist youth I used to question this focus on one moment in the life cycle—the match. Why so much cultural anxiety about who would mate with whom?

Decades later, from the vantage point of a Mom with five kids (and finally being a feminist elder), I get it. Launching the next generation is essential to civilization. It matters a lot how families form. So much depends on the union of sperm and egg, from genetics (huge) to co-parents' compatible or incompatible child-raising styles (sometimes relevant and sometimes not, depending on whether sperm and egg donor are planning to co-parent or not.) Societies provide traditional guideposts to help people channel themselves into new families, guideposts such as dating customs, engagement, marriage and baby-making.

In my own life, that sequence of events didn't feel quite right. I knew I was ready to parent way before I felt ready to partner. My vision of my own life always included passionate parenting and I did not see marriage or even partnering as a necessary step to achieving that vision.

In the mid-1980s, in my mid-twenties, rooted in a strong women's community, I started making plans to launch my family. My own childhood had essentially been positive: I was the oldest of five daughters, raised by a wonderful mother who was steeped in knowledge about child development and who loved mothering. She taught me by example to live by my priorities. Her priorities included taking her children to Mississippi at the height of the Civil Rights Movement to live and work for a few amazing, formative years. She was starting a radical statewide Head Start program, designed to infuse economic opportunity as well as early childhood education and comprehensive social services into very poor communities with "maximum feasible participation of the poor" in running their own programs.

Aside from those years in Mississippi, we lived in Washington, D.C., where my father was a journalist, my mother worked on early childhood policy, and we kids absorbed the ethos of the Civil Rights and Anti-War Movements in the nation's capital.

My parents divorced when I was seven, but remained friends. A typical dinner scene in my teenage years included my father and his girlfriend, my mother and her boyfriend, and seven kids (the five daughters plus my mother's boyfriend's two boys) all engaged in lively political conversation around the long, redwood dinner table. Eventually, my father remarried and my parents moved into separate realms with friction between them. I absorbed various models for a workable life.

Raising kids was one of my major life goals. I wasn't opposed to being in a partnership, although there was no particular person with whom I wanted to make a family. Starting where I felt ripe and ready and being open to what unfolded from there made sense to me.

When heterosexual couples have babies there is a default assumption about how they got the baby: probably a penis entered a vagina allowing sperm to meet egg. Or maybe someone else's penis and vagina, sperm and egg, met and the baby came into the family by adoption. Most people rely on these tidy assumptions without giving much more thought to the details of conception. People hearing about my family have to think more. Where did the sperm come from? Where did the baby come from?

Once, when I was speaking on a panel about alternative family formation, someone in the audience asked, "How do single parents or same-sex couples get babies?" I responded, "There are lots of ways to get babies." Everyone laughed because life used to be so simple.

In telling my story I've found that people are both curious and squeamish about the details. While conception is a universal human experience in that every person was once conceived—not to mention that many also participate, themselves, in conceiving new life—the particulars of a conception story may be unfamiliar and even uncomfortable. I'm happy to share my story, which these days is less and less unique as more people make babies in more different ways. Even so, I'm a little worried about being attacked because of people's discomfort with life choices that differ from their own. My hope is always that my story will help create more understanding and contribute to tolerance of the wider world of possibilities of creating family.

I was in my mid twenties, preparing to be a member of the clergy, when I started looking for a sperm donor. My education, class background and race empowered me to think about what kind of family I wanted to build. Even though "the world" didn't always approve or understand, I felt privileged to have inner freedom and external support as I started making plans to start a family.

The word "queer" was not yet in common use, and that term was not one that I applied to myself, but the concept behind it did express my identity—an out-of-the-box identity, a living-life-on-your-own-terms identity. I loved some women and I loved some men. Gender was not the main focus of attraction for me so "bi-sexual" was never a term that spoke to me. At the time I was ready to start a family, I didn't have a partner of either gender with whom I wanted to make and raise a baby. So there were decisions to be made.

At that time, I was preparing to become a Rabbi. The world of organized religion was pretty straight and narrow: there was not a single publicly gay or lesbian leader of a mainstream congregation in the Jewish world. When I applied to rabbinical school, the admissions committee—in an attempt to weed out deviant applicants—asked, "Do you plan to have a family?" I knew that in their minds "family" meant a husband and shared babies. I definitely planned to have a family, in my own way, and enthusiastically answered, "Yes!" I wasn't exactly challenging the norms, as much as stretching them to be more inclusive.

I preferred to have a known sperm donor because I believed that kids like to know where they came from and my future child would be no exception. My lover at the time was the wife of a world-renowned rabbi, both of whom practiced Orthodox Judaism. She reminded me of a gorgeous goddess—a voluptuous beauty who was smart and funny. On the outside, husband and wife looked quite traditional, she with her hair bound under the Orthodox head covering and he with the ritual fringes hanging down from under his shirt. But people can be less conventional than they look on the outside. It turned out that Talia and her husband, Jacob, had an open marriage and both of them invited me into their innermost lives. They actually wanted me to join their family for the long haul, but I was focused on making my own family. I was acutely aware that in planning my own life I was making choices for my children-to-be, and their well-being was uppermost in my mind.

One day, helping Talia organize her kids' bedroom, I was discussing my desire to start baby making. She said, "You should ask Jacob if you can use his sperm. He's really good at making babies." They had three beautiful kids together, and he had older kids as well from earlier marriages.

When I spoke to Jacob about donating sperm to "help me make a family," he immediately said "Yes!" He was a Holocaust survivor and he understood that this was about creating new life—this was good. We didn't even discuss logistics until later. Choosing someone to be the father of my unborn children was a big deal and I was ecstatic.

It turned out that more than one person was ready and willing to help us become a family. I had another friend, a young professor from

Swarthmore College, who offered to be my donor. Although I didn't end up using his sperm, he was close to the family for our early years, until he moved to Europe.

From the beginning I knew that I would be the parent of my child. I would be responsible for executive management, funding, nurturing. I didn't expect Jacob's participation, but he was welcome to be involved if he wanted to be. We had complementary needs: he wanted clarity that he would not end up raising another child as a hands-on parent, and I wanted clarity that I would have all authority as the hands-on parent. I chose a donor with care to protect my parenting rights, knowing that I was ahead of the curve of social understanding. I did not want to have to defend myself or my family building choices in front of a judge who was used to nuclear, heterosexual families.

It felt a little funny to be thinking about possible future complications at such a generative time of pure intention but I think family makers do need to be smart as well as inspired. My heart and my mind told me that Jacob would be an ideal donor. He had beauty, brains and good health, and he was at a stage of life in which he was completely not interested in raising another child. We were clear that being a donor and being a Daddy are two different things. He proved to be an excellent donor because he respected our agreement and honored my parenting rights.

At our first meeting to make a baby, Jacob brought a turkey baster. In those early days of alternative feminist family making, our babies were called "turkey baster babies," because sperm could be transferred using a turkey baster. After we had introduced sperm and egg, he said, "You should put your legs up so the little swimmers get where they are going." I lay on the bed with my feet vertically resting on the wall. In reality, there were more efficient methods than the turkey baster, but I was touched at Jacob's open mindedness.

Once pregnant, I faced the alarmed reaction of the board of directors at the congregation where I worked as an educator. They considered me an "unwed mother," and had a lengthy discussion among themselves about whether to fire me. Finally, they decided that they had hired me to be an educator and I had done an exceptional job starting an innovative religious school for them, which had grown from five students to more than 100 during my tenure. The Board decided not to fire me and instead gifted me with a stroller.

There was still lingering negativity, though. The president of the congregation confronted me after religious school one day, saying, "You are supposed to be a religious and moral leader."

"I *am* a religious and moral leader," I said.

Years later this person apologized to me, in print, confessing that she hadn't been open enough in those years to different life paths. And that same person's child now lives and works in the transgender community with full support from the parental generation. These days, my denomination also wholeheartedly embraces diversity of family life.

While pregnant, I continued my rabbinical studies, working toward my ordination and also a Master's degree in Urban American Studies, while also working for the synagogue part-time as an educator. Though there was no depth of economic security in my life, I had supported myself for years and was willing to live simply. I mostly had confidence that somehow by juggling priorities and making trade-offs, I would be able to support a family.

Every now and then, though, I'd experience a gap of faith and have a good, panicked cry about how I would manage. I'd pick up the phone and call my good friends Joanna or Felice or my mother. It was at those times that I was especially grateful for the community of friends and family that surrounded me. They were wonderfully supportive and had confidence in my ability to take on this mission. My own mother never doubted for a moment that I would be a great Mom and would manage to support my own family.

My father, whom I adore, took longer to endorse my life choices. The paradigm of a single woman intentionally making a family without a man was new to him. Once, I asked him what it meant to him to be a man and he replied, "To be a provider." That conversation gave me insight into how I could live my life without invalidating his life, but rather creating another path—not better or worse, just different. Being in real relationship with him meant tempering any arrogance I had that my way was a better way.

In figuring out how I could make single parenting work, I knew that having resources that matched the needs would be crucial. If the need was big, the resources had to be big. My Yes had to be stronger than society's No. I knew that if I was facing discrimination for my life choices, I needed an extra-strong support foundation to affirm my life choices. Preparing to be a single Mom, I built my community by taking care of other people's kids. My friend Merle's son, Sammy, and I had Monday afternoons together for years. I brought friends and family together for meals and rituals; I cooked meals, drove and ran errands for those in need. When I became a Mom, my community responded in kind with an outpouring of meals, hand-me-downs and offers to babysit. The feeling of having needs met with abundant response just made me want to be there even more for my community. We created a circular flow of blessings.

Rosi was born in the summer of 1987, with sparkling black-olive eyes and one little curl on the top of her head. She was the most beautiful, alert, present baby I had ever seen; I was beyond-belief in love. It was amazing how this nine-pound bundle of baby instantly transformed my life, and made me into a mother—a role I've never regretted for a second. From the moment of her birth, mothering has been central to everything I do. Decisions about employment, time, money, food, adult relationships and everything else were from then on filtered through an impact-on-Rosi lens.

We moved into a limited-equity co-op that is committed to affordable housing and racial and economic diversity. I still live there today. At the time, I rented out one bedroom to help pay the bills and get a bit of mother's helper-ing. The day the renter moved in I felt totally ambivalent about whether I wanted to share the little bubble of baby-and–Mama. Rosi and I were in an idyllic bonding phase. Little did I know how well the arrangement wth my renter would work out.

At first, everything about mothering was startlingly new. How to nurse the baby, how to encourage her to sleep through the night, how to walk my dog, Griffin, with a baby, how to race home from seminar before the childcare person had to leave. It was like that stage of learning to drive when you grip the steering wheel and focus every ounce of attention on staying on the road. As with driving, mothering rapidly became a comfortable instinct.

My precious baby girl and I would sprawl on the rug, she doing her baby work of babbling and learning to grasp toys, with me inches away doing my graduate student homework. After the exhausting early weeks of caring for a baby who woke up every couple of hours to nurse, I settled into a rhythm with my little one, elated to have begun the parenting adventure.

The roommate, Sarah, turned out to be fabulous with little Rosi. We'd take turns rocking the baby almost-to-sleep in the rocking chair at night. At the last moment before she drifted off, I liked to lay her down to put herself to sleep so that she'd develop the skill to self-settle. As a ncw Mom, every second of parenting felt significant and Sarah was amenable to my desires. She was about my age, running a little business that she had started, and hoping to meet a man to marry.

As we lived together and cared for the adorable baby, Sarah and I became lovers—never with a plan to be life partners, but just a nice romance on the home front. Sarah told me, "This apprenticeship in motherhood is so valuable. I'll be a better mother when I have a kid, because of this experience." She did indeed become an excellent mother a few years later.

Family friends took Rosi for two-hour blocks of time when I went to work, which meant I only had to pay for a few hours of childcare a week. The Director of Practical Rabbinics at the rabbinical school would wear Rosi in a baby backpack while I attended one class. In some ways, my little girl was a community baby, but with me very much at the center of her life.

Room For More

❧

When Rosi was a toddler, I started making plans for a second child. My mother had had four children under the age of four (and much later a fifth child). I wanted a pack of kids close in age that could play together and support one another. Passion for motherhood clearly does not correlate with the number of children one has; this was simply my own vision, rooted in my own childhood experience.

By this time, Jacob's travel schedule was so demanding that it was hard to overlap in the same city at my fertile times. We decided to freeze sperm in a sperm bank across town. Jacob and I would go, make deposits, and then when I was ready to withdraw, I'd go pick up a huge cannister filled with liquid nitrogen and a rack with mini-tubes, each containing one-fifth of an ejaculate. The whole process was expensive, time-consuming and inefficient.

Talia and I researched acquiring the freezing equipment for ourselves. She spent hours on the phone (this was before the Internet) investigating the option of deleting the middleman—the sperm bank—from our process.

We got hold of a farm equipment catalogue, reasoning that if farmers could routinely inseminate cows, we certainly should be able to use the same equipment. I felt strongly that getting pregnant shouldn't have to be an expensive, medicalized procedure. The *Nasco Farm and*

Ranch Catalog: Worldwide Service to Agriculture arrived in the mail, all 277 pages of it. A goat, a cow, a rooster and a horse were featured on the front cover. After flipping through the pages on livestock identification and home butchering, we finally located the section on equipment for artificial insemination, which we preferred to call "alternative conception."

Meanwhile, my Rosi was toddling around, touching forbidden items and telling herself "No, no, no!" in her high, sweet voice; traipsing across the room with a stack of underpants necklaced around her throat; wearing her Mickey Mouse ears and green sunglasses; earnestly stuffing socks into a tattered pocketbook. Soon, she was eyeing my full platter of breakfast saying, "Mommy, let's share." Often, Talia's four-year-old joined us, and he and Rosi played together.

We decided that buying the equipment would be quite possible, but maybe it would be easier to choose a different donor who was more available than Jacob. Getting pregnant again quickly was more important to me than having the same donor for each child. Jacob understood and introduced me to a student of his whom he recommended as a donor. Jack had also survived the Holocaust, as a young child, and now he was a creative, successful musician studying to be a rabbi. When I asked him about donating sperm to help me make a family, he immediately said "Yes." He, too, understood that this was about the miracle of creating life.

In the course of helping me inseminate, my roommate, Sarah, and donor, Jack, fell in love and married a few years later. Sarah had always said she intended to marry a man, so I was emotionally prepared and supportive when she told me her feelings for Jack. Each of us was moving forward with our own life plan, encouraging one another along the way.

Partners appeared when I least expected them: Talia and I faded out as lovers, but continued a close friendship; Sarah was roommate and lover for a year and a half before partnering with Jack. Then Rebecca and I met when I was five months pregnant with Raffi. She lived in Brooklyn with her two kids from a marriage she had ended. She had also left behind the very traditional Judaism of her childhood and was seeking a new home community. Talia, Merle, Rebecca, some of our kids and I all went to Perkiomen Lake, near Philadelphia, on a hot day in July. Rebecca and I, with my big pregnant belly, stood in the shallow water while two-year-old Rosi splashed nearby.

After that day, Rebecca would call me up, long distance, and say things like, "We talk with each other better in person than on the phone." I was not expecting romance, so it took me a while to register that she was courting me. Rosi and I visited Rebecca and her kids in Brooklyn a few times. The kids ate plump, Brooklyn knishes and playfully taped band-aids across one another's bodies. Rebecca and I debated whether we should let them use the whole box of band-aids— was this teaching wastefulness or was it endorsement of happy play?

Later that year, after we had become lovers, Rebecca moved with 7-year-old Yonah and 9-year-old Nava to my neighborhood. Our kids became best friends who loved spending the night at each other's homes. Rebecca and I, basically each single-parented our own kids in our own homes, four blocks apart, with lots of happy overlap. We shared the same simple delights: spending hours watching flamingos at the zoo, choosing representative animals for every family member— "Rebecca's an elephant, Julie's a deer, Rosi is a bunny rabbit. No, maybe Rebecca is a bear." We played lots of Charades, In the Manner of the Adverb, Doctor-Doctor-Please-Come-Quick and Murder in the Dark. We hiked, camped, built fires and explored the woods. We two Moms spent countless hours processing kid dynamics and strategizing with each other about child development.

I had great affinity for Rebecca as a person and as a mother. She was so positive and encouraging with her kids and also thoughtfully inter-vened when she thought that would help them grow. A classic example of Rebecca's positive parenting happened when her daughter, Nava, was eleven. Nava arrived at the top of their staircase, calling downstairs joyfully to her mother (whom the kids called the Hebrew word for mother, "Ima," pronounced Eema.) "Ima, I got new shoes. Look!" She was balanced precariously on awful, gaudy, gold shoes. Rebecca took one look at them and responded enthusiastically, "Oh wow, they are *so gold*!" I loved Rebecca for that.

We talked on the phone all through the day and every night before bed and we spent Wednesday and Saturday nights having adult-only time together, usually at my house because my kids were younger and fell asleep earlier in the evening while her kids got to have a popular teenage babysitter and enjoy popcorn and videos.

"I wish we had met each other earlier," Rebecca once said. "Then we could have started this together." I sometimes had that same sentiment, but usually I liked our arrangement in two nearby homes. I was surprisingly committed to Rosi being an oldest child and not a submerged step-sibling in a blended family of Rebecca's and my children.

A bigger apartment opened in our co-op building, one with three bedrooms and a balcony. This was when Rosi was six months old and I didn't yet need all that space. I agonized over whether the extra space was worth the extra money. To move or not to move? Would I really need the space? Me and one baby and a roommate did not need that much space in the short run, and finances were always a consideration, but I was imagining how my family would grow. I decided to make the move and we eventually did expand to fill every inch of the new apartment. Looking back, I can't even fathom how I ever could have hesitated to take the bigger space. Sometimes, thinking big is hard.

Raffi was a winter baby, born in December 1989. When I held the naked newborn baby covered in birth fluids on my chest for the first time, I knew that a maximum amount of new love had been born with this baby. He was as precious to me as anything on this earth could possibly be, and yet he delivered a huge challenge into my lap. I was coming out of a long stretch of years living primarily in women's community. My friends and I were intent on re-valuing the worth of women and we were woman-oriented, even though some of us had male partners. I had always felt that if I had a boy I'd rise to the occasion and be a wonderful mother for him. But when Raffi actually arrived, I was suddenly massively insecure.

It didn't help my state of mind that during the first ten days of Raffi's life, the weather was below freezing with a bitter wind, and my apartment's heating equipment broke down. Rosi came down with bronchitis and a double ear infection. Baby Raffi snuggled contentedly in his magenta bunting, a gift from Joanna, while I held Rosi in my lap, letting her watch kid video after kid video, which we usually never did because I valued play time more than screen time.

I had two overwhelming sets of questions: Had I ruined our lives by having a second child? I felt guilty, as if I might have betrayed my firstborn by bringing a second child into the family. She was a trusting two-year-old with a heart full of faith, and suddenly her mother had delivered a new child into her family. Rosi, herself, was excited about the idea of a baby, but I knew she had no idea what a sibling really was. How would she learn to share the easy, intimate, perfect closeness that she and I had had for the first two-and-a-half years of her life?

My second question was how could I possibly raise a son? My life was exceedingly woman-centered and most of my family-of-origin consisted of women. How could I possibly guide this wiggly baby boy into manhood? Would he be dominated by females and fail to find himself? Would raising a boy be a thankless task because boys have to separate emotionally from their mothers in order to grow up?

My tears flowed into Rosi's mop of curls as she sat on my lap watching videos. When my rabbinical school friend Jonathan came to visit, I confided in him about my worries that I wouldn't know how to raise a boy. Jonathan was a bearded, guitar-playing rabbi-to-be who had thought deeply about what it meant to be a man. I asked Jonathan, "How is this little boy going to grow up?"

"You'll love him so much you'll accept the biggest challenge of your life —letting men into the inner circle," Jonathan said with great kindness.

Taking that wisdom to heart, I stepped back to assess the situation. I was reassured that there was nothing I couldn't love about the cute little male mammal in the bunting—he was just my baby, and I knew what to do with babies. He was a young human being and human beings do best when they have strong, caring, life-long mothers. Every human being needs both connection and independence and this little boy would need both of those as well. I finally concluded that the single significant definition for a boy was a human being who is going to grow up to be a man. (These days, with greater understanding of gender fluidity, the choices are even more wide open and I would now say that a baby boy is someone who is definitely going to grow up to be an adult human being.) Jonathan and my mother both pointed out many examples of men who grew up and stayed close to their mothers.

My mother Polly had come for a week to help with the new baby. I calmed myself by realizing Rosi had everything she needed; Raffi had everything he needed. The furnace would be fixed. Spring would come. All of us would have time to grow together. I would start right there, right then, with that little baby and grow it from there.

My mother and I sat on my sofa figuring out how to spell Raffi's name: Rafi or Raffi or Raphi? Polly's theory was that Rosie had five letters in her name so Raffi would want five letters. When Rosi was seven, in an act of self-definition, she took the "e" off her name and has had four letters ever since (even though her Aunt Lizie jokingly offered to pay her to reclaim the "e.") The number of letters in my kids' names turned out to be one of the non-issues in their childhoods, as none of them cared at all how many letters each had in their names.

With two children, the first couple months were intensely demanding. I was hyper-focused on making sure that every moment of sibling interaction went well. People in 12-Step programs say "one day at a time;" I was struggling through 10 minutes at a time, literally watching the clock as segments of time ticked by, only barely managing to manage everything. I cared intensely that every moment of the new siblings' time together be as good as possible. Just as with my first child, before long I integrated the new parenting challenge, which became an easy routine, at least while Raffi was in his jovial infancy.

Soon after Raffi's birth, Jack and Sarah helped me get pregnant with a third child. Baby Zoe joined the family in 1991. For each of my births I had been surrounded by a core circle of beloveds that included Talia, Moon, Joanna and Felice. My friend Susan, a brilliant activist and domestic artist, hovered lovingly in the background, ready to create living room curtains or a pot of stir fry, whatever was needed. My sister Lizie was there too. Now, Rebecca prepared the very first message my third baby would see, a card saying "Welcome to a wonderful world, sweet Zoe."

When I went into labor with Zoe, the group gathered again. Things moved quickly and soon I was howling in the back seat of Joanna's car as we drove to the birthing center at the hospital. Talia reminded me to ride up over the pain. The nurses were grumpy that night because there had been more dead babies than live births. They wouldn't let all of us into the room so my friends rotated in and out.

When Zoe was born she didn't look pink the way my other two babies had looked soon after birth. She had a husky, purple-ish tone that didn't seem right. I kept saying to the nurse, "This baby doesn't seem to be getting enough oxygen," but the nurse was busy delivering the placenta. Finally, forty minutes after Zoe's birth, a team of pediatric emergency specialists whisked her away into the NICU. Felice took credit for saving Zoe's life, although that's not exactly how it happened.

My baby, who had been born bleeding into a lung, was struggling to live. The extent of oxygen deprivation was unclear. At that moment, it didn't matter to me. I knew I'd love this child and raise this child up no matter what cognitive or physical impairment she ended up with.

For more than a week she lived in the NICU. My mother stayed with Rosi and Raffi and my friends ensconced me in a little hospital apartment so that I could be on-site with Zoe.

With me riding a wave of momentous love and support, months passed before I let myself fully realize how scary the aftermath of Zoe's birth had been. Only months later did I weep with relief and exhaustion that we had survived an ordeal. Zoe seemed to be fine. There's a prayer in Judaism called *benching gomel*, when you stand at the Torah and say words of thanks for coming through a hard time. In my own way, I prayed that prayer.

*   *   *

Our bigger apartment, spacious, sunny Apt. B202, where all my kids would spend their childhoods, was slowly filling up. I say its walls are like the walls of the ancient Temple in Jerusalem, which were said to have expanded to hold however many people needed to be held. The co-op has 48 units filled with friendly neighbors, a few cranky characters and kids of all ages. There's a large courtyard in front, where we collectively plant flowers, and a football-sized, fenced-in backyard, where anyone (like me) who wants to grow vegetables can have a garden.

The space available to my kids for play was beyond anything I could have managed on my own. I don't earn any equity by living here—the value of the building goes up but the residents don't benefit financially from that increase. The equity stays in the building and in the community that lives in the building. But since we collectively own the building, and no landlord is trying to profit from our housing, the cost of living here is affordable. The next generation will also be able to live here for affordable prices.

When Rosi was a baby, Sarah lived in what we called the Big Room, a master bedroom with its own bathroom, for another year after our move and then moved away to marry Jack. They, and their son David, have remained extended family, as my own family grew outward in concentric circles. Eventually, my three kids shared what we called the "blue-rug room." One bunk bed held Rosi and Raffi and a crib held little Zoe.

When the kids were a little bigger, I built myself a medieval-style bedchamber, with curtains to draw closed for privacy. I created it in what would have been the dining room wall. We call that room the Family Room since, in addition to my bed, it houses the washer and dryer and laundry area, a huge toy shelf and a corner for general over-flow junk such as boxes of files and photos.

Visitors would ask me, "Why don't you give yourself a bedroom?" I had the whole apartment and I wanted the kids to have the bedrooms. Even so, most of my kids shared rooms with one another for most of their lives. When I first offered 10-year-old Rosi a room of her own, she preferred to stay in the communal bedroom with her siblings. A whole year later, she finally agreed to have her own room. Raffi and Zoe got their own bedrooms for the first time when they were college students.

I think Americans overestimate the amount of space human beings need for living, and in estate-style homes families may lose the human connections that come from living closely in shared space. Nevertheless, I sometimes experienced the down side of a fully filled home—I didn't have ample privacy for my own social life; our storage space was limited; and as the kids grew older it became harder for the meticulously tidy child to share a bedroom with the wondrously sloppy child. We each had to sacrifice some personal preferences in the name of the communal good. I think it worked out pretty well.

Life Works

❧

I was a single parent, but I didn't feel alone. My women's group was intimately present in our lives during my early-parenting years: Moon, Susan, Talia, Joanna, Merle. My family-of-origin was also closely connected. Beloved sister Miggie, just 11 months younger than I, even moved in with me for three years after Sarah left to be with Jack. Miggie was completing her internship and residency in psychiatry, but always found time to help around our home. She painted a wild jungle on the wall of the kids' room in bright, primary colors. She sorted laundry and had a gift for mending. Years after Miggie married and moved to Chicago, when one of our garments ripped, the kids would say, "Send it to Aunt Miggie!"

Miggie invented the Second Adult Phenomenon. Those are things that only get done when a second adult is around, such as wiping the grime from behind the garbage can. The first adult makes sure the kids are fed and clothed and loved. With a second adult on the scene, a wider range of tasks can reasonably be accomplished. Later in my parenting career, I had occasion to delve deeply into the nuanced differences between a second adult versus a second parent.

Three adults seemed to me an even more perfect number for a parenting team because there are three full-time jobs required in parenting: earning, nurturing and arranging. Somehow, a family needs income; the kids need direct care; and a million arrangements need to be made for things like doctor appointments, play dates, birthdays and school. People assume that a solo parent is "one down," but a bigger conception of what is needed might let us see that even a two-parent family is underserved.

I wasn't the only one creating family in nontraditional ways. Throughout the country, solo Moms and two Moms and solo Dads and same-sex, partnered Dads were baby-making. In my city, I joined a lesbian Moms group to find other families that had some variety. There were about a dozen of us with kids around the same age, although because of different choices of schools and different neighborhoods these kids actually had less of a presence in one another's lives than I would have liked.

Life wasn't perfect—that there is a hole in the donut is always part of the truth, and you always have the option of focusing on the donut or on the hole in the donut. During my early mothering years only one of my four sisters had kids yet, and my mother was protective of my sisters' stages of life, not wanting my kids to dominate family scenes. On our frequent visits to D.C., I had to whisk my early-rising little ones out of the house at 6 a.m., so as not to wake up the rest of the household. By the time there were 18 grandchildren, and all my sisters had their own children, no one was worrying anymore about who woke whom up.

Another strain in my family of origin was that I wanted my father to step in as a strong male role model and be a close grandfather for my kids, but I had to really work to achieve that relationship. He had never had a grandparent and he had a younger, new wife who probably was not thrilled by the never-ending demand of family relationships from his previous marriage. My relationship with my Dad and my dream of a close relationship between him and my kids were hugely important to me. I never gave up on us and worked and worked on improving our relationship.

We exchanged a series of loving and honest letters to sort out past miscommunications. He was deeply concerned that I was unintentionally saddling him with possible future financial responsibilities and I was hurt that he would assume anything of the sort, since I had been completely self-supporting since the age of 22, and didn't rely on him at all for my family's operating budget. We both persisted in reaching out for connection in spite of gaps in our understanding of each other.

These days, my father is one of my biggest champions, frequently expressing his love and admiration. He grew into a cherished grandfather for the kids, who truly adore and admire him, and his wife, Wanda, has also given them her best. Wanda remembers every birthday; she teaches the kids complicated card games; and never fails to put in a good word for her alma mater, the University of Michigan, although she hasn't yet convinced any of them to go there. I appreciate how the two of them are an example for my kids of devoted companions in a happy marriage of many decades.

With the help of beloveds, I survived high-stress passages of family life such as the time when Rosi was a feisty four-year-old, Raffi an acting-out two-year-old, and baby Zoe was just two months old, I discovered virile, athletic lice leaping through the wispy curls of my newborn's hair. Just then my mother called on the phone from Washington, D.C.

"I can't talk. I'm having a nervous breakdown," I told her. "We all have lice."

"I'll be there in three hours," she said.

Three hours later, she appeared and helped me survive that epidemic. For the second lice infestation, some years later, Merle and Billee stayed up till 2:00 a.m. helping me wash every single garment and sheet in the house. Lice was one of the worst afflictions of my parenting years.

Another time, guests from out of town were about to arrive—friends of Miggie's who wanted to talk about making babies through alternative conception. Raffi had a high fever and was gasping asthmatically on a pillow; Rosi and Zoe didn't look too perky, either.

"I just don't think I can pull off an evening of adult entertainment," I confessed to my sister.

She shed her hospital scrubs, whipped up a gourmet feast in about 20 minutes while I tended to sick children, and the guests walked into an idyllic scene of deceptive calm.

Overall, 1 was immensely grateful for family and friends and intensely devoted to the task of mothering. There was great joy for me in mothering my three little ones. They would follow me around from room to room as I did housework, building "forts" with all the blankets in the house, nestling together on boats at sea or on spaceships zooming through outer space. Even when Zoe was a non-verbal infant, Rosi and Raffi included her in their play. "Zoe's the cook," they'd declare as she cooed and randomly waved a wooden spoon. Later, when the girls wanted to play house they'd make their energetic brother play the role of "Scuppers the dog," or he could be a hunter who was out hunting (roles he does not remember fondly).

I poured my heart and soul into family life. One-on-one time with each child every day for at least a few minutes, and in longer blocks of time at least once a week, was a top priority for me. I wanted the time to support and witness each child's growing selfhood. One-on-one time made it possible to notice each individual and to be present in relationship with each one. I spent time just being with each child as they played like the time Rosi sat in the sand box molding wet sand while Raffi was with a baby sitter and infant Zoe napped.

"This is a castle. It's for the Bad King," Rosi explained.

"Let's make the Bad King go away so you and me can live there."

"Okay," she said, adding, "And Raffi, too."

"Me, you and Raffi can live there."

"And now I'm going to build a castle for before Raffi was born and just you and me will live in it," she told me.

*   *   *

My partnership with Rebecca was deep and supportive, but it was also a complicated decade of our lives. Both of us faced high demands on the home front coupled with economic insecurity and different visions of our futures. I was still riding the momentum of intense family-making, and even with three children I realized I wasn't done yet. Mothering truly felt like a calling, like the centerpiece of my life's work and the reason I was here on earth. I wanted a fourth child. Rebecca, on the other hand, had not chosen single parenthood. Fabulous as she was as a mother, she was ready to move out of the early childhood years and have more of a grown-up life for herself. She was adamantly opposed to adding one more child to our mix. We eventually parted ways over our inability to bridge this difference.

We separated and I experience separations with brutal intensity. I had to live through my own inner tumult while doing my best to carry on with steady-state parenting. We decided to keep our kids closely connected. I'd have one or both of her kids over for dinner; she'd have different combinations of my kids at her house. Rosi developed the tradition of spending the second-night Passover seder each year at Rebecca's house and I'd take Nava every fall to the Poconos for the High Holy Days. But while our children remained close, I wanted as much space from Rebecca as possible in order to reorganize my heart.

What felt most alive for my future was planning for a fourth baby. I assessed the possibilities for getting pregnant. Both of my donors now lived in distant states so I needed a new plan for this fourth child. I was able to find a man, through networking, who was open to being a sperm donor. Paul was a friend of my friend Jonathan. Unfortunately, he lived four hours away from me, which presented some logistical challenges. He seemed to be a great choice: an open-minded, vigorously handsome and intelligent man who had talents ranging from professional-level musicianship to star power as an athlete. He had been captain of the tennis team at Stanford in his youth and was now the dean of a liberal arts college. We figured we could work out the logistics.

Paul would drive two hours; I'd do the same and we'd meet in a cornfield in this beautiful place under the full moon. My cycle happened to coincide with the full moon. Soon I was fielding an intense range of emotions—ecstatic to be pregnant again and deeply grieving because Rebecca and I were separating.

Just about three months into the pregnancy, I lost the baby-to-be, compounding the loss and sadness of that time. I reached deep to find resources for excellent mothering even through my own hard times. The inner life of a parent does not cease just because we have dependents.

After the miscarriage, my donor, Paul, went on to become the donor for my dear friends Felice and Felicia in the conception of their spectacular daughter, Shira. A few years later he married and became a father of two girls. Recently, Shira told me: "I'm really close to them. I think of them as cousins." I appreciated how donor insemination could create sprawling networks of connection.

I still mourn the child I might have had. After the miscarriage, with my own fertility no longer at its peak, I decided to adopt. I took out a bank loan to finance the exorbitant adoption fees, sandwiched in my mental budget between the end of re-paying my own rabbinical school loans and a day in the distant future when I imagined I'd start needing college loans to send Rosi to college. The adoption loan was worth every penny of debt to me since I consider the gift of raising a human being to be priceless. I stepped through the adoption door with zest, slowly recovering from heartbreak.

Jonah Alejandro, born in 1996, in Guatemala, came into the family and was as popular as a puppy with the big siblings. My friend Joanna's wise words, "You get the kid you're supposed to get," felt right on target. Little Joey toddled around, saying "Boom boom boom," earning himself the nickname "Jonah Alay-boom-boom." He was as deeply connected to my soul as the babies I birthed.

Four years later, in 2000, Mozelle, whom we nicknamed Mozi, also born in Guatemala, joined the family as an infant. I did not want one child to be isolated as the only brown-skin child in the family, or the only one who came into the family by adoption, or the only one born in a different country. It felt important to me that Joey and Mozi would have each other to help normalize their experiences.

Now with five kids and me in the three-bedroom apartment, we were using every single inch for multiple, creative purposes. The living room was simultaneously our family space, our dining room, my rabbinic study, a classroom where I taught a religious studies class on Sunday nights, and the guest room where my mother obligingly slept on the homey sofa when she came for one of her frequent visits.

Being an adoptive family was both exactly the same as being a family formed by birth and also completely different. We became a multiracial family and a new, unexpected adult partnership unfolded for me that took me beyond being a single parent for a stage of life. But that's a story for later.

My donors have both been extraordinary, the best I could imagine. The kids have relationships with these people, but in no way were they Daddies. We called them "donors." When the kids were young the donors would send holiday cards and birthday presents; they'd visit, they'd call. They were a background presence in our lives, although none of the kids put much energy into developing those relationships.

The option was there and still is. If anything, the donors have been eager to augment their genetic contribution with the gift of legacy—wanting to pass on stories and treasured items even though they are in peripheral relationships in the kids' lives.

There were definitely times when each child would have liked to have a hetero-normative family with two, opposite-gender parents living under one roof. Having a donor made them different. Even if they were well-adjusted to their own lives, which included donors, they sometimes minded being different. Kids in general like to be unique within their comfort range, but they don't like to be different. A kid might want to be the only one wearing all purple, or choosing a particular topic for the art project, but they might not want to be the only one with a single parent. As the diversity of family formats increases, there is less and less a standard of Typical versus Different. I even feel reluctant to use the words "mainstream" and "alternative" since in reality the alternatives are becoming the mainstream. But in those years there was still a dominant culture of heterosexual, partnered parenting—at least for most kids some of the time.

I tried to make space for the full range of my kids' feelings, even though I was sensitive myself about my choices. I cared so strongly about providing a good life for these little children. Critics of "alternative families" think that kids can only do well with two parents, one a man and one a woman, married, living in the same home. They worry that the kids will feel an absence if they live in any other family format; the kids will feel less-than and do less well in life emotionally and academically. Some skeptics expressed concern about a mother who had various lovers rather than one long term, monogamous partnership. My Dad and his wife were among those who wondered how well a single parent could do. Indeed for some people, these alternatives are Plan B and they wish they could have the more traditional format. I didn't want to dismiss these concerns just because they were critical. I wanted to parent with open eyes for what was true.

So when Raffi was a wild preschooler, was he acting out because he was confused about whether he was the man of the house? Or because he missed a big dominant man to help contain him? Did he need my empathy? Or did he simply need my guidance in learning to self-regulate? Maybe there were elements of all of the above.

Sometimes I think adoptive parents or single parents or same-sex parents feel defensive about our differences from the old-fashioned norm and we over-read into our kids' feelings and behavior the effects of our choices. We think they are suffering from missing a Dad, or from abandonment about being adopted. Sometimes that might be true, but it's also true that there are many other possibilities to explain whatever is going on. Maybe the child had a fight with a friend, or is getting sick or is hard-wired for anxiety.

On the other hand, it's easy for a parent who is so aligned with what's best for the kids—with their happiness and wholeness—to underestimate their emotional struggles. For a parent to see a child having a hard time can be so painful that sometimes we manage to be oblivious. I didn't want to project my own concerns onto the kids and yet I did want to be attentive to what was real for them. Understanding my kids' behavior and choosing helpful parenting responses helped me learn to guide hundreds of other parents when they faced similar complex situations.

Every now and then I'd ask the kids, "Do you ever wonder what it would be like having a Dad live here?" Or, "Can you imagine what your birth moms are doing right at this moment?" My intended message (which may at times have felt to the kids as if I were forcing my agenda on them) was that no conversation is taboo and they didn't have to have a party line about our family. I wanted to stake out a range of topics, put them boldly on the table, and be able to be with each child's real-life experience of joy, sorrow, sadness, yearning and questioning.

One of the ways I've communicated pride to my children about our family story is to label people who don't understand adoption or gay rights or different family structures as "ignorant." There are people who say all sorts of insensitive and sometimes even awful things about other children's families—"Why didn't your birth mother want you?" or, "Everyone has a Dad; why don't you?" I wanted my children to see that it's the other person's ignorance that's the problem. The other person might be misinformed or have limited experience with this life variation. I wanted my kids to feel in-the-know, that they had inside information and could educate others.

In my early parenting years, I did feel defensive about my choices because they were seen as so alternative by many people. I felt pressure to have a "perfect" family in order to prove that non-traditional paths were perfectly okay. Other people would complain that their three-year-olds didn't sleep through the night or their eight-year-old refused to do homework, and I smugly asserted that my kids had No Problems. Only when I saw how well my family was doing did I come to relax and trust that I had nothing to prove. I grew to understand that I was allowed to have challenges and problems just as any parent has. I no longer felt that I should hide or minimize them. There was nothing that needed to be defended or marketed.

I've mostly had huge confidence as a Mom—much more than I've had about partnering. In the partnering realm I seem to need an inordinate amount of reassurance and kindness whereas in the parenting realm I've always had an inherent inner solidity. Being flexible, being resilient, being a problem-solver, being completely dedicated to the task are all qualities that I've cultivated and that have informed my mothering.

In any life, at a given moment, a human being is only able to experience a part of what is possible. You can't be a back-to-the-land organic homesteader and also a corporate lawyer at the same time; you can't live in a Tibetan monastery in India devoting yourself to Buddhism and also take care of your ailing mother in Queens. Some people have a spiritual life, some don't; some have sex with a mate, some don't; some have a dog, some don't. Making peace within myself about my own capabilities and limitations helps me be fully present as a mother.

The less I live in worry and anxiety about not being good enough, the more I can do the best job that I can do. There are things I'd like to give my children that I can't give them in my particular life—the example of a long-term partnership for instance—yet I'm quite proud of what I am able to give them. They are very lucky to be surrounded by grandparents, aunts, uncles, cousins, Mom's ex-lovers, the new partners of Mom's ex's, donors, father figures, God-siblings, community....I have given them a web of amazing human connection even though it is not limited to traditional lines of a family tree.

With the kids turning out to be pretty okay human beings, each developing nicely into their own potential, the skeptics also relaxed. My family has had a lot of stability: we've lived in the same place for decades, I've been the parent on duty for decades, we've been integrally involved in community life for decades. Even with some non-traditional realities, in many ways family life is pretty routine for most families most of the time, mine included. We spend a lot of time living the repetitive rhythm of family life: feeding, bathing, transporting, snuggling, guiding, comforting, giggling, clothing and then doing it all again. There's a lot of laughter, love and learning and also times of sadness and struggle.

Years later, Rebecca and I are best beloveds again and the kids are still extremely close, sibling-ish. Zoe and Nava have a weekly phone date and whoever is around goes to cheer Yonah at half-marathons.

I am so proud to include Nava and Yonah as my children and proud to be claimed by them as one in a collection of their mothers. They understand that each mother has a unique relationship with them: their Rebecca mother raised them and their other mothers each have special family roles that include sharing graduations, birthdays, holidays, news and blues and recoveries. We've had to invent language for who we are to each other. I call Nava and Yonah my God children, even though Yonah says "I don't believe in God." They call me their Greenbean. Rebecca and I call each other "First Responders," as in who do you call when the car breaks down. Rebecca's partner of many years, Barbary, has also been integrated into the family circle.

Through it all, I believe my kids are growing up with a Mom who is a real human being living a life that involves choice and consequences. Because no one set of choices is right for everybody, my kids, too, will need support, guidance and inspiration in finding their own workable paths. For them and for others, I am glad to share this version of family-formation and the discoveries that have come my way on this parenting journey.

My life is not a fairy tale where the story comes to an end with "happily ever after." It is a contemporary saga in which I am an active agent, a writer of the script, a maker of decisions. No one will rescue me, but also no one will determine my fate. "Freedom is a constant struggle," says the folk song from the Civil Rights era. Yet freedom is also a path of consciousness, contribution and happiness.

WEALTH

Being Rich

❦

"Mama are we rich?"

"Yes, we are rich."

My family has enormous privilege compared to billions of other people in the world. We have clean drinking water, live in a relatively peaceful country, and enjoy the prospect of continued stability. As an educated professional, I move in middle- and upper-middle-class and even wealthy orbits. My kids expect that they will have professional options when they grow up. Yet, in the context of this privilege, some months it does feel like a miracle that I—primary provider for five dependants—am able to pay all the bills.

I have managed to raise my children with at least the illusion of solid middle-class stability. My intention is first and foremost to help my kids experience the abundance in our lives before we get into the complexity of the global class system and the places where we have more or less than others. I look around at my comfortable apartment packed full of books, stuffed animals, toys, fresh fruit and electronics and think, "My God, what an illusion this all is." It all depends on me being able to earn the income to fund this life, month after month. There's no guarantee that I'll be able to do that next month or next year and if I can't, will it all be gone? I have no inherited wealth, no trust fund, no stream of income from a partner committed to me and my family. But I am able-bodied so far and I have good friends and I have caring family. In case of an extreme emergency, I don't think we'd be out on the streets.

When I pay the bills each month I feel a swell of happy pride that I can provide for my family. Juggling all the priorities and options is like playing monopoly, only it's the real thing. Money comes in, money goes out; I have great satisfaction in seeing the fruits of my labor support the people I love.

When the kids ask about our economic status I always compare our privilege to the rest of the world. I talk about African squatters who hike four miles to get a bucket of drinkable water and Indian peasants who work ten hours a day for a bowl of rice. Why look at the small part of the pyramid above you and feel deprived when you can look at the vast base of the pyramid below you and feel lucky? Then I add, "In the United States, we're in the middle."

I try not to communicate any stress about financial demands to the kids. They sometimes experience limits because of our finances—we can't afford everything they'd like to buy—but they don't need to experience worry and anxiety about it. Worry and anxiety don't make the finances any different; they just add to the hardship.

I believe money should be there to serve a person's values, not to poison us with stress. I've noticed that most people seem to live in a way that stretches them financially to the limit, or even beyond, no matter what their economic status. One friend of mine has millions of dollars, which she uses to support important non-profit work. Yet, she used to suffer because her brothers, who use their money to make more money, are richer than she is. How we feel about money is all relative.

Sometimes, as I clear away the little plastic toys scattered all over the floor, or sort stacks of paper clutter or eye the heaps of clothes sitting in my kids' closets, I remember nostalgically the days when I lived with a typewriter in my right hand, a guitar in the left and all my other worldly possessions in a pack on my back. How much of my time do I now spend managing stuff? Some days I want to veto a single new item entering this house. Yet, we live modestly compared to most people we know.

A wealthy adult student of mine sweeps in once a week for her lesson wearing gorgeous, fine-textured garments from all over the world. She lives on an estate with horses and has an indoor swimming pool. I'm so grateful that she wants to learn what I can teach because through her tuition I can fund one child's private-school tuition. We love each other. One day she wrapped me in a bear hug and said, "Julie, I wish I could be as marginal as you."

It reminded me of the Yiddish proverb: "It's no curse to be poor, but it's no great blessing either."

People's lives are different. I'm not a child of the Mumbai slums scavenging for cans to recycle. I'm not the inheritor of a fortune sitting on a philanthropic board to participate in its disbursal. I have my own economic realities and choices. I often work with and for people who have more than me—swimming pools in their backyards, family vacations to Italy, expensive summer camps for the kids. As long as I am paid fairly for my services, I don't feel resentful of their fortune. Some of them have much harder lives than I have in non-monetary ways, and some of them are lucky in non-monetary ways.

I also often work with people who have less than I have—who are dressed in ratty clothes and who expect that the heat will go off at the end of the month. I don't feel guilty for my good fortune, either. Resentment, envy and guilt don't change anything. Those feelings just slow us down from making a better world. So when those feelings arise I shift my gaze toward other realities that let me see the bigger picture. This ability has kept me sane in a world of wild gaps between the part of me that is a "have" and the part of me that is a "have-not."

In my younger parenting years, my family was poorer. I was still a rabbinical student when I had Rosi. We were living on income from my quarter-time student internship and some student loans. I was so fiercely committed to family making that I thought to myself, "If need be, I'll work behind a dollar-store counter to support this family." (Back then, we called them five-and-ten-cent stores.) In the late '80s, there was a lot of job discrimination in my field against gay and lesbian people or anyone in any kind of non-traditional family.

Right after I graduated from rabbinical college, I applied for dozens of jobs directing religious schools. A non-discrimination policy had recently been passed at the rabbinical college, after years of hard work by me and other activists, stating that there would be no discrimination against applicants to the rabbinical school or against rabbinical students for being gay, lesbian or bisexual. The problem we faced, though, was that no work had yet been done to educate and support the congregations who would be hiring the college's graduates. Those congregations knew about the non-discrimination policy and they were frantically seeking ways to make sure they did not end up with a gay or lesbian rabbi. Any non-normative family was suspect.

Search committee members were aware that it was against the rules to ask directly about the marital relationships of people applying for positions. So they found devious ways of obtaining the information they wanted: "Would you bring your husband to dinner before the service?" I was asked regularly. When I called a member of a search committee for a prospective job, I regularly got the response, "Oh you're the single parent. What are you planning to do for childcare?" My heterosexual, married friend Marc, also about to graduate from rabbinical school and applying for rabbinic positions at the exact same time, was never asked that question. "I have no idea what we'll do for childcare," he confided in me.

Even though I had top credentials as a Jewish educator, I was unable to get a job within a one-hour radius of my home. Rosi was two, I was pregnant with Raffi and I needed work. Pushing through mounting panic, I cast my mind about for possibilities. Finally, out of dire necessity I decided to launch my own project, a dream I never would have attempted if I had had any other choice. These days, there are wonderful programs that mentor and fund young "social entrepreneurs," as I would now be known. Back then I was on my own as fundraiser, program director, outreach staff and dean of students, all rolled into one.

The idea was to start a Jewish Renewal Life Center to bring spiritual seekers to Philadelphia for a year of immersion in Jewish living and learning. Participants would take five classes to learn about traditional and innovative ways of being Jewish. They'd each have an internship where they could put those spiritual ideas into practice. And they'd be integrated into a Jewish community living by the sacred cycle of the year.

The Life Center was a severely under-funded labor of love, but it was a fantastic project. Terrific people came from all over the world to learn with us. Some of them became life-long friends. At a time in my family's life when it would have been easy to become isolated— me being a single Mom with a house full of very small kids—there were people in and out of my home at all times, surrounding us with community and transforming their own lives by being part of our community. My living room was the administrative office, classroom and worship space for the Life Center. Finances were weak, but there was passion, joy and meaning in this work.

In addition to running the Jewish Renewal Life Center, I did the bread-and-butter work of a rabbi. I married couples, named babies, conducted Bar and Bat Mitzvah ceremonies and buried the dead. This work was also deeply satisfying as I took part in meaningful relationships with so many different people and held open the door to meaningful religion for them. People who had been marginalized by mainstream Judaism—same-sex couples and interfaith couples— sought me out because they knew they would be welcome.

I did not think of my work as a business, but more as a mission. This compromised my ability to put bread on my family's table. Eventually, as I faced the higher and higher expenses of raising my children, I realized that I would not be able to support this growing family if I didn't think of my work, at least in part, as a livelihood. I started thinking of my freelance rabbi work as a "rabbinic private practice," which meant charging higher rates for my services and higher tuition for the Life Center.

After 12 years of running the Life Center, I turned the work over to other organizations and found a part-time pulpit with an open-minded congregation that would provide a steady income. They became my new community to nurture and tend. By then, attitudes toward difference within the Jewish world were beginning to shift and this special congregation and I warmly embraced.

When Joey was two, I also enrolled in a training program in Marriage and Family Therapy that I could attend part time over five years. (Zoe was just old enough to be dropped off with Joey at Joey's daycare at 8:00 a.m. She would take Joey in and then walk one block up the street to her neighborhood public school at 8:30 on the one day a week that I needed to be in class by 9:00.) I was excited about new challenges, but sad not to be able to continue with the Life Center project, which I had passionately birthed.

Because of the meager financing of those early parenting years, there were times we couldn't afford the treats I wished I could give my kids. When I passed the bakery with my little children, I would have liked to offer them a lovely muffin or chocolate-covered strawberry, a raspberry tart or gingerbread man. But I had to be the voice of maturity. "No love, not now." Because paying the gas bill was more important than those treats, we could only feast our eyes. There were moments like that, but overall I was quite happy to dress my kids in hand-me-downs (Rosi called it "Shopping in the closet," where we kept big bags of high-quality giveaways), to visit nearby family for vacations and to invest in the early childhoods of my children by being present with them instead of working every minute for money.

One day, nine-year-old Zoe had a craving for Kentucky Fried Chicken. I wanted to support what she desired. It's good to know what you desire. I also knew that we were down to the last few coins in the wallet. We made it an adventure. "Let's go see if we have enough coins to get a chicken wing and maybe a biscuit. It might work out." Our coins added up to three dollars and nineteen cents. At the drive-in window we dialogued with the teller, "If we add a mashed potato will it be over our budget?" With each additional item we could afford both of us squealed with glee. When we drove out of there with a small meal we were both so pleased.

Rosi, by age 13, had two after-school jobs, one working for a neighborhood artist and one helping out in the religious school. She could now buy her own clothes, which was good because I could never keep up with her knack for style and fashion. Often she created her wardrobe out of scrap material and hand-me-downs. The last time I took her shopping for clothes, before she started buying her own, we stepped into the department store and were both overwhelmed with all the tantalizing possibilities for a spring outfit. I told Rosi how much we could spend that day. She naturally wanted clothes that surpassed that limit and I would have loved to buy her what she wanted. But I also needed to make the payment on the car, the insurance and the school loan, and have enough left for groceries. To splurge on clothes would compromise the other needs. I was acutely aware of the intricate entanglement of self-esteem and consumerism in this culture. We learn that to value one's self means to buy the latest, best, newest, coolest. How could my daughter feel completely valuable, completely worthy, without having the material markers that society imposes? That day in the mall I started a conversation with my daughter that we have had many times since.

"My love for you is infinite, but my budget is not infinite," I explained. "When we come into this store it's tempting to want everything. When I look around I start wanting things for me, too. So I really know how you feel." She nodded with understanding. We were on the same side. We were supporting each other in the face of limited budgets and sparkling capitalist displays.

For her summer birthday, I promised Zoe that she could choose a new swimming suit. We made it a fun mother-daughter project, pouring over catalogues, discussing each suit and finally selecting one that she liked. Later in the summer we visited family friends who had a swimming pool and a daughter the same age as Zoe. Zoe had forgotten to bring her suit with her so the other little girl offered to share one of hers. She spread twenty swimming suits out on her bed for Zoe to choose from. I don't think any of those suits were as meaningful to that child as the one birthday suit that Zoe had chosen with her Mom. Less was more.

We lived on the richer side of the class divide as well. When I traveled in Guatemala, I was wealthy. The coins in my pocket, casually donated into a beggar's hand, fed a Mayan family for a week. The upper-middle class in Guatemala sat in Pollo Campero, the equivalent of Kentucky Fried Chicken, while bands of impoverished, barefoot children peeked in the window. As I bought beautiful, hand-woven cloth in the market, local residents watched the vendor with envy and the woman tending the stall told me I was supporting her family for a month. In Guatemala I was part of an elite, privileged echelon.

In the privileged caste, I joined friends in thinking through ethical behavior from that vantage point. Once Felice, her life partner Felicia, Zoe and I visited Jamaica. Wherever we went, we were badgered by dozens of salespeople proposing prices that we could see were double or even quadruple the going rate for whatever activity we were considering, and yet the prices still felt totally affordable to us, coming from a different economy. Felicia and I were of the opinion that we should just pay whatever they asked. We had the money and they needed it. Felice and Zoe were adamantly opposed to that. "They're business people. They expect you to bargain. You are being condescending not to engage in the bartering. They won't take a payment that's less than what they need."

We had heated debates on the beach about the correct approach to interacting with the Jamaicans. Felice also held a strong principle that she wanted to work primarily with females, assuming that women use resources to feed and educate their children, not to gamble or drink. Donations could buy solar heaters for women in Darfur so they wouldn't be raped while gathering firewood or, micro-loans for Indian weavers who could work at home and support a family.

Our class privilege was entirely relative. Back at home, I took my family to a fundraising concert one evening at the conservative synagogue where my children attended religious school. The kids were excited to be staying up late for this special program. We paid for our tickets at the door and walked in. Close to the stage were the highest-priced seats surrounding tables heaped with tantalizing food and party favors. The next tier of seats had food but no party favors. Behind that there were tables with small snacks, meager compared to the feast that was available in front. And in the back, where our tickets took us, we found chairs with no tables, no food and no toys. The other concertgoers were my fellow community members whose children were growing up with my children, the people with whom I pray regularly, many of whose children I teach on Sunday mornings. I watched my expectant, innocent children taking in the economic stratification.

Some of the wealthy patrons hadn't even bothered to show up so there were plenty of empty seats. I sat my family in the front row and offered them the food and the party favors. Afterward, I wrote a letter to each person on the planning committee and received back apologies and statements that the arrangements had been unintentional and would not happen again.

When my family qualified for financial aid because of income level and family size, the family got a boost. Some years, the kids received reduced-price lunches at public school or state-subsidized health coverage. Even though I am wealthy in Guatemala, in this country sometimes I dance on the safety net. Other times I buy an extravagant dress for Zoe's Winter Ball or send Joey on Outward Bound, which costs a fortune. We eat organic vegetables sometimes, but not always, because they cost so much. I can't afford to feed my kids vegetables if each broccoli head costs as much as a tank of gas.

Class is not simple because just about all of us experience both more privilege than some and less privilege than others. We live the utter complexity of class. I think we can still make a difference in helping kids understand these issues by how we frame our own experience.

Do you compare yourself to those who have more or do you feel the abundance of how lucky you are not to have less? If you are feeling "less-than" financially compared to the people you surround yourself with, a helpful antidote can be to read some of the classic books about people living in real poverty. This literature is so important as a reminder of what's true. If you are one of the people in the situations described here, you can feel affirmed that someone is paying attention. Examples of such books are *Random Family* by Adrian Nicole LeBlanc, who lived with poor people in New York for 10 years; *The Corner* by David Simon and Edward Burns (who then based the brilliant TV series *The Wire* on this material); and *Beyond the Beautiful Forevers* by Katherine Boo, an award-winning, firsthand account of life for children in the slums of Mumbai. I could go on and on with this list, but those are some suggestions of books that have helped me keep my own life in perspective and know where a difference needs to be made.

Even when my financial resources are stretched thin, the kids have grandparents, aunts, uncles with resources. They go to the theater and get birthday presents. We have a consciousness of belonging, of possibility. My friend Felice once told me, "In my life, being working class meant not being able to dream." My kids can definitely dream.

"Mama, are we rich?"

My older and younger kids have been raised in two different classes: the older ones, especially Rosi, grew up with a strapped single Mom, which perhaps instilled the frugal values she has. My youngest ones are coming up in a family with more discretionary money and they expect a more lavish lifestyle. They assume that when we stop at a rest stop on the highway, we'll buy drinks, or that every holiday means new clothes.

I think much of the modern world loses the richness of human interconnection by housing the core functions of life within small family units. Financial stress burdens the providers and often trickles down through the family system. To counteract this nuclear isolation, to create wealth of all kinds, family leaders actively need to pursue counterstrategies.

One way of creating wealth for your family is to expand and deepen your web of relationships by building meaningful connections with grandparents, neighbors, family friends and those in need of healing or extra support. Abundance is about so much more than money. Last week, I was feeling alone, unconnected, unneeded. This week, I've been full-up happy. When I looked at the difference between the two weeks I see that this week I was on call to help make a graduation party for a friend's child, to take dinner to a family dealing with a medical crisis, and to host an extended family member passing through town. Being needed in this web of interconnection fills my own sense of abundance.

Money is part of abundance. In my friendship circle we have at times helped each other out in ways that cross the money boundary. (See section on Sharing) Felice pointed out that doing this financial sharing within our friendship circle was all well and good, but we mostly know people who are fairly privileged and connected to affluent professional circles. After all, we were often sharing the expenses involved with non-necessities, or maybe things that begin to seem like necessities only to privileged people, such as finding a school that's the right fit for your child. Felice said we should take care of our own friends and community but also be conscious of giving to people elsewhere in the world with whom we aren't already connected. It's also good to contribute to projects that empower poor people in other parts of the world.

It's true that no amount is too little to help someone somewhere. Twenty-five dollars can buy a hen for someone who can then feed the family nutritious eggs and, if they have access to a rooster, raise and sell chicks. I loved it that for Rosi's *bat mitzvah* my friend Joanna "gave" her an endangered Orangutan, and for Raffi's *bar mitzvah* his donor, Jack, gave him the gift of feeding an Ethiopian child lunch for a year. A nice thing about wealth, whatever level of it you have, is that you get to be generous. When I ponder what will probably be my under-funded old age, the part I feel the least happy about is that my ability to be generous in material ways will be limited.

Ultimately, our mission is to make a world where resources are shared in equitable and sensible ways. A step along the way is to expand our sense of what abundance means so that we don't need to strive with greed for more, more, more. Whatever amount we have, we have some power to instill values about the meaning of wealth.

Too Much

"No, that's enough sugar."

"No, we're not going to buy that."

"No, we already have too many."

Living in a culture of Too Much creates a parenting challenge. How can I help my kids make satisfying choices to have Enough in their lives and to ensure that others have Enough in their lives? How can we avoid being co-opted into the consuming, greedy mindset, preferred by corporate capitalism, of "Want, want, want! Buy, buy, buy! More, more, more!"? This mindset rests on the inculcation of a slight feeling of deprivation in kids from a young age. Parents are enlisted in creating that sense of deprivation by having to say "No" all too often in the face of endless sales pitches. One of the things I do not enjoy about parenting is being the meanie who is constantly set up to say "No."

It's not that I mind setting limits or saying no, on occasion, to my children. Setting limits is an expected part of parenting. But we live in a culture of surplus on overdrive. This culture juxtaposes an overwhelming array of tempting, alluring consumerist choices and sets me up as the guard at the gate.

I do not want to be the guard at the gate. What I want is to be an ally to my children, nurturing what is developing and growing, guiding what needs to be tamed, celebrating each one's unique self. I realized early on that my intention to be an ally was mightily undermined by the relentless consumerist, materialist society that surrounds us. I could easily be forced into a role that I don't want to be in unless I'm willing to buy my children everything they fancy, feed them everything they crave and inundate our family life with Too Much. Unless I'm willing to let happen whatever happens, without taking any leadership as a parent, I have to say "No" way more than I'd like to. That's what I mean when I say I'm being set up to be a meanie.

With Too Much hounding us at every juncture, the danger is that kids will feel deprived even in a world of abundance. What a paradox that psychic deprivation and mind-boggling material privilege live side by side. Witness the very privileged child who complains, "I never get anything I want. Everyone else gets what they want." Worst of all, parents get co-opted into the role of depriver by constantly having to say "No, no, no!"

I want to be in the role of saying "Yes!" to my kids. The reason I'd rather mostly say yes is that I trust they will then internalize a sense of generosity and well-being from which they will develop their own mechanisms for saying yes and no within themselves. I want them to become their own champion choice-makers—of course making pre-dominantly wise, reasonable, nutritious and appropriate choices!

There is a gap between me saying no and my kids developing the skills to self-monitor, self-manage and make good decisions. My simply saying "No" doesn't make me feel good and it doesn't help them develop the thinking and the skills needed to be their own decision-makers. My challenge as a parent is to structure situations—set them up so that my child and I are not on opposite sides of a request. I want us to face the issue together, on the same side, going in the same direction. And I want them to experience me not as a gatekeeper, but as a supportive guide in decision-making. "Let's think this through. If you spend your allowance on this toy, then you won't have it for the school store on Monday. What are you thinking about that?"

If I let the culture of Too Much polarize us, it wins. How do I stay on the same side as my child? How can we be allies in the face of way, way Too Much—too much stuff, too many calories and too much advertising bombardment? How in this high-pressure cultural cacophony of Too Much do we teach our kids to make good choices and feel fulfilled? How can I help my little children manage desire when ads promoting every new toy and gadget surround them? How can I help them manage peer pressure to own the latest brand?

Since I want to be in the role of saying "Yes" to my kids as they develop their own internal compasses to say yes and no within themselves, I need to prepare myself and them for interfacing with the culture of Too Much. Over the years, I developed these More Than Ten Commandments to guide me in the world of Too Much. They have been useful in helping my children navigate a demanding world that intertwines the formidable advertising industry with peer pressure and youthful desire.

1. Choose the child's peer group with care.

Making wise choices about my child's peer group sets the context for our experience. Putting my child in an elite private school or a public school in a wealthy suburb will pose problems related to surplus wealth. My child will be comparing him or herself to children who have designer clothes, toys, computers and luxurious trips. There may be good reasons to put a child in such a school, but I want to consider carefully what I'm getting into. If I make the decision to place my child in a neighborhood and/or school with a large wealth factor, I try to balance that with other experiences that convey a more varied picture of socioeconomic realities.

I'd rather have my child experience herself at the top of a pyramid of privilege than at the bottom. Isn't it better to look down that pyramid and realize how lucky you are than to look up and covet the lives of those at the oxygen-scarce pinnacle?

When my child complains about our relative class position, I want to be able to say, "We know people who are richer than we are and who are poorer than we are."

That was one of the reasons I wanted to keep my kids in the public schools as much as possible. This was a challenge because we live in a distressed urban area where most children never learn to read at grade level and a shocking percentage never graduate from high school. I wasn't so worried about academic achievement because my kids, coming from a home where education is highly valued and supported, were likely to live up to their academic potential. I was more worried about boredom, self-esteem, racial tension and safety.

Some families live in areas where even the public schools are bastions of privilege. A challenging question is how you can make sure your child experiences diversity of race, class and family structure. It is good for kids to see a full range of human experience and, if possible, to have intimate experiences with difference. Awareness of diversity opens options for your child to be a unique individual and also prepares your child to live in a global, multicultural world.

Each of my kids spent two to 10 years in the urban public schools, and they each also had the experience of excellent private education for at least a few years. Each setting presented its own challenges. Zoe, attending an elite private academy, had to live in two worlds: the world of her family, which lives in affordable housing and sometimes shops at Walmart to save money; and the world of designer clothes, weekends at Broadway shows, and gifts of sports cars at the age of 16. Each year virtually all the girls in her class returned from spring break with their hair braided from trips to the Caribbean.

On the other hand, Joey, attending the neighborhood public school, developed prejudices against African-Americans because the students there were mostly from poverty backgrounds with unenlightened attitudes about gay people, militarism and the environment. No matter how many times I tried to help him separate skin color from consciousness, he was convinced for years by his limited, but intense, personal experiences that all black people were rough and ignorant. Now both Joey and Mozi attend what they call "a rich school," where second-graders have iPhones. Mozi is disgruntled that she doesn't have an iPhone.

Your child's peer group will have a big impact on what your child sees and expects. No doubt you are checking out your choices and weighing the strengths and weaknesses of each choice in terms of your values. Good luck!

2. Reframe your child's request in order to say "Yes."

One strategy to manage the world of Too Much, is to reframe the issue so that you are holding the reins of the discussion. My child looks at the dazzling display of candy in the check-out aisle and asks, "Can I buy the candy bar?""

"Yes, you can buy it for dessert. Where shall we keep it till then?"

"Can I buy the Sweetie Tweeties?"

"Yes, when it's Valentines Day, let's choose some of this kind of candy."

"Can I have the Twirly Magic Cornucopia?"

"That would be nice for your birthday or for a holiday."

I hope that I am helping my child direct desire into appropriate channels for fulfillment. Rather than being the victim of the conversation, I try to take charge of the direction in which I want to steer it.

My friends playfully tease me, mimicking a child's voice: "Mom, can I have sex with my girlfriend?"

"Yes, honey, when you're 35."

3. Orient kids before entering stores.

"You're going to see a million toys in here. I'm sure you'll see lots of things you want. So don't get the Get Me Get Me Gimme Gimme's." I can relate to the Get Me Get Me Gimme Gimme's because sometimes I get them myself. I start fantasizing about wanting the next generation of electronic device or I accompany my child to buy the hiking boots he needs, only to fixate on sandals that I don't need. I'm experiencing a form of material lust, greed even, that is promoted and rewarded in this society. Each of us has to find our own comfort zone with ownership and acquisition and each of us needs to be aware of when we trespass that zone. There is no one right answer since each one of us has a unique configuration of resources, values and needs.

My kids have internalized awareness of what I call the Get Me Get Me Gimme Gimme's and can occasionally point out when they see me operating with that attitude. It's good to be checks and balances for one another. We keep one another true to our values (or at least to what I hope will one day be the values of my children.)

4. Make a plan as a way to help you take charge in the culture of Too Much.

Even though you are surrounded by a culture of Too Much, making your own plan of action can help you avoid being subservient to it. "In this family, we buy the children special things for birthdays and certain holidays. At other times, we help you save your allowance or earn money to buy what you want."

"Can I have the Darling Dangling Doggy?"

"Yes, you can have it if you earn money from chores and save your allowance. Let's see how much you need to save...."

I find it helpful to plan ahead with the kids as a way of channeling and managing desire. "We're going into the supermarket. We're going to focus on buying healthy groceries. Each of you can pick one sweet treat for after dinner and you can pick one special thing for a lunch box."

Of course, there are still the inevitable queries about buying Kool Aid and sugary breakfast food.

Even though I sometimes feel besieged by the onslaught of undesirable options, I can reference our original plan, "Our plan is to buy healthy groceries. Ask me something I can say 'yes' to." This strategy shifts their attention slightly toward finding things that I will approve and we walk out with products more in line with what I actually enjoy buying for the family.

"We're going into CVS to buy these three things: toothpaste, vitamins and soap."

The glittery stickers beckon, but I stick to my plan. The problem is that I have to be really careful myself not to buy on impulse. I have to model sticking to the plan.

Now and then when I want something I'll discuss it with the kids, make a plan, save the money, and go on an expedition to get it so that they see the whole process articulated and modeled. When one of the kids sees something in a store and wants it on the spot, I offer: "Let's talk about that and if you really decide you want it, we can make a plan to buy it."

When we have a strong foundation of making a plan and sticking to it, an occasional spontaneous exception is all the more fun, especially if I, the parent, initiate and offer something unexpected. Passing a yard sale, Mozi and I notice an adorable stable set with a little horse sitting in a cute barn. She is startled and delighted when I ask her if she'd like me to buy it for her.

Some things are bigger than a child can buy on their own. Maybe these are things that can wait for the future. Say to the 11-year-old, "Maybe you'll get an iPod for your next birthday." There's value in helping a child earn, wait and plan. Instant gratification isn't the best builder of character.

5. Emphasize values more than budget.

Your child says, "You could buy it for me if you wanted to."

"I want to focus on paying for our home and our car and good food and happy celebrations. I want to give some to others who aren't as lucky. There are lots of other things we could buy, but these are my priorities."

"But Mom, you have enough money."

"I do have enough money and I have to choose the most important ways to spend it."

"But Mom, I think buying this is important."

"When you are a grown-up you'll get to decide how to spend the money you earn. You'll figure out what's most important to you."

Some of my friends struggle with a budget that does not have natural limits. They have enough money to buy virtually whatever they want. Felice says to me, "We really could buy Shira everything she wants. So how do we explain that we aren't going to do that?"

"Well, why don't you want her to have a shopping cart of new outfits when you go into the clothes store?" I ask.

"It's just not our value to buy so much stuff, but she likes clothes and we have the money. So why shouldn't she get what she wants?"

We ponder this question. "This is a question more about values than about money," we decide. "The conversation with Shira has to be about values even if she's posing it as a money issue."

In families with two parents, it is common for the parents to have differing values about how much to give the kids. My friends Peter and Penny got into a big fight in the aftermath of a shared agreement that Peter would take their 13-year-old son on a shopping expedition to buy a suit for an upcoming family event. Father and son returned, happy to have accomplished their mission. When Penny looked at the price tag on the suit she went ballistic. "I said 'a suit!' I didn't mean something equal to the down payment of a house!"

"You said 'a suit.' I bought him a suit."

Choosing family values then becomes a relational issue between parents calling on them to attend to their own communication and decision-making processes.

6. Structure desire.

Identify times in the year when gift giving and receiving is expected. This will help structure desire; kids will have a psychic place to put their longing, an internal calendar to help them self-organize. Birthdays, holidays, graduations and anniversaries are all appropriate. In my family, on Passover we give little gifts in exchange for the kids finding and handing over the hidden *matzah*, which allows everyone to complete the Passover ritual. For birthdays, each child gets a Big Brother or Big Sister gift on the birthday of the younger one whose entry into the family made someone into a big brother or sister—a custom I designed originally to temper the older sib's predictable jealousy on the birthday of the younger sib.

7. Ally with your children's interests.

Engage with kids about what they want. You can build your relationship, exploring their interests and fantasies, even if you aren't going to buy them what they request. I want to ally with my child's interests and desires, rather than dampen them.

"Yes, that's such an interesting Ninja Turtle outfit, gladiator sword, super race car, etc. etc. Who would you like to play that game with? How would the game go? What side do you want to be on? What would you do with it? How fast do you think it goes? Which color/version do you like best?"

It's a balancing act for a parent. I want to affirm my child's interests and desires without succumbing to frenzied consumerism. "I like you to have what you want, honey. Yes, I can see why you'd want that."

"Mom, can I get the Dragon Buster Double-Edge Light Saber?"

"Well, honey, it does look interesting. What game are you imagining playing with it? Who would you like to play that with? Would the other player need a light saber too? Or if they didn't have one, what else could they use? What do you like about the light saber? Yeah, it does look shiny and sharp. Did you ever get to use one at somebody else's house?"

"Mom can I get the WW2-xformat-fullscreen-Wydiebuster electronic thing?"

"That sounds so interesting. What features does it have?"

Still, more stuff enters my house than anyone needs. I think wistfully of Laura Ingalls Wilder, author of the *Little House on the Prairie* series, living in her log cabin and cherishing her one book. It was a major event for her to buy a set of little white cards with a picture on each. We have sets like that piled up in drawers, lying on the floor, in the art cupboard, behind the bed. The kids have notebooks and game books, coloring books and sketchbooks, many of them with a page or two used, then the book is discarded, or simply added to a heap of something that might be looked at again if not for the ongoing deluge of stuff.

8. Sometimes say no.

In the book *The Power of a Positive No*, William Ury of the Harvard Program for Negotiation explains how saying no is really saying yes to your own integrity. He is focusing on the world of business and political negotiations, but the word "No" is also an important part of good parenting. Our kids need to know who we are and what we stand for.

Some things are against my values and my child will never get them from me, no matter what. In our family we don't buy guns or weapons. The kids are allowed to make whatever they want using cardboard, carrots, scissors, glue, string or whatever inspires their imaginations. My sons have created all sorts of clever military toys, hand-crafted with diligence and creativity. Beg as much as they want and they still don't get Nerf guns, bb guns or any other kind of gun. (The one exception when they were younger was the little water pistols for the swimming pool, which I called "squirters," not "guns.") When they became older teenagers, my sons and I made decisions collaboratively about buying violent electronic games and gadgets.

For other parents the line may be drawn on certain food items or on what kind of movies it's okay to watch. Kids register that you are expressing your caring for them, that you are doing your best thinking about what's good for them, even if they don't like your verdicts. Being able to press up against your limits can even be strengthening for them, although it might not be much fun for you.

Knowing that a parent is able to say no is reassuring to children. They feel more secure knowing that you are strong enough to say no to the dangers of life, however you define them. Being able to say no when an occasion calls for it is different from being set up by the culture of Too Much to constantly say "No, no, no" in the face of an advertising and peer culture pressing for more, more, more. No is a part of parenting, but the greater part of parenting, ideally, is yes.

9. Give in.

Sometimes, you need to give in and get something that isn't what you want to be getting because as a parent you are balancing multiple values. Sometimes my kids want something—say for a birthday—that is an expensive, gimmicky, unnecessary item. Because I value my child and my child's wishes, sometimes the greatest gift I can give is to give exactly what my child wants, even when it isn't something I care about her having.

Similarly, when my child needs to give a gift to a friend who has more than everything she needs, I don't value giving an expensive birthday gift, but I do value my child having a sense of belonging and being appreciated in her peer group. If this gift for a friend is important to my child, I might prioritize respecting her social sense over my own aversion to excessive materialism.

I admit there is a slippery slope here. How much do I try to keep up with the Joneses? And what if the Joneses' community lives at a level that I can't possibly match? In her private school, Zoe learned quickly that her family could never afford to reciprocate the lavish gifts that the peer group tossed off. Zoe developed a knack for creating the most meaningful personalized gifts for her friends: a treasure box full of items representing intimate inside jokes; a novella written by Zoe with her friend as the heroine; a hand-made blueprint for life for a graduating senior. Zoe's friends considered her gifts priceless. Still, I spent more money keeping up with the Joneses at that school than I like to remember.

10. Differentiate between love and money.

"My love for you is infinite but my budget is not." In a materialist world, spiritual values such as love are enmeshed with the material value of things. Things come to represent connection, worth, caring and commitment. Think of a wedding ring. Think of the message behind expensive beauty products. A parent can help children untangle the material and the spiritual.

11. Let the kids own the process of buying.

Earning money and deciding how to spend it helps kids evaluate worth and make trade-offs. When my kids became young teenagers it was their responsibility to earn spending money for entertainment and for much of their wardrobe. In our community, they babysit, shovel snow, help in the market, walk dogs, carry groceries, move furniture, help solve computer problems. They also can earn some money at home for extra chores. They experience pride and joy in earning and spending their own money. When spending, the child still has to clear the purchase with me, though. They don't have the right to buy anything they want just because it is their own money. Joey can't say, "Mom, I'm buying a BB Gun because I saved up the money myself." Even if he's using his own money, he has to abide by the family purchasing framework: we buy things that contribute to peace.

12. Articulate your own thought process in making decisions.

"Here we are at Staples and the bakery is right across the street. I love it when we get a treat there, but I'm also thinking about the brownies that you baked for dinner dessert. So I think it makes sense to save our treat for after dinner, you know?"

In our culture of Too Much, food often becomes the focus of insatiable desire and overconsumption or underconsumption. Helping a child make wise choices about food involves the same approaches that are discussed above for non-edible things. For example, just as you choose your child's school environment, you choose what food choices will surround your child at home. You get to choose the school. You get to choose the groceries that will stock the refrigerator and the cupboards at home. You choose your young child's milieu. The More Than Ten Commandments can all be applied to food.

In my family, children younger than 13 are expected to eat vegetables every day, sweet treats only at dessert time and generally go with the program of family meals at meal times. My hope is that by early teenage-hood they will have internalized these self-regulating patterns sufficiently to make their own good choices. It is a privilege, in our family, to be in charge of food choices once you are a teenager. Even though I err at times, my intention is not to remind my 14-year-old to eat his broccoli every evening, and not to comment when he stuffs candy into his pockets as he runs out to skateboard.

It's a challenge to inculcate self-regulation in the face of plenty. I can recall one particular day of Too Much. My seven year-old ate a sugary breakfast product in the morning, cupcakes at school for a child's birthday, candy after school that a friend gave her, a lollipop at the dry cleaner's and another that the bank lady gave her, and now she is asking me about dessert after dinner. It was a feast of sugar all day, but I had to be the one who said "No." I would have liked to have been the one to give her a treat. Instead I said, "Did you have five vegetables today? Let's count. Well, if not, what could you have now to make you ready for dessert?"

13. Fill your lives with non-commercial activities. Create your own culture!

The more you create culture within your own family and with friends and with community groups, the less your kids are available for the predatory commercial culture of the United States. Here are some examples of what families can do together:

Sing songs (There's a great family song book called *Rise Up Singing*).

Build play forts with blankets, sheets and pillows. Have pillow fights.

Play board games and card games. (Make them silly if competition is stressful). Check out the high-quality German games full of strategy and creativity for older kids

Play games with balls of different sizes, indoors and out. Make mazes for marbles.

Run, tag, tackle, throw, catch, kick, bat, wrestle and roll down hills.

Light sparklers, play flashlight tag in the dark, watch a moon eclipse or shooting stars.

Cook, bake, decorate, invent concoctions. Learn a new kind of cooking such as making sushi.

Volunteer with community groups that are cleaning up the earth, or feeding the homebound or anything else that helps others.

Make art projects with glue, markers, paint, glitter, popsicle sticks, velvet appliqué and more. Paint a wall with colorful handprints. Fingerpaint the bathtub walls. Use your broken kitchen dishes to make a mosaic.

Read out loud. Listen to story recordings. Make story recordings. Write books.

Create a salon for haircuts, mani-pedis and hairdos.

Make paper airplanes, origami and paper dolls. Use perler beads and make jewelry.

Learn magic tricks and dress up as magicians. Put on shows.

Plant gardens, water, tend, harvest; help a neighbor do it, too.

Build sculptures out of scrap wood, pinecones and sticks, and other found objects.

Clean the house together to raucous, loud music; play hide and seek while you clean house.

Lift weights, stretch, do yoga and exercise together.

Take a hike or go biking. Go camping. Build a bonfire. Swim.

Make funny videos and laugh at them.

Raise pets: play with pets, discuss pet behavior, groom your pet, document your pet—if a long-term pet is too much, borrow pets from the school on spring break or foster a pet in need.

Explore your neighborhood or city. Find free culture at the library and in other public venues.

Do a science project; find books at the library with hundreds of simple projects.

Sew, quilt, embroider, crochet, mend, make stuffed bears, table-cloths and doll clothes.

Learn a new language and watch favorite DVDs in the new language. Read childrens books in the new language.

Play with mud; play with water; play with cornstarch; make home-made play dough.

When you do not have time to be involved in every single project, find friends who share your values and who will take turns organizing projects; or give kids ideas and direction and set them loose to create their own homemade culture. If you don't like projects, try putting on good music in the background or a podcast that is interesting to you and secretly listen while you engage. Take my friend Merle's reassuring words to heart—when I complained to her how bored I got sitting on the floor playing with my three-year-old, she said, "Julie, there's no one who could possibly be as interested in playing with a three-year-old as another three-year-old."

If you don't think you're creative or skilled, that doesn't matter at all. Do it anyway!

14. Choose rewards carefully.

Make sure the rewards you use reflect your values. I try not to use food as a reward because food should be about nourishment, not vali-dation. When you use material things as rewards, you elevate the value of material things. Some alternative rewards include:

~ privileges such as getting to stay up 15 minutes past bedtime

~ choices such as whether to have dinner inside or outside; what the menu for dinner will be

~ activities such as getting to play a board game, or spend extra time with Mom

When one of my kids was little, I had a big bag of colorful buttons that I used as rewards throughout the day to help my child manage ADHD. Those buttons meant exactly nothing—they didn't gain my child anything or represent anything other than themselves. But my kid loved achieving a button.

A Family Counterculture

A family counterculture speaks back to corporate, consumerist, out-of-control America. The counterculture values self-management, homegrown production and collective well-being. The way to get there isn't to run a police state authorizing this and forbidding that, but to guide children gently toward internalizing patterns of behavior that work for life. You inculcate your family's counterculture and all of you will have less need to consume corporate culture. The more my children get to be thinkers and decision-makers and the more I get to say "Yes" about food and stuff, the more the kids and I will be aligned and our family culture will prevail.

When kids come from families that make thoughtful, reasonable decisions about buying, they are more likely to be able to reproduce the lives they came from. When your child steps out into a first job, eventually, the bar on lifestyle expectations should not be so high that it seems unobtainable. Expectations of a constant supply of new electronic equipment, restaurant dinners, wardrobe updates and travel undermine motivation to start where you need to start, which is at the bottom of the earning ladder, and build a successful life. You don't want life to be so easy at home that your child has no incentive to build a life of their own.

Children's experiences making decisions about how much is enough will also prepare them to make decisions about using drugs and alcohol, riding in cars with friends who have been drinking, and the many decisions revolving around sex and sexuality. They are building internal character by grappling with what they want and whether and how to get it. They are learning to be independent of what corporate America tells them they should want and want to be. They are strengthening themselves for the life-long practice of making choices. Thinking of it this way, I actually appreciate all the many, many choices assaulting us every day because I understand that we are engaged in a life practice of choosing well—choosing to have minds of our own!

Enough

❧

In the world of Too Much, ironically, no one has enough; no one is good enough. One antidote to this sad state of affairs is seeing more of the world through travel, by watching documentaries and by reading. It's crucial for children to learn about the varieties of human living conditions and the range of opportunities—and the lack thereof; and the different meanings of deprivation and of fulfillment. Broadening the horizons of consciousness has a huge effect on one's sense of abundance.

After I witnessed families of 10 sleeping together in one room on shared mats, I could never be invested in whether my children had their own, separate bedrooms. I could listen to my kids' feelings, complaints and wishes without having any guilt that they were actually deprived. I had no need for them to feel the way I did or to agree with my perspective; but I could parent without feeling guilt around these issues.

By the time they were teenagers, my kids would play with me: "Mom, we were born in a barn! B202 (our apartment) is such a ghetto!"

Zoe would say, "Mom, when I talk about not liking my bedroom, why is it that you always start comparing it to African huts and saying how lucky we are?"

I think by then they secretly had a streak of pride that their circumstances, more privileged than some, less privileged than others, were just fine.

To reinforce that pride I sometimes tell them, "I'm glad my children are not spoiled."

"Mama, are we rich?"

Years ago, I wrote a small sign for my living room that reads:

We Are Rich
We are rich in love, caring, family relationships,
Kin connections, in always having enough food, in always having
enough water, in always having enough heat.

WE ARE RICH
In ideas, in play, in fun, in problem solving, in humor, in peace-making
and in generosity.

This little sign was part of our environment, but I never specifically pointed it out to the kids. I was pleased one day to overhear Mozi quoting from that sign, explaining to a friend that richness isn't just about things. I didn't even know that she had noticed the little hand-written sign that had been tacked on a corner wall for years.

Engaging in the creation of a counterculture requires parental clarity and leadership; requires parents to invest in character formation even while recognizing that we are not all-powerful crafters of personality. While not omnipotent, we do provide important foundation, scaffolding and influence for growing children. Parenting matters. We can help our children find pathways for good living even as our ability to shape character is threatened in this particular society. We need to work hard, and work with our kids, for what we value.

As we engage in values-based child raising, I hope we are finding paths of integrity even in out-of-control corporate culture. Family countercultures can grow into whole community countercultures as you find like-minded people to share your activities. You become models, then, for others who are looking for ways to consume less and engage more. We have to make active choices to resist the dominant culture and to construct our cultures of choice or else our kids will be inducted into a culture of debilitating greed and unsustainable consumption. Family by family, we begin to change the world.

Spiritual sages teach that a person should appreciate 100 blessings every day. I would never leave "enough money" off my blessing list. Money is a useful form of wealth that makes possible so much of value: a home, nutritious food, health care, good education. Money is definitely important, and yet it can obscure the many other blessings in life.

When I pay attention, I realize that so much of my wealth is experiential and relational:

- When I put my foot into my favorite sneaker every morning, feeling the ultimate comfort of a perfect cushion, and I feel pure joy.

- When I build a bed-nest with four-year-old Joey and we pretend to be eagles.

"Here, my little baby eagle, here is a nice mouse for you that I caught in my beak."

"No, Mama. Eagles catch food with claws, not beaks."

"Okay, then let's be lions in our cave under the covers."

"Okay, Mama, but lions live in dens, not caves."

- When I reach my 44th birthday and both my parents are alive and very well. What a blessing to be in my mid-forties with two healthy parents.

- When ten-month-old Mozi crawls vigorously across the room to me, dangling her toy duck from her mouth because all paws are engaged—so sweet, so ridiculous.

- When I draw on the bounty of psychological resources to talk myself through hard spots. I tell myself, "This isn't a good time to evaluate your life. You're tired and cranky." Or, "Don't despair of never having love. Today you're sick in bed and wishing someone would bring you soup."

- When I officiate at a baby-naming ceremony and a power greater than me flows out to touch these people who are moved and healed.

- When I read the news over cappuccino because it makes me feel true to my heritage, to my grandfather and father the journalists and my mother the writer.

- When a partner and I reach the other end of a hard discussion and feel the visceral sense of grace, relief, gratitude and connection between us.

- When I immerse in a hot bath, admire the sprouts in the garden, hear the friend on the phone, read the thank-you card, utter a prayer.

- When I read, think, sing, share, dance, hike, love, cry, comfort, create, pray and play.

• When I write these words.

I want more *and* I want less *and* I have enough.

I am poor and rich and in the middle.

"Mama, are we rich?"

"Yes, my love, we are rich."

STORIES

Narrative Parenting

One day, when my Raffi was three, I was taking my three small children to the doctor's office for their annual check-ups. We had to cross a busy street and Raffi impulsively dashed into the street, right in the lane of an oncoming car.

"Raffi! Stop!" I shrieked.

He obeyed, freezing within an inch of the car, whose driver had slammed on the brakes in the nick of time. I've told that story to Raffi many times over the years.

When I tell the story of Raffi almost getting run over in front of the doctor's office, I have a choice of how to present it. I could focus on why I didn't have a better grip on my three-year-old's hand as we crossed the street, or why he didn't have the sense not to dash into traffic. But the useful, relevant part of the story for Raffi as a small child was that he had listened so well. As I told him that story dozens of times over the years, it reinforced the message that good listening kept him alive.

The stories we tell our children are treasures that can help build a family. Stories can reinforce character and values, create bonding experiences, defuse tensions, normalize difficulties, inspire hope— the list of how valuable stories can be could go on and on. There are also stories to watch out for, stories that can undermine your family's well-being.

Stories are told already in our families, with and without intention. Children frequently hear our take on things, our interpretation and memory and selection of what to share. They internalize our worldviews from toddlerhood on. This information helps shape their self-image and lets them know what gives us pleasure, what interests us, what we value in our society. Since stories have a tremendous impact on growing children, this is a place where parents can bring consciousness and creativity.

I call this Narrative Parenting. You are creating a narrative that helps your kids make sense of their lives. The term Narrative Parenting came from studying storytelling in other fields, namely theology and family therapy.

When I was in seminary I learned about a way of talking about God that wasn't based on intellectual analysis and logical consistency. This approach to God was about experiencing God's presence and sharing those experiences. In seminary we all wrote spiritual autobiographies, asking the question, "Where have I experienced God in my life?"

Many of our autobiographies barely mentioned God. Instead, they were about nature and family, birth and death, transcendence and social justice. For many students, God was present in these experiences. This approach to theology, called Narrative Theology, made sense to us.

A few years later, studying family therapy, I learned about two New Zealand family therapists, Michael White and David Epston, who developed a method of working with individuals and families called Narrative Therapy. They noticed that their clients were coming to sessions with a problem encapsulated in a story about the problem. For instance, a parent might say, "Nine times out of ten, Johnny has a tantrum when he doesn't get what he wants." Narrative therapists listen carefully to the story told by the family, listening between the lines for different ways of telling the story that could lead to change. The therapists want to hear about the exception—the tenth time, when Johnny manages not to have a tantrum. What was different that time? And how can the family build on that success?

Just this week, I had a couple in my office telling me, "We only had one good conversation in the whole week." We spent the rest of the session talking about what they learned from the successful experience of that one good conversation. Who was able to initiate and how did they do it in a way that elicited responsiveness? Who was able to be responsive and how did that feel? Where could they apply this new information about successful conversations to make their conversations go better more often? We all learned a lot from exploring more deeply what worked instead of getting stuck in the problem story.

Parenting is a realm that can use good storytelling just as much as the realms of theology and therapy. Narrative Parenting is the art of using stories to help raise good human beings. By stories, I really mean every word that comes out of a parent's mouth, because knowingly or not, our words become stories in our kids' minds.

Through our own words, we are implanting a literature full of dialogue, morals and punchlines within our young ones. The more intentional we are about what we say, the more freedom we have to implant the stories we actually mean to give to our kids. You don't have to be a theologian or a therapist to embrace the idea that what we say to our kids matters.

When and Where

Narrative Parenting happens whenever we directly or indirectly tell a story that our children hear. Stories are told during car rides, at bedtime, the dinner table, overheard phone conversations, fireside chats with grandparents, ritual moments such as birthdays, confirmations or weddings. We are already doing Narrative Parenting whenever we talk, so we might as well craft stories to highlight character strengths and possibilities, human resilience and responsibility.

Choosing Usable Stories

In choosing what stories to tell, we have an opportunity to think about the messages we want to convey. What part of the story is useful? Historians talk about recounting a "usable past," not just every detail of whatever happened in the past. In thousands of years of history, so many things happened: people woke up and built fires and harvested food and signed treaties and invented technology and baked bread and discovered new territories and raised children and stitched clothes and had wars; how does one choose how and what to tell about what happened in history?

To make sense of the endless data of history, historians explore themes and patterns that are relevant to life today. They select their material based on what will be helpful, usable and relevant to us today. Like historians, we parents mine our own experiences and education to construct a "usable past"—a relevant story, for our own children. I imagine most of us have a good sense of what is useful and relevant to our particular child. Does this child need to stand up for himself more? Does this child need to think through the consequences of an action? Would this child benefit from seeing that she is a valued friend? Would it be helpful for this child to see that all human beings make mistakes, and that we recover and move on?

We have a wealth of sources for stories. We can tell stories of family lore—every family has such stories—or make up our own creative stories, which gives us the opportunity to tweak the characters and plot for strengthening qualities in our own child that we want to encourage. We can also choose story recordings such as Books on Tape that have both interest and value for our families.

Stories about Real Life

My friend Moon described an upsetting experience to our women's group one evening. Moon had been sitting at her kitchen table, drinking from a mug of hot tea with her new daughter Mira on her lap. Mira must have been about eight months old, recently brought home from China. Suddenly, Mira's little baby hand grabbed the hot mug, splashing scalding tea on her tender skin. Moon was awash with guilt. This infant had been entrusted to her for life and already she had allowed the baby to be injured. We listened to Moon's feelings, comforted her and then started talking about how to tell this story, especially in years to come, when this might be a story that little Mira would hear. Was the core of the story a neglectful mother allowing her child to grab a mug of hot tea resulting in burning a baby? Or was the core of the story a mother who quickly responded to her baby, called the doctor, learned that infants develop new skills every minute, grew with her baby, understood that accidents happen and didn't lose faith in her ability to be a good parent?

Parents have the opportunity to pay attention to what we are communicating in our stories. When we tell stories about painful parts of history, whether it is personal history or political history, we can lift up elements of kindness, courage, and justice. We need to think about what message we want to share and make sure we're sharing that message. The difference between random story-sharing and excellent Narrative Parenting is our own consciousness as leaders.

Stories that Help or Harm

Even though I surrounded my little children with all kinds of diverse families, much of the classic literature for very young children, especially in Rosi's early years, portrayed heterosexual nuclear families as the norm. By the time Rosi was two, she was projecting a heterosexual nuclear family onto her universe—a family that was very different from the single-parent family with donor in the background that was hers.

"This is the Daddy block and this is the Mommy block," Rosi explained to me as she played.

While visiting the Natural History Museum with her same-age cousin, Lindsay, whose Dad "is in heaven," I watched the two girls with solo Moms run through the exhibits saying, "That's the Daddy gorilla; that's the Mommy gorilla. That's the Daddy elk; that's the Mommy elk." I was pretty sure these animals did not live in nuclear families and I was absolutely certain that Rosi's play blocks did not come in gendered and mated sets of two.

I was concerned about how Rosi was making sense of the discrepancy between her family and the families she saw in children's books. It felt like the dominant culture was undermining my parenting choices, and making my daughter feel that her different-looking family wasn't "normal." I told myself that on the positive side, Rosi was learning a useful language that would help her social life, since so many preschoolers start their make-believe games with, "This is the Mommy; this is the Daddy." The words were a kind of formula that initiated play, and she had mastered the formula.

When she was a little older, we encountered another set of stories that worried me. Rosi went to Jewish religious school where she was taught the classic stories attached to Jewish holidays. First there was the Hanukah story, with the bad king Antiochus who wanted to hurt the Jews; then the Purim story, with the bad king Ahashverosh whose evil prime minister wanted to hurt the Jews; and finally the Passover story, with the bad king Pharoah who wanted to hurt the Jews. I was alarmed at the way all these stories made the world seem like an unsafe, hostile place for Jewish people. I didn't want Rosi to grow up feeling like a victim. In the same way that I had to wrestle with exposing my kids to classic sexist stories such as The Three Bears—Papa Bear with his great big voice, Mama Bear with her medium voice, and Baby Bear with a little tiny voice—I struggled to find value in the stories of our religious tradition. On the one hand, I didn't want to shield my child so much that she was unaware of standard cultural stories; on the other hand, I sure didn't love a lot of those stories.

Being playful with the stories helped some. We could tell the Three Bears with the Mama Bear coming in the door first, then Papa Bear, then Baby Bear. We could mix it up a little, change the power dynamics. With the religious stories we could amplify the courage and heroism of the characters who stood up to the bad guys—Queen Vashti, Queen Esther, and the Egyptian princess, Batya who rescued Moses as he floated down the Nile.

Eventually, I came to feel more comfortable with classic stories about horrible things happening to the Jews. I saw them as inoculations, preparing my kids to cope when bad things actually do happen. Now the kids would have story templates planted within: "Yeah, bad things can happen in the world and the good news is here we are and all is well." The bad-king stories prepare kids for bad things that do happen sometimes, and I hope they instill a sense of resilience rather than paranoia.

The biblical tradition, in addition to having a bunch of bad kings, also holds positive stories of adoption, blended families and triumph over family troubles. The story of baby Moses is one of the best adoption stories around: his birth mother, Yocheved made a plan to keep him safe; his forever–mother, Princess Batya, raised him in the palace. He actually spent his first years with his birth mother acting as a wet nurse and his forever mother as parent. Because of this, Moses knew his roots as a Hebrew and also had a taste of privilege in the palace. From these two heritages, Moses was able to become a great freedom fighter.

Sometimes it's possible to use disgustingly violent or sexist stories as jumping off points for bigger discussions. "What did you think about the way so and so was treated in the movie?" But I think the culture offers way more of this kind of entertainment than is healthy for growing young people. As long as you can reasonably shield your child from some of the garbage in the entertainment world, you might as well take the opportunity to do so. By the time you have teenagers, you may need to make more compromises rather than engage in a censorship battle.

Stories Not to Tell

We shape our children through our stories whether we intend to or not. Even very young children listen to the stories we tell about them and internalize self-image from our stories. From the time a baby is 18 months old, we need to be aware of telling negative stories about him—how he refuses to go to bed or what a terror he is with the dog. He is learning who he is and he's learning what kind of behavior elicits our interest, if not our pleasure. When we repeat a story about his misbehavior or difficult traits, those little ears are soaking it up and believing it.

"I'm really worried about his language development."

"My partner has no idea what he's doing with the kids."

"She'll probably grow up to be a prostitute."

Kids listen to the stories we tell about other family members and about other people and absorb messages we don't necessarily intend for them. I was surprised to learn that Rosi felt pressured to be perfect when she heard me telling stories about the incompetent insurance agent or "low-IQ" sales clerk. When I really thought about it, I wasn't speaking with much tolerance or compassion. I could understand how she would feel bathed in judgmental expectations even though I had no intention of judging or pressuring her.

We might also think twice about talking to a friend on the phone within our child's earshot about how awful it is to deal with the "ex," or how we don't trust the day care center. Stories can build compassion, confidence and wisdom, or they can implant worry, confusion and self-doubt.

Whenever my kids are within earshot, everything I say I try to say with awareness of their presence, their receptive ears and fertile sense of self. Grownup conversation and jokes are for grownups and it's important to shield kids from those confusing messages that can be misunderstood.

One day, Max who was an intelligent middle-school child with delayed self–control, saw a baby squirrel on the lawn and without thinking he grabbed it by the tail. The squirrel immediately sunk its teeth into Max's finger. It was quite a sight to see Max swinging the squirrel around and around, trying to get it off his finger. The episode ended with the squirrel being bashed to death and its brains taken to a lab for a rabies test. Max told the story again and again at every family gathering for weeks after. He was rewarded with tons of interest and attention for the sad, irresponsible behavior that a conscious parent would not choose to reinforce.

Yet, the experience had also been traumatic for Max, and sharing traumatic experiences can be healing. One sentence offered by the parent at the end of every story would have made a huge difference. Max might even have internalized the sentence and started offering it himself. "And that's how Max learned never to grab a wild animal." When we pay attention, we can edit our kids' inadvertent negative narratives.

Probably a lot of us have similar, if not quite as dramatic stories. When I was 10, I visited neighbors who had a parrot. The neighbors warned, "Don't stick your finger in the cage; the parrot might bite." I stuck my finger in the cage and the parrot did bite. Maybe the moral of the story for me was that there were certain things I had to discover for myself, even when grown ups were there to give advice.

"Head Stories"

My Dad used to tell my sisters and me spy stories. We lived in the Cold War era when the news was filled with constant scheming between the United States and the Soviet Union. In my family we called creative, make-believe tales "head stories," because they were spun from someone's imagination.

Dad would gather his batch of little girls onto the sofa and regale us with made-up tales of the preposterous characters Bugspray Pictureframe, Dirty Underpants and Stinky Armpit. These guys rivaled the intrigue of the most talented real-life spies. I don't know if my Dad intended to play lightly with the tension people lived with under the threat of nuclear holocaust and the potential destruction of life on Earth, but the stories had the effect of taking current events—which we children might not have even known about in detail, but which infused our atmosphere—and making them fun and playful. The last such story was told when I was about 11, and I remember them all with delight.

Treasure Cup stories were a highlight of my kids' childhoods. Rosi, Raffi and Zoe were the heroes and heroines of these stories, which involved a secret chalice that was kept hidden in Grandmother Polly's creek at her farm. In the story, wherever they were, the three kids could hold hands and call the cup to them: "Treasure Cup! Treasure Cup! Come to us. Treasure Cup! Treasure Cup! Come to us." Then they could choose a place for the cup to take them, and in that place they usually had to solve a problem.

I made up the stories off the top of my head as I drove on long car rides, but I had some parenting considerations that I wove into them. Cooperation among the three kids drove the action—they called the cup together, they had to agree on a place to go or agree on how to take turns choosing different destinations. Sibling rivalry was explored, problem-solving modeled and co-operation rewarded in my stories.

If I felt that Zoe, the youngest of the first three kids, wasn't being listened to enough, in my story it would be Zoe's idea that saved the day. Only when the fictional Rosi and fictional Raffi listened to her was the story's problem resolved. If I thought Raffi was feeling left out in real life, a Treasure Cup story would have him playing separately and the others begging him to join them for a Treasure Cup adventure.

The stories were interactive and involved a certain amount of choice for the listeners. The kids in the story travelled on a mattress that flew high in the sky. As they relaxed on the comfy mattress they could conjure up whatever food or drink they wanted. Each child would order their delicacies, and into the story these choices would go. "Would you rather deal with a flood or a forest fire today?" "Would you rather help find a lost child or get food to hungry people?"

For years, walking Joey to preschool and then elementary school, I told Joey "Johnny Bat" stories. My real life Joey was an adorable young guy who had a hard time managing his impulsivity. The fictional Johnny Bat was a little black bat who encountered one situation after the next in which he made mistakes as a result of his lack of self–management. But then he had a second chance and managed better the second time.

In each Johnny Bat story there were two parts. First there would be a recounting of the trouble Johnny Bat got into. Then he would experience the same situation or choice again and the second time he would handle it well by making better choices. In one story, Johnny Bat gobbled up the fruit the family was saving for dessert and then the second time around he remembered to wait to save the fruit for dessert. In another story, Johnny Bat played with his sister's forbidden toy and accidentally broke it; but the second time he stopped himself from taking her toy and was pleased to be invited to play with her and the toy later. Once, Johnny Bat kept playing outside when he was supposed to fly into the cave for bedtime, but the next time he had a chance to do it right.

Young children are forgiving listeners. Our stories need to have a certain amount of engaging drama and maybe even silliness, but they don't have to be strong on plot or craft. I stopped telling my own stories to my kids when they reached the age of critical analysis, probably around 10 years old. I wanted them to remember these childhood stories fondly and without mockery.

Redemptive Stories

The best stories have some redemptive element that offers hope or resolution or justice. They may be complex, messy, realistic or cryptic, but they should be more than bleak renditions of distress. What's the point of creating a story if you aren't going to add the intelligent human concept of redemption? Life can be harsh, and I believe the purpose of a story is to provide support to human beings living it. The support comes in the form of message such as:

"Lots of people go through these things."

"We're all in this together."

"You never know what the outcome will be."

"You have choices."

"There is love in the world."

"Things will turn out okay." Even a story that conveys "I care about you so here's what not to do in life," has that redemptive message. We're telling each other to live and learn, and reassuring one another that, like Johnny Bat, we can do it better.

Some stories help give kids perspective. Experiences that aren't actually fun when they are happening can become important stories: the time the car broke down a few hours from home on a dark road in the middle of a dark night before we had cell phones. Or the time the dog disappeared and was found hours later, after frantic searching. Or the time we had no heat or electricity for three weeks in the middle of the winter.

"Remember the time we drove ten hours to the Outer Banks and then Hurricane Felix came along and we had to evacuate the next day?"

"Yeah, remember the 19-hour traffic jam?"

"I remember taking a wrong turn off the highway and being so proud of myself for figuring out the mistake after only an hour. I could have driven all the way to California by mistake!"

"Remember when Lindsay threw up all over the car seat?"

Stories like these, fashioned from normal life hardships, teach courage, resilience, problem solving and humor. In retrospect, it's possible to open up the original experience, give it a larger framework and find meaning in it that might have been elusive during the actual moments of stress, whether it was a flat tire or chemo, grieving at a funeral or enduring some other difficult experience.

In addition to giving perspective, stories can connect the past and present in meaningful ways.

"You are so good with animals. I imagine your birth parents must have had a gentle touch with animals."

"Your ancestors were brave pioneers and you've inherited that quality."

When Raffi calls from college feeling overwhelmed about a looming deadline for a 20-page paper, he tells me, "I feel stuck. I feel like I've bumped up against a wall and I just don't know how to reach my goal. I'm so stressed out." I recall for him the story of a past success on a different playing field.

"Raffi, I'm picturing how you play Ultimate Frisbee. You just find a way past all the defenders and get that Frisbee to the end zone. It's awesome! I think you'll find a way through these academic obstacles, too."

Not only can stories lift up experience into a bigger realm of values, connection and human understanding, stories can also plant seeds for the future.

"You love banging on the kitchen pots. Maybe when you're bigger you'll get to play a musical instrument."

"I saw how you taught the little kids that ball game. I could imagine you being a gym teacher when you grow up."

"Wow, you solved my computer problem. Maybe you'll have a job someday being a technology inventor or fixer."

This linking of the present to the future is helpful in making the grown-up world not some unfathomable, mysterious challenge, but a continuation of what the child knows and does today.

One final way that stories are redemptive is in building a community of shared memory and meaning. Someone once told me that when she was a child her family was economically poor. They couldn't afford a lot of trips or cultural experiences. Their cousins grew up in a much more privileged life, always traveling somewhere or going off to camp or lessons. But when this observer looks back, she thinks her experiences were richer than the cousins' because of how her family processed them. Even an overnight in a state park became a shared family story. Lingering over memories, reflecting and re-telling, extends the experience itself and builds community through shared memory.

Redemptive stories give perspective, find meaning in adversity, plant seeds for the future and build community through memory. These stories enhance our lives by bolstering human compassion, optimism, humor and hope. They are stories to grow on.

Collective Stories

When I was eight years old, in 1965, my family moved to Mississippi to take part in the Civil Rights Movement. For two years we were part of a dramatic, intense fight for freedom. These powerful, formative experiences became a significant part of the family lore. After those two years, we moved back to Washington D.C., and my mother decided to add a child to our family. (These days we would call Gwen's father a "donor," as there never was a plan for him to stay in the picture.)

My little sister Gwen was born in 1968, a year after our return from Mississippi. That did not stop Gwen, as she grew older, from claiming our family's civil rights experience, which had become an essential theme of the family that shaped our family's identity. Gwen had never been to Mississippi, yet she inherited memories and stories so that she frequently said in her growing-up years, "When we were in Mississippi."

Taking on the stories of your people reminds me of the way Jewish people talk during Passover, saying, "When we were in slaves to Pharoah in the land of Egypt." Being in Egypt and participating in the liberating exodus from Egypt were life-changing themes for the Jewish people, which became the greatest freedom story ever told. The biblical book of Exodus describes the miracle and events of that liberation. People around the world who experience oppression—from African slaves in the U.S. South or Tibetans oppressed by China—have used this story to express their own freedom struggles. "When we were slaves to Pharoah in the land of Egypt," is an important marker of Jewish identity, one that reminds us to care for the stranger who may be a poor person today or an immigrant or even someone who is a bit strange to us.

Not even all the Israelites who lived at the time of the Exodus events experienced it in the same way. Some of them had never gone into Egypt in the first place and some of them never left Egypt in the Exodus, choosing to stay behind. Nevertheless, the story of leaving Egypt became the personal creation myth of Jewish peoplehood, owned by all Jews, whether or not we were actually physically there or even alive in that generation. My sister Gwen was participating in the greater story of our family when she claimed Mississippi as part of her own personal story.

Both the mythic/historic narrative of a people and personal historical narrative are important. Hearing stories from grandparents about their lives and times is such a valuable inheritance for children. Grandparent stories root them in time, give them a longer view to which they feel connected. The story of a child's family's past, going back a few generations, is important. If there are no grandparents alive or nearby, maybe it's possible to find some elders in the community with whom they can forge real relationships, elders who share something in common with your family such as being immigrants or being members of the same church/synagogue/mosque or living in the same neighborhood.

My grandmother Piggy (her name was derived from a young niece's inability to pronounce "Peggy") told me stories of her personal heroes: Sigmund Freud, Carl Jung, and John Dewey. Their teachings shaped Piggy's life in Greenwich Village in the '20s and influenced her in her life's work, which was the field of progressive education. She talked to me about being a socialist and traveling through revolutionary Soviet Union to learn about new ways of organizing a society. I felt rooted in recent history when she told her stories to me.

Connecting kids to our own stories gives them a personal history. Where did you come from? What have you been through? What events were memorable turning points? Kids will be interested in things such as (if we are partnered) how did we meet? How did we decide where to live? As a single Mom it was important for me that my kids hear these types of traditional partnering stories from others, since I didn't have one to tell. I wanted my kids to internalize a range of partnering possibilities. Sometimes I'd ask my kids' aunts and uncles to tell stories about their courtships.

An even bigger story of humanity also helps us live our lives well, which is why great literature, television and film can be an important part of civilization. I wish my kids lived with Bible stories in the same intimate, passionate way they live with Harry Potter or *Star Trek*. Popular culture has much more of a social grip on their interests, I suppose because it's promoted and hyped in a way the Bible isn't. Imagine if each Bible chapter had a multi-million-dollar publicity campaign and a national conversation surrounding it? But then I think of how oppressive this norm would be for minorities from non-biblical traditions and I understand why the "dream of a common language," as the poet Adrienne Rich called it, is problematic.

Our own society is in flux right now, not having a single shared story because the story we thought we shared turned out to be Western-centric, and biased toward white, heterosexual males. Now a diversity of stories is radically more inclusive, but there is no longer a canon that every educated person perpetuates. (Zoe is telling me there is still a canon, only now it is more accurately referred to as "The Western Canon.")

Still, literature, both biblical and non-biblical, opens doors for young people and reading aloud together is a wonderful family activity, even after all members of the family know how to read and could take a book off to a corner by themselves. Children's librarians in the public library are terrific resources for finding books that will interest the individuals in your family. As you read together, you can use what you read in your parenting.

Stories that Make Parenting Easier

I read my younger kids all the Miss Piggle Wiggle books, marvelous stories about an eccentric wise woman who helps kids overcome problems. In one story, a little girl has a problem with sassiness, always talking back. "I'm not gonna do it; you can't make me!" Miss Piggle Wiggle applies the solution of giving her a parrot who mimics her until she improves her language.

When my Mozi reacts to routine parental comments with opposition, "No, I don't want to clean my room," or "No, I'm not going to take a bath," I tell her I'm going to give her a parrot.

"But I like parrots," she says.

"Yeah, but you wouldn't like to clean up after it."

Now we are joking about parrots rather than antagonizing each other.

Having read *Little House on the Prairie* together, when it's cold outside we tell each other, "At least it's not minus 30 degrees and you have only your long underwear and feather quilt to keep you warm."

The Maurice Sendak story-rhyme about Pierre whose constant refrain is "I don't care," has served my family well by helping us turn conflicts into poetry.

"Rosi, we have to get the art project off the table 'cause we're having guests for dinner."

"I don't care," says eight-year-old Rosi, who is engaged in gluing little wooden sticks to a cork structure she has created. "I don't care."

"Then you're Pierre," I say lightly as I help her safely move the project.

Our mini conflict of needs has been elevated and is now framed by an understanding that "these things happen to people," parents and children don't always see eye to eye.

When I studied the Bible and other ancient religious texts as a young woman, most of the stories were told by men, about men and for men. Struggling to find a place for myself in this tradition, I embraced a wonderful Hassidic teaching about the black letters of the Bible, which are written on the blank white space of the parchment. The black letters represent what has already been revealed while the white spaces represent the canvas upon which we write the unfolding stories of our own lives. We are writing the texts with our own evolving lives.

As we write these life texts, none of us really lives just in the moment. We are repositories of a wealth of experience and we hold within us seeds of great potential. Our choice is how to articulate this past, present and future with consciousness for our kids. Parents get to help link the past, present and future through intentional storytelling. Our Narrative Parenting is a formative and meaningful way to help kids make sense of their worlds.

A life skill that many of us parents want to impart to kids is to be able to find the silver lining in life, to have a positive outlook. Literature of all kinds, whether classic or homespun, can point our kids in the direction of creative coping and enjoyment in life. We are in a position to help our kids see the world as a place of promise and our human journey as one of growth in awareness and competence. When our stories for children incorporate themes of hope, problem-solving, acceptance, connection and forgivingness we launch human beings into the world prepared to make it a good place.

RELATIONSHIP

Partnering

"I wonder if you would be interested in adding one more child to this family with me as the donor and the Dad."

Len and I were standing back-to-back in my sunny, cluttered kitchen as I washed Passover dishes and he returned them to a high shelf for next year's rites of spring.

Len was in his forties, almost seven years older than me. Physically fit, with a rainbow *kipah* atop a head of long grey ringlets, he had come to learn in the Jewish Renewal Life Center, the program that I founded and directed to immerse spiritual seekers in living Judaism. Having experienced the best that gay male life had to offer, he literally gave everything away and came to Philadelphia for a year of immersion in Jewish spirituality.

"Been there, done that," he told me about his previous life. Now he was seeking God.

By then I had had three children with my two wonderful known donors and I had recovered from mourning the miscarriage with the other donor and decided to adopt. My relationship with Rebecca in its primary partner-lover stage had ended, and as I emerged from that sorrowful time, the idea of adopting a fourth child seeded new hope and excitement. My kids were 10, 8, and 6 and I was in the final stages of bringing the new baby into the family. The time frame of international adoption was so variable that I hadn't been very public about my plan. I didn't want the world talking to my kids about it before anything definitive was in place.

Standing in the kitchen that day, I took in Len's question about becoming a donor and a Dad in this family and I told him about the baby about to arrive. He and I had had fun taking the kids to climb trees behind Philadelphia's Art Museum, and another time visiting the cherry blossoms in the nation's capital. When I told him about the new baby about to arrive, he maintained his interest in moving into deeper connection with my family and I was intrigued.

Soon after, as his year at the Life Center came to an end, Len needed a place to live. We began to talk about him renting a room in my apartment. We barely knew each other, but I felt my heart's desire begin to intermingle with his—he reaching for family and I welcoming a potential best friend in parenting. Something I had not sought before, a potential parenting partner, felt right at that time. Saying yes to Len living with us was an experiment in my mind.

I thought we were moving slowly. I didn't make any promises and couldn't yet answer his question about becoming a Dad to my children. I thought we could live together, see how it went, and not jump to naming anything. Working on expanding the family through adoption opened me to considering adding a Dad as well. My babies who would come into the family by adoption would have lost their birth-parents and birth culture and I liked the idea of growing additional family connections for them and for all of us. I thought there would be ample time for discussions and decisions with Len down the line. Sometimes you just open your heart to saying Yes to what life presents and I responded to Len with that instinct.

I brought baby Joey home days after the Life Center year ended and Len moved in. All of a sudden we were caring for a darling toddler together. Joey wobbled around the living room, practicing first steps as Len and I, surrounded by four kids, quickly stepped far beyond that first tentative landlord-tenant agreement.

Caring for a baby together was an astonishingly intimate experience for me. Never had anyone other than me taken one of my kids to a doctor's appointment. Having another adult cook dinner for us in our own home was remarkable. (I cooked broccoli every single night. The first time Len cooked dinner for the family, there was no broccoli. The puzzled kids asked, "No broccoli for dinner?") The act of passing the baby bottle back and forth as we handed over the child felt wondrous to me. The wonder had to do with this other adult, who was not being paid and who had no formal reason for being there, who was joining me in the care of this precious new family member.

As Len and I opened to the possibility of making family together, internalized hetero-normativity pressured all of us into certain assumptions; from a hetero-patriarchal perspective, didn't every single Mom have an empty space at her side for a Dad/mate? The kids, young as they were, and I, had inevitably absorbed the model of Papa and Mama and baby makes a family even though that model wasn't the model of our own lives. One day Rosi was looking at a picture in a magazine of a Mom, a Dad and some kids and she said, "This looks like our family."

"How is it like our family?" I asked curiously.

"Here's the Mom. Here's the Donor. And here are the kids," she said.

"What about our other donor and our birthparents?" I asked. We just couldn't be crammed into a standard format.

Now Rosi suggested "Len can be the Daddy!" That seemed intriguing to her until she noticed the ways that family life was changing with Len's presence. Len and I engaged in adult conversation, sometimes he wanted to make decisions about things or had needs to add to the mix of our complex dynamics. As Rosi's enthusiasm diminished for a Dad-like person's presence in the family, I noticed another issue specific to first-born kids that might have been operative. From being a first-born child myself, I could understand the tendency for an oldest child to feel like the partner of a single parent even when the parent does not see the child in that role. When the parent has a real, live adult partner, the first-born child can feel usurped. As a Single Mom committed to very primary relationships with my kids, I also wondered what Len's role could be in our family.

At Joey's baby naming ceremony, with my blessing, Len read a short piece he had written, asking, "Am I this baby's Daddy?" We had no plan about what was unfolding, only a willingness. Later, my sisters were mad at me for not letting them know about the onset of an important new relationship in my life. But to tell the truth, I was making moment-by-moment decisions as possibilities unfolded and I myself did not know where we were going.

Although single parenting had been an extremely positive experience for me, I was grateful to have another care-giving adult in the house. His presence made possible many more "Second Adult Phenomena," such as having extra time to attend to my older children even as we integrated the baby into the family. With Len's help, I was able to continue to spend a few minutes alone with each child every day and a block of time, eagerly known by the kids as "Private Time," with each child one-on-one every week. I liked having a new friend who was also attending to this family's life.

My priority for the year was integrating relationships, especially weaving this new baby into our web of family relationships, and attending to each child emotionally as we moved forward. My priority was not the dishes, the toys, or the laundry on the floor. I even had an edge of testiness—could a new adult really handle my family life? With other kinds of helpers, such as babysitters, I tried to minimize the demands on them by having dinner all ready, or ordering in pizza so they wouldn't have to cook. I sometimes made play dates at someone else's house for one or more kids so the babysitter would have an easier task. They didn't really have to mastermind the show. But for better or worse, I didn't ease Len into the reality of family life in those ways. I needed to see whether he could really be present in this family's often messy, always lively life.

Managing family life was a constant act of triage, of choosing the absolute top priority for the next moment. Neat stacks of folded and sorted laundry that emanate domestic order do have an appeal for me but they just weren't at the top of my priority list. I had to earn money to support the family; buy groceries, haul them up to the apartment, put them away, cook food and feed the family, and then do the dishes. I counted as priorities giving calm attention to each child, planning necessary and festive events for the family, and enjoying them. In the face of all this, tasks like folding laundry sunk to the bottom of my To Do list.

I would wash and dry the clothes and then dump them in a clean heap from which each child transferred their own belongings into a heap in their own area. The kids and I didn't fold or sort or put clothes in drawers or closets. These happy heaps of clothes were certainly functional, if not traditional. Everyone had clean clothes to wear every day. But what felt like joyful family building to me looked like physical chaos to Len.

At first, Len had no clue what it took to keep family life afloat. It was easy for him to be critical. I had no clue how chaotic it felt to him. It was easy for me to be unsympathetic. Neither of us had any way of communicating with the other about what was going on inside us even though the motivation to grow into family was strong.

We danced this dance of early family making without finding a way to talk about it. We were two very, very different people who didn't know each other or our own selves well enough. We had completely different assumptions, but didn't even realize how different our expectations and perceptions were. We had no language for communicating, and stumbled along through trial and error. It was as though he spoke

Ugaritic and I spoke Banshee. His was a language of deeds: "Who else's kitchen floor would I wash? Of course I'm committed!" I craved a language of process: "How can we co-create a life together if we never discuss it?"

Amazingly, Len and I persisted, growing in forgiveness, trust and our ability to cherish each other. After that first year, he sobbed in my arms, "I can't do this." It wasn't clear exactly what he was saying he couldn't do, but I was glad in the moment for the authentic connection, even if the content of what he was saying was an ending.

We separated for two years. I didn't yet have big expectations of who we were to each other or how long our relationship would last—our platonic partnership truly felt experimental to me. So now I easily single parented again, he lived in a tent in a meadow in a different state, meditating, reflecting and earning his keep by working at a retreat center. I made sure the kids saw him periodically, but we were not in close touch. The older kids were used to having housemates live with us for a period of time who then moved on so it wasn't unusual to them that Len was gone. We'd had Sarah when Rosi was a baby, then my sister Miggie for three years, then there had been a Life Center student named Ellen for a year, and Life Center graduates Karen and Reuben each for a summer. To me though, there was too much unexplored potential in Len's question about being a Daddy for our journey to be finished.

One Monday, three-year-old Joey ran a high fever. Zoe was bursting with anticipation over my promise to chaperone her third-grade class to the ballet the next day. Torn between needing to care for little Joey and not wanting to disappoint Zoe, I called Len at the retreat center four hours away. We hadn't talked in months, but on hearing my need, he said, "I'm in the car," and he arrived four hours later.

Joey lay in bed, limp and burning up. The dramatic evidence of his illness was good for Len to see because it would have been hard for him to believe that the child had been sick the next morning, when

Joey had bounced up, raring to go and racing around the house with supersonic energy.

I had asked for help and Len had responded gallantly. The incident re-opened my willingness to connect.

Three years after Len had first asked about being part of this family, when Joey was four, I answered his question—"Yes, you can be the Daddy for Joey." I asked him if he'd like to join me in raising another baby. He'd join the family as a significant person to each member. He said yes and I started the adoption process to bring Mozi home.

Our original parenting agreement was a rudimentary verbal construct. We agreed on three things, with no details explicated: I would be the primary parent including having full custody and all responsibility. He would be called Daddy. We would share the adoption debt. We optimistically called ourselves Parenting Partners. Every one of our agreements morphed and developed way beyond our original words, not in any linear or graceful progression, but with multiple lurches and detours. What was exciting to me was trying to build a new family relationship that was loving, growing, and fulfilling even though it did not follow a standard model.

As Len and I moved into a deeper, albeit undefined, connection, primal issues for both of us ignited. Now I did have expectations and therefore disappointments. I found myself acutely sensitive to his emotional absences. I lived in the rhythm of his feast or famine cycles, soaking up his attention when it was available and pining for it when he disappeared for weeks on end. I marvel now at how I, a person who had lived so happily as a single woman for so long, suddenly felt the most intense loneliness I've ever felt. I did not want to be romantic with Len. I wanted the kind of best friendship that is so common in the lesbian world and I did not realize how hard this would be to develop with this celibate, gay man who came from a different world.

The positive side of my yearning was a deep willingness towards sharing myself and my family with Len. I was proud of myself for letting this man into our lives. I had to ask myself, as perhaps one does at the beginning of any major relationship, if I was brave enough to risk having my heart broken. As a fierce mother lioness, was I willing to offer up the tender hearts of my young ones? I watched carefully, registering that Len caringly built a relationship with each child in the family, not just with one or two. I was definitely not willing to sacrifice the well-being of any of my children in exchange for having a man in the house.

Without some kind of primal emotional bonding, it was clear to me that a person does not become a family member. I had lots of helpers during those years, often bartering to meet the family's needs: babysitters, roommates, family friends, grandparents, house cleaners, carpool drivers, the kids' teachers and coaches, the building superintendent who did repairs around the house. What made someone a Parenting Partner?

We weren't trying to be a couple, but it wasn't clear how to be family without something pretty emotionally intense happening. The emotional quality of our partnership was couple-like. Neither of us had other lovers. He had chosen a path of celibacy long before he met me and I was in no significant sexual relationship when I met him. Despite our mutual motivation, and our alternative structure, we faced many of the same challenges to intimacy that "typical" couples face: different expectations, different assumptions, different styles.

He would say, "I get so angry about the socks. I'm just not that evolved. It's the heap of mismatched socks that gets me."

"It's just you and me, each of us fragile and vulnerable doing the best we can. I'm not any more evolved than you."

"You're not? Uh-oh."

"That's why the Bible teaches that the teaching is not out there in the heavens or far away across the sea. It's right here in our mouths, in our hands. It's in the socks."

I was trying to reference our shared holy text, a resource we both valued, but he just thought, understandably, that I was preaching.

I tried to explain how I see parenting as consisting of three components: nurturing the children; funding the family; and making executive decisions about things like schools, play dates, household rules. I considered us to be Parenting Partners in name only because neither of us knew how to partner and he was just growing into the role of parent. I grandly graced him with the title "Parenting Partner" even though I didn't see him as a full parent or as my partner. My question was could we grow into the title we were generously using? Could we really become Parenting Partners, inventing what that meant even as we tried to do it well?

Both of our visions, while un-discussed, seemed to be bigger than our initial agreement. I was frustrated that he thought of himself as a Daddy, but wouldn't join me in the parts of parenting that were bigger than childcare, such as thinking about schools, managing the kids' living space and paying bills. Yet paradoxically, he felt left out, as I learned much later—marginal, like I didn't make room for him to be fully a part of the family. Did he assume that I would hand the kids over to him, a relative stranger, and immediately share my power with him as instant parent? I needed us to grow together.

Our original covenant, such as it was, did not give any detail as to how we would negotiate these issues. Our basic agreement did not state that we would even share decision making or financing, other than paying back the adoption debt. The term Daddy was undefined and could mean anything from a mere title to a life-long Nurturer-Provider-Executive Decision Maker. I wanted to talk about all this, but he interpreted my need to talk as a critical message to him that he needed training in parenting. I was incensed that he wouldn't let me share my feelings and ideas.

So many of us, me included, never had the model of our parents' successful relationships from which to learn. My parents were unable to give me this. They were married for 11 years, in their very early twenties, during which time they had four children. They gave me many, many gifts, but staying in an adult love relationship with each other was not one of them. As Rabbi Goldie Milgram points out, "We are all intimacy challenged."

As is typically the case in relationships, seeing Len's disabilities was so much easier for me than seeing my own limitations. I couldn't find a way to communicate my desires, ideas or needs in a way that could be heard by him—everything I tried bashed into a wall of hurt or offense on his part. I couldn't find a way to create the safety he needed for him to share his inner life and he was unable to guide me. We were in a relationship where the rules were unwritten. We both wondered, "What is this relationship anyway?" It wasn't a marriage, we weren't lovers, we had no written agreement or formal commitment, and he wasn't biologically or legally connected to any of us. Did I even have a right to expect anything at all of a Parenting Partner? I did not like living in this limbo, where I felt I had no standing or right to need or expect anything; I had no place at the table to discuss my concerns and I hated having them dismissed at every turn. Yet there was also something that felt mighty good in the joining of our forces.

I wondered whether there was some way that I was unintentionally shoving him into the role of husband, someone who was supposed to partner me in a mutual way on emotional, psychological, economic and other fronts. That model of one partner being the be-all and end-all who can fulfill every need doesn't work for heterosexual marriage and it couldn't work for our alternative arrangement either. But how do you weave someone into a family—really become family together—without a deep emotional interconnection?

Now and then I'd come home to find that Len had cleaned the house. The kitchen sparkled, toys were stacked, once he adorned the table with purple tulips. I could call him on my way home to ask if he wanted his favorite Dunkin Donuts coffee. I could make sure he had three hours a day to be on his bike. Every day I felt that I was giving him the most precious gift of all: family. Each act of kindness seemed to multiply good will.

We were crafting a unique relationship focused on raising children, a relationship that felt like family, that was immensely supportive in many ways. Even though my friends asked how I could make a life with Len that did not include sex, this was not really my main question. Sexuality is such an important part of life but it doesn't necessarily have to be interactive and it may or may not be a part of relationships that are very primary. You can have an incredible sexual life with yourself (a truly undervalued kind of sexuality). I wasn't committing to excise sexuality from my life in its expressive, interpersonal forms so now and then I wondered what role I would create for sexuality in my life when so much of my energy was invested in a Parenting Partnership with this particular man.

I wished there were more stories of other people who walked their own non-traditional, creative paths before us. I did reach a depth of connection with Len that would naturally for me flow into touching, even lovemaking. When we were emotionally disconnected and not communicating well, touching would have been another pathway into honest encounter—a way in, like prayer, that can be beyond words. Yet in the Venn diagram of our lives, sex was not a place of overlap. I realized that I wanted connection with Len, but sex with Len was not at the heart of my primary desires.

Really what I craved most in the body realm was physical affection, such as hand holding, hugging and snuggling. Len and I were both free to have sex with other people if we chose to, although we were so engaged in family life with five children that time for that was scarce.

There were only a few times during these years that I was sexual with others and he maintained his celibacy. In a day to day way, wondering about the role of sexuality in our lives was a very background question while the foreground was incredibly rewarding daily, shared family life. The joy of raising a house full of kids filled me with such abundance and constantly called on me to grow new understandings of myself and of others. To encompass my love for Len, I no longer felt like "lesbian" was my only self-definition. I didn't love Len romantically, I loved him deeper than romance in some way, and "lesbian" felt like a part of my identity but no longer the whole of it.

"That's strange," 12-year-old Rosi pondered, bountiful dark curls spread over her pillow as I tucked her into bed, "Joey and Mozi have a gay Dad and a lesbian Mom."

"Well, Sweetie, " I said, holding my own new sense that being a lesbian is part—a proud part, but not the whole—of my love orientation, "We're a queer family." I tried that word, though I didn't love its sound. But I loved the concept behind it—the idea that we get to create lives that work for us, not lives that conform to a mold that might have worked for someone else. It's a case of life fluidly growing me into identity rather than identity defining life. Later, my kids would proudly embrace their own identity as "Queer Spawn."

Rosi swung like a pendulum from being the biggest advocate of Len as Daddy to being nastily resistant to him. I felt certain that my own solid relationship with Rosi would foster good family relationships as time passed. There was no one more precious to me on the face of the earth than my first-born child, my Rosi. Len was distressed by her behavior, which included a few stuck-out tongues and raised middle fingers. He wanted me to advocate for him, ally with him and confront Rosi. I took a more elastic approach, which was hard for him. I rode the waves of our collective of personalities, early on avoiding going up against Rosi. I trusted her to work through what was hard for her, which I imagine might have had something to do with an oldest child feeling displaced when a single Mom has a special friend.

After six months, when Rosi was becoming a young teenager with her own alluring social life, I had a heart-to-heart talk with her. I said, "Rosi, I think it's fair for me to get to have a friend and I really want you to support that, just like I support you having your friends." The developmental moment was right. Rosi was ready to hear me, and from then on she and Len have gotten along well. We had surmounted some of the hazards of a blended family.

In the months before Raffi's Bar Mitzvah, it became increasingly important to me for Len and me to clarify for ourselves who we were. At a Bar Mitzvah we would be presenting our family to the community, so who was he in our family? What message were we giving these children and also our community? Was Len a Daddy or was he a Nanny? He did lots of caretaking, but I didn't feel met by a peer who related to me through discussion, reflection, planning and problem solving. I continued to be solely responsible for all the expenses of family life. I wanted a steady-state connection with an adult partner—not one riddled with such a seemingly ambivalent quality of on-again, off-again. I felt like I was on a roller coaster surviving what felt to me like swings of his emotional presence and absence, his yearning for intimacy and avoidance of intimacy.

Confused, I asked him again and again to be part of a conversation with me about my concerns, but I couldn't engage him; to him I was "just a lesbian who wants to process all the time." Month after month went by without any discussion about issues of great concern to me. I tried repeatedly to raise my questions, with mounting frustration. To me he seemed distant, unconnected, shut down. I'm sure I seemed emotionally demanding to him. While I had helped scores of couples overcome this exact dynamic, whatever skill or wisdom I had was not welcome in my own relationship.

With the kids he was warm and constant, joking with each one individually, helping family life happen. We got through the Bar Mitzvah with flying colors. I carefully signed the invitation: "Julie, Rosi, Raffi, Zoe, Joey, Mozi and Len," not wanting to leave him out and having no idea or input from him on how best to include him.

Our inability to talk with each other was building into a crisis. Should I drastically change my expectations that we were parenting partners? What would this look like to the kids? Had I made a disastrous decision to bring this man so close to the heart of my family? I had especially given him to Mozi, the youngest, whose heart would be torn apart if she lost this man. I was torn apart knowing that I couldn't survive in this relationship as it stood, and yet I didn't want to disrupt the loving relationships the kids had evolved with him. I wrestled mightily with how to balance the conflicting needs of different family members.

I asked myself if I could find a place of freedom for myself in the relationship. When I feel my own personal agency, I suffer less and can be much more compassionate toward others. I wondered if I could gently shift my gaze without making a sudden move or obvious disruption. I needed to step away from what seemed like his sullen rage. I stopped trying to talk with him about things that I cared about, stopped trying to involve him in decisions about kids' schools or activities. I still suffered through his painful behavior with me, but I felt freer than I had when I wanted something that he couldn't or wouldn't give me. He wanted to be a parent, not a mate; but in this family the only invitation to be a parent required building a strong relationship with another parent. Little three-year-old Mozi suffered seeing the tension between us.

Years later I learned that during those difficult nine months, when Len seemed so totally shut down, he had tears behind his eyes at every moment. He was just trying to keep them in. He was living in his own world of pain and anger, neither of us able to reach or soothe the other.

What seemed to me to be coldness and hostility was the wall he had learned to build when he was overwhelmed or scared.

After nine months of my emotional shift away from this relationship, Len agreed that therapy could help us and I found a wise, older-woman therapist, probably in her eighties, who had an impressive resume of experience. Her wrinkles alone were enough to reassure us that we were in good hands. We used that sanctuary for years to learn how to enter the universe of the other. She provided a safe space where we could begin to share what was true with each other.

We were two "others" who had chosen each other for powerful reasons: we wanted to share love for the same children. We weren't soul mates. We weren't lovers. We didn't fit into a box called Marriage. We used the word Parenting Partner, but constantly bumped up against different desires and expectations about what that meant.

So who were we?

Slowly, wonderful interconnections grew. When Mozi arrived, Len had left his retreat center and moved a few blocks away from us. The kids could walk easily back and forth; we were in and out of each other's homes, communicating many times a day by text, e-mail and phone and spent time together many times a week. We learned to reconnect quickly after upsets, to make small *tikkuns* or corrections, to live with an attitude of forgivingness.

Especially as the mother of sons, I valued having a man with whom I could work through my own "man" stuff on an adult level, bypassing the unconscious proclivity to work it through on my male kids. My internalized sense that men were a bit fragile and maybe a bit misogynist and couldn't handle the full strength of a woman was now being challenged by Len. The pathetic idea that a man should mainly be a cash cow, a provider, rather than a caring nurturer and emotionally responsive peer, tainted my ability to see a male human clearly, much as I longed to relate to a transformed male. Here, in my adult relationship, in partnership with someone who was also growing and changing, maybe we could transform that corruption.

Moms benefit from focusing on these issues with another adult—a partner, a friend, a therapist, a sibling—so that our gender "shit" that we invariably carry as human beings in an imperfect society doesn't get dumped on the next generation. Single Moms need to make special efforts to find adult partners for parenting consultation because we don't have the natural opportunity over coffee every morning or on the shared pillow at night.

Len and I literally had to learn to feed each other. In the early years, he would cook food that seemed odd or incongruous to the family. He'd put tofu in the chili and served potato chips as the vegetable. I couldn't feed him, either. I knew he was a vegetarian, but had no idea that meat on the table grievously offended him. It took him years of silent suffering to let me know. I also couldn't tell him what I liked or wanted because he was so insecure feeding a whole family that he'd melt down. Maybe he became more confident as a parent; maybe I became more sensitive in talking to him. Somehow, we learned how to feed each other, which resulted in years of delicious, pleasing family meals.

I had to learn to stop blaming him and instead to take radical responsibility for having chosen him, exactly as he was, for my own deep, unconscious reasons. Not only did we both desire to build family, which was an obvious passionate point of joining, but also each of us had our own less obvious reasons for choosing the other.

From my childhood I had learned to be an extreme over-functioner, which meant that in choosing a partner to mesh with myself, the only choice had to be someone perceived by my unconscious self as an extreme under-functioner. That's what would allow me to feel "at home." So my loyal unconscious, entirely unbeknownst to me at the time, chose someone who would not threaten me even as my conscious frustration was that he wouldn't step powerfully into the partnership as an equal peer.

From my point of view, he wouldn't act like an adult with me and I was so darn frustrated about that. I had to learn that I had chosen him precisely because he didn't challenge my autonomy. I like a lot of freedom and a partner's intimacy-avoidance at least guaranteed me that, although it posed other intolerable problems. As my own understanding deepened, I realized that my struggle was between my own conscious self (wanting a peer) and unconscious self (wanting mainly to preserve my own empowerment) rather than between me and him. It's always helpful to find the work that is your own work, rather than the partner's, because then you actually have agency to do something about it. I was happy to understand my own choices and shadow sides better.

I imagine he had his own inner struggle between a desire to be a responsible, fully engaged Daddy and a total aversion to living the life of his own father, who had dropped dead of a heart attack, literally working himself to death, at age 51. So here we were, like all adult family members, with our internal puzzle pieces and the relational puzzle pieces and the generational puzzle pieces and all the demands of kids and life. Both of us were committed to growing as human beings; both of us had strong spiritual paths and incredible perseverance; plus, the stakes were high because the intricate, intimate heart strings of five children were tightly intertwined with our progress.

Slowly, I let him in and Len stepped up. The more he stepped up, the more I let him in. We built trust, through hard, hard work. We grew toward health—less over-functioning and less under-functioning and more partnering. Two steps forward, one step back, our drama— which felt so dramatic internally—played out against a very routine backdrop of caring for kids. No one ever missed a dentist appointment or forgot the carpool. School forms were sent in on time and play dates were planned. Skinned knees got tended, bedtime tucks provided, fears calmed, jokes shared. Academic and athletic efforts were championed. Amazing conversations about politics, ethics and social issues flew around the dinner table every night.

To the three older kids he was "L." Since he was not "Daddy" to all the children in the family, we invented "Len Day" to take place near Father's Day. Each year we'd surprise Len with something special on that day. One year it was a planter full of brilliant magenta petunias. Another year we made maroon tee shirts for each member of the family saying "Happy Len Day." When we had to give a title to the relationship between the kids and Len on school forms, we'd write "Father Figure."

When I was particularly baffled by this man in my life, I tried thinking of him as an alien from outer space about whom I could ascertain two things: he was friendly and his intentions were good. My job was simply to be as kind as possible. My kindness and his kindness were like water for thirsty plants, helping each of us blossom.

Eventually, I saw that we had reached a place where our relational challenge was more spiritual than psychological. I had better understanding of myself, and of him, of our backgrounds and wounds, gifts and strengths and my questions rippled into how could we cultivate the resources to live with those realities? No further insight would make things different; the ways that we worked well in a family were wonderful; the things that were frustrating, disappointing and challenging would stay frustrating, disappointing and challenging. My relationship goal now was to live with the good, the bad and the middling. My spiritual practice became one of "staying in."

My new mantras were, "It is what it is," and "I am *in* this relationship." Rather than reacting to what was hard, I chose to accept it and focus on living with my own integrity and best self. What happens when you stay in? What happens after you would have broken up but you didn't? I developed skills in riding up over my frustration at our different paces and our different willingness to dialogue about our lives. When I felt unmet emotionally, I shifted my attention to the many privileges of a partnered life.

I was enormously proud of what we were able to create. Growing in beloved relationship truly felt like God work. We were reaping the rewards of learning how to bring both strength and vulnerability to this relationship. There were weeks when I lived in bliss that I was living my unique dream. He had committed to staying present in our relationship without wild swings of connection and disconnection. I had committed to including him fully, not alienating him by talking as an expert or preaching my opinions. We came to love each other dearly, to be quite primary in each other's lives, to truly share a family.

I loved the feeling of being on the inside of a caring relationship with someone who knew where I was throughout the day and who thought constantly of small ways to please me. I loved caring about a primary adult beloved, sharing companionship and a valued project. Although I continued to be the prime funder of the family, our standard of living was higher with his added input; logistics such as carpools and rides to tennis lessons were phenomenally easier than when I was a single parent. We found areas of shared interest: long walks in the woods, modern dance performance, good books and podcasts and our love of Judaism. Rich enjoyment bubbled up from the stability and love informing the family that Len and I had both created. Family life in all its voluptuous, voluminous velocity flowed around us, through us, over us.

My attention was involved with intense parenting of five children. I spent my time finding the right schools for each one at each stage of life, addressing emotional and learning needs, maintaining the home nest so all of us could flourish there. Surrounding and upholding this family life was my own meaningful work as rabbi and therapist.

The quest to love well is the most important spiritual work we can do, and each one of us has a story to tell about our attempts and mistakes, and the wisdom we gained from the journey. We get one life to live, and who is an expert on living a life? It seems to take a lifetime of attempts and mistakes and learning even to have a clue. As you grow and move through different life stages, your relationship needs and abilities change. Can you reinvent the relationship? Or tolerate it in its earlier stage even though you long for something different? Or do you need to part ways as primary partners? Rabbi Sheila Weinberg says that we are always halfway between Jerusalem, the Promised Land, and Chelm, which is the village of fools. Because our adult choices about relationships form the context of our kids' lives, these choices have huge import for our parenting.

In our second decade of developing our partnership, I came to think of Len and me as "we." We had travelled a rocky road, but the reward of all that hard work was that we did become partners in many aspects of parenting, including caring for the kids, sharing expenses and making many executive decisions. I was so grateful for his utterly practical reliability, his delightful and irreverent humor and his steadfastness in returning to try time and again. I was so grateful to have the opportunity to gain deep self-knowledge and grow in primary relationship. Our parenting was definitely enriched by having two minds thinking well about the kids.

No doubt Len has his own version of the story. I do not claim to speak for him.

Conflict

Raffi, age 12, is sitting at the computer when I approach him to say he has five minutes till bedtime. He ignores me. I nudge. He ignores me. I nudge. He looks up at me and says, "Fuck you."

I am shocked. After an obstreperous preschool period, my son has been superbly cooperative and sweet. No child of mine has ever spoken to me like this. Those kinds of words aren't even used in my home. Trembling inside, I feel panic that this is the beginning of an out-of-control adolescence. How will I, single Mom, handle this man child who is almost taller than I am and is clearly pushing into new territory?

I grew up in a conflict-avoidant home of nice girls. Each of the five sisters glided into a unique specialization that pre-empted competition: I was the intellectual, Miggie the artist, Katie the philosopher, Lizie the jock and poor Gwen had a hard time for years figuring out what was left over for her. (Now she's an editor with a Ph.D. in English literature.) My mother both nurtured our specialties while also communicating to us that we were whole human beings and could develop multiple aspects of ourselves. We found it more convenient not to be whole human beings, but rather to specialize—at least during the years when we were packed together in the family home.

Once we grew up, we expanded our selves such that Katie, the philosopher-poet, actually became a successful scientist; Lizie, the jock, became a public health analyst; Miggie, the artist, went to medical school and became a psychiatrist; and I, the intellectual, became a spiritual leader. Leaving the nest allowed us to claim the counter-selves that hadn't had the space to grow in the childhood home, each of us becoming a more well-rounded human being. As kids we mostly didn't compete; we didn't fight physically or with words. We were nice.

But conflict is a natural part of human life. It's there and it's going to be coped with one way or another. My awareness of the value of conflict grew slowly as I learned from my relationships and my professional training. These days my heart yelps with joy when certain kinds of conflict erupt because such good things can come from exploring what's real. I don't enjoy storming, defiance, bickering or straight-up fighting anymore than the next person. But it no longer makes me feel the surge of rising blood pressure, the ferocious escalation of reactivity, the hardening stomach knot accompanied by feelings of shame, and the blaming self–talk—"What kind of a parent must I be if my children are acting with such antagonism? What have I failed to do?" I now, at least sometimes, appreciate the aperture that a disagreement—an unwanted difference—creates for improving relationships.

Use an Authoritative Sense of Self *and* Hardcore Skills

In facing conflict fruitfully, I've needed to stretch my internal attitude toward conflict as well as my external skills for handling conflict. Being a nice little girl who grew up under patriarchy, I found that the challenge of finding an authoritative voice—not dominating, as in having power *over* another person, and not helpless, as in avoiding my own stellar power—took some time. (In a seminar on tools for organizing, a leader asked, "How much power do you want to have on a scale of 1 to 10?" Some people chose 5. I chose 10. The feminist writer

Alice Walker claims that the single way in which most people give up power is by believing they don't have any.)

Performing a leadership role in my family means claiming my power and my authority, even when the patriarchal social system undermines women and tells us we shouldn't be strong. I can have a lot of impact on how and where conflict takes place. My leadership shapes the ways my family deals with the tensions and upsets of life. The internal sense of my own authority, grown in resistance to society's sometimes subtle but definitely demeaning messages about women, wasn't enough—standing alone—to make much difference in my family's life. I needed skills, hardcore skills, which I learned by trial and error.

Standing with Raffi at the computer, my heart is pounding, adrenaline coursing. I know I need to calm myself down, but I have no idea how to handle this. On the one hand, I look at that kid, at any of my kids, and I just feel infinite love, tolerance and understanding. On the other hand, I really don't want him to be a brat or treat me badly.

Slow Down and Think!

Cultivating an ability to slow things down turned out to be a gift for me and my family. When interactions move more slowly, both the child and I have the opportunity to consider choices. One way to slow things down is to leave the conflict for the moment until the intensity of emotion settles down. Another decelerating option is to repeat something the child said and ask, "Did I get this right? You want to stay up for 15 more minutes?" Or, "Let me make sure I understand: you'd like to go to the concert with your friends and no grown-up?"

I aim for a neutral tone, not antagonistic or sarcastic. I'm letting the child know that I am trying to understand them and I'm buying time for both of us to communicate thoughtfully. During that pause I ask myself, "What is really going on here?" Reacting emotionally, with rage, sadness, frustration, annoyance or even despair, or feeling embarrassed, defeated, helpless and hopeless are options, but I guide myself into different territory. An underutilized resource for parents is the mind. What do you *think* about the situation? Because you are more mature than your child, it is up to you to hold onto clear thinking, even when your child can't.

As a thinking parent I am asking:

- What behind-the-scenes factors could be motivating this behavior? (is this child tired, hungry, stressed?)

- What expectations should I have based on this child's developmental stage? (Certain ages are known to be more oppositional than others, certain stages are all about kids differentiating themselves from you.)

- When does conflict erupt? Are there noticeable environmental triggers such as sitting in the car together, or the period right before dinner when everyone is hungry?

If you have an analysis of your situation, problem-solving becomes easier. Parents as leaders need to stretch our minds to think well about our families. Our ability to think clearly is a huge resource for us.

In the face of my 12-year-old's "Fuck you," I need to buy some time to calm myself down and then reflect on the situation. Walking away, I say, "I expect you to be off the computer in five minutes."

Once calmer, I think to myself, "Yes, he's on the verge of adolescence; yes, it is late at night and we are both tired; yes, he is highly motivated to do what he is engaged in without distraction. No, it is not helpful for me to extrapolate from his rude words that we will travel a rocky road in years to come."

Yet Raffi and I have reached a threshold that cannot be ignored. Distancing myself in the moment is a good choice, but I want to address what just happened between us and I don't yet have a plan for how to do it.

See the Problem Through Close-Up and Long-Range Lenses

The wise parent is both fully present in the interaction and at the same time has a bird's-eye view of the bigger picture. That's the difference between the child and the adult. The child is probably fully, entirely, *in* the moment of upset or resistance or sassiness. You, as the adult, have a bigger perspective. If you're losing that bigger perspective, as I was with Raffi when he swore at me, then you know you need to slow it down. Slowing things down allowed me to find support to help me think through the situation and find a constructive response.

As I walk away from the conflict with Raffi, leaving him with the expectation that he will cooperate and giving him space to do so, he also ambles away from the computer. Once the kids are in bed, I take the advice of the great Jewish sage who told all seekers to "Find a teacher." Even teachers, especially teachers, need teachers. My teachers include therapists, clergy, support groups, great books, friends and family. The first person I call that night is critical of me.

"You treat Raffi like a prince! No wonder he thinks he can talk to you like that."

Maybe that feedback could be helpful at some point, but it isn't helpful in my time of great upset. Empathy and ideas for how to strengthen my ability to guide Raffi and address our conflict constructively are what I need now. I know it's my job to keep seeking support until I feel confident to take the next step with Raffi. Instead of criticism, I need listening, good questions and brainstorming. Advice also can be helpful, but sometimes I just need my dear friend Felice to ask me open-ended, empathetic questions. "What are you worried about?" she asks when I call, distraught.

"What message do you want Raffi to take away? How do you think he can best hear that?"

Having guides as you grow in your parenting is a wonderful resource and maybe you will guide and support others as well. We can all call forth the authority in one another. We can help one another slow down in our interactions and draw more on our thinking abilities. We can help one another hold the close-up lens and the bigger-picture lens at the same time.

I decide I want to act boldly with Raffi, to do something dramatic that will make a strong impression. I don't want to do anything puni-tive, but take action that lets him know I am serious about a standard of respect in our relationship. The next day I drive to his school in the center of the city and pull him out of class. He's not expecting me. I don't tell him why I'm there right away. I take him out to lunch.

"I need to talk with you about something that happened last night."

He looks up, curious.

"Don't ever say 'Fuck you' again to your mother. It is not okay."

"Okay," he says.

"I treat you with respect and I expect to be treated with respect. You can have whatever feelings and thoughts you want, but I don't want to be treated in a mean way."

He responds to my confidence and clarity. At the end of our lunch he says, "Can we do this every day?" I breathe a sigh of relief as we walk back to his school.

Sometimes, Move Closer to Conflict

I take my kids on the overnight Amtrak train to visit my sister Miggie's family in St. Louis. I am so excited to take my five little ones on this big adventure to see their cousins Emma and Hoben. In the sleeping car, each of us has cozy fold-out beds that become part of the compartment walls during the day. I feel so snug in these little quarters with my family squashed in together. We have a layover for a few hours in Chicago. It's Christmas day, and all the shops near the train station are closed. Our only option to find a meal requires a hike in the freezing weather five blocks to the single place open in all of downtown, a Dunkin' Donuts. The area feels desolate and seedy. One of my kids cranks and fusses and resists coming on that walk until I am seething with frustration. We are all hungry; I want to go get food, and I can't leave this young person alone in the train station.

A counter-intuitive strategy for dealing with conflict is to move closer to the person you're in conflict with rather than pulling away. Often, conflict comes from something other than oppositional disregard. Maybe the child is anxious, or wanting your attention. Being bratty is one behavioral possibility, although the outcome—your negative reaction—is probably the opposite of what the child wants and needs. If you can hold the bigger picture that children are reassured by connection, you can reach deeper than the unacceptable behavior. You can't reward the behavior in the moment, but you can find ways to connect in spite of it.

At the moment in Chicago, I was thinking, "When we get to St. Louis, all I want is to put my resistant child in a room far away from me and not have to listen to more arguments." But in a flash of inspiration I realize that if I draw this child closer to me, he'll calm down and we'll get along better. This defiance could be based on inflexibility about transitions and anxiety about new situations. When we got to St. Louis, I had this child sleep in the same room as me, drawing him closer, reassuring him quietly with steady presence. The connection to me was grounding and allowed this child to settle down and be his usual sunny, fun, cooperative self.

Human development specialists have big names for the way kids become calmer with calm, connected parenting. It's called attachment theory and attachment parenting. I learned through personal discovery that these ideas make sense, although on the negative side I've seen these theories used in practice to smother kids' ability to self-soothe and find their own footing. Kids need to be held close and also given the space to make their own way, and it is our lucky job as parents to find the delicate balance between the two forces.

Plan Ahead, Make a Plan

As the parent, you probably have observed predictable patterns of conflict with your kids and you may be able to use your insight to prevent future conflict. Sometimes, just having a plan helps family life run more smoothly. For instance, having a plan for who sits next to whom at the dinner table and in the car relieves the stress of kids trying to grab the choice spots and bickering over the unfairness of the outcome. Without a plan, stress levels are higher, people are less reasonable and the climate feels more toxic. When the subject is something you aren't heavily invested in, such as who sits where or who gets the blue vitamin, the kids might as well make the plan. They can figure out a system to rotate turns in the front seat of the car, at the dinner table next to a parent and in the distribution of coveted blue vitamins. Kids with certain special needs especially do well when they know the plan in advance. The less flexible your child is, the more it is likely that routine and advanced planning will help things go smoothly.

As the parent leader, you are aware of who pushes whose buttons and you can do behind-the-scenes planning to relieve tension. When one child is going to get a special birthday present, I sometimes take another child aside, enlisting them collegially in the surprise. They get to be an insider helper, which can temper envy. Similarly, co-opting the child who is most likely to disrupt by giving them a special job or a say in the decision-making can earn you some peace and quiet. That's how Raffi got to be the "drummer" at our Friday night candle-lighting ceremony and that's why Joey got to pick out the surprise guinea pigs for Mozi's birthday present.

There are times when you can make plans to reduce the sibling stress in kids' lives, which hopefully will reduce conflict. You can plan after-school and weekend activities that purposefully keep them from overlapping at home; you can find activities that are unique for each child and allow each child to shine (which is probably why my mother helped my sisters and I to develop our self-chosen specialties); and you can arrange the sleeping quarters in your home so that each child has a private area even if it is within a shared bedroom.

Reactions to change often generate conflict, and you can sometimes plan to ease into change rather than letting it abruptly confront children. Of course, sometimes you can't ease gently into change and you just have to do the best you can. But you might as well help kids gracefully manage the changes you can predict because doing so will reduce tension in family life.

Let's say you've decided that you want the kids to start loading and unloading the dishwasher, but this has never been a part of their duties. You want to enlist their cooperation, reduce resistance and end up with more team effort around the house. Pegging changes like this to markers in the year can reinforce change: New Year's Day, birthdays, beginning of summer, beginning of school year. Weeks before the change, you start planting news of the upcoming change. "On the last day of summer, we're going to start our new school year by stepping up with family responsibilities. The kids are going to take turns loading and unloading the dishwasher. You guys can figure out how you want to divide up the days and the tasks. We can talk about it at dinner."

If there's protest you stand firm, "Yup, it's a new year and everyone is a year older and more capable so we're all going to pitch in." The calendar helps hold your mandate, giving it a bigger context.

Privileges can also be pegged to the calendar. At the beginning of the school year allowance gets raised. When someone turns eight they get a private overnight trip with a parent, when they turn 10 they get a pocket knife. Thirteen-year-olds get to hold the steering wheel on the country lane at Grampa's house. Scaffolding responsibilities and privileges like this helps give kids a sense of momentum and purpose in their growing.

Endorsing both inner growth and outer growth supports this affirmation. You can measure your child's growth every six months on the wall and comment, "Just like your body grew, I can see you growing on the inside too in kindness and responsibility."

Consult with the Parties Involved Before Predictable Times of Conflict

In addition to having a structured plan that makes conflict less likely, consulting with people ahead of potentially conflictual situations can make a difference. Even if your child or children are very young, they like to know that you care about their desires, preferences and ideas. This is not only conflict-prevention, it also communicates respect. Not every single little household task has to be a matter of discussion and consensus decision-making (I remember the time my friend Sarah said to two-year-old Rosi, "Time to put your shoes on," and Rosi said, "Let's talk about it." That seemed to be an unnecessary time for talk.)

In general, finding time to consult kids is an important part of leadership. When people own a decision, they are less likely to balk at, disrupt or react to its enactment. Including the parties involved in a consultation about a decision, is helpful even when you will make the ultimate ruling, and even if the decision doesn't go the way the child wanted. At least you can acknowledge their feelings and wishes even when you can't accommodate them.

Conflict Between Siblings

I imagine I am in good company as a parent who dislikes spending time with my kids when they squabble and bicker (although isn't it interesting that I don't mind nearly as much when it's someone else's kids squabbling and bickering!) Having to endure accusations shooting back and forth, mean jabs and unkind words, "He did this," and "She did that" is definitely unpleasant. These sibling interactions are exhausting to my psyche, grating on my nerves and eroding my morale. The kids seem to feel the same displeasure some of the time, while at other times they actually seem to find joy in their barbaric interactions.

Littermates of puppies, bears and lion cubs wrestle, pounce, cuff, snarl, bite and pin each other, trying to establish their pecking order. Most animals assert a hierarchy of dominance and submission. This fact gives me solace as a parent, reminding me that competition and conflict are natural. In the animal kingdom, a hierarchy that establishes peace is allowed to stand (even when it means the runt of the litter doesn't get fed as well and may even die). But in our families we actually disrupt the stability of a hierarchical system, for very good reasons, when we endorse each child's entitlement to equal rights.

Research shows that neglected children often get along very well with their siblings. In lieu of parental support, they turn to each other with cooperation and empathy. At least when my children fuss with each other I know they are not only acting in line with their animal natures, but they also are not neglected!

In the course of all that roughhousing, kids learn survival skills that toughen them up for the world, teach them how to shield themselves and forge ahead with strength. Sometimes, only-children find a cousin or playmate to take on this intense sibling role. Raising kids in too "nice" a way prevents them from acquiring some useful life skills. In sibling play or best-friend play, kids learn to stand up for themselves.

They learn that they are strong enough to handle difficulties and that they have an inner core that can't be hurt.

These skills are valuable, but I don't want to listen to them toughen each other up with obnoxious behavior. I can't ignore this behavior, though. As the leader of the family, my job is to be in charge, to make sure no child is actually going to endanger the body or essential emotional well-being of another. The child expressing noisy or disruptive anger annoys me more than the provoker and I might be tempted to blame that one, but when I really dig deeper it often becomes clear to me that siblings can mutually annoy each other. Taking time to reflect, rather than leaping into immediate reaction, helps me see the deeper dynamics.

Let's face it: siblings have the capacity to truly bother each other. Whatever fantasy life a parent has of darling children who are best friends at all times is likely to be shattered by the reality of the rambunctious, passionate, infuriating nature of real relationships. The blessing is that despite the ups and downs of sibling life, siblings are a lifelong resource for one another and potentially will find future joy and connection in these relationships. In many families, best friendship— playing together, confiding, enjoying the other's company—co-exists with rivalry and tension.

In fact, the more emotional engagement there is in a pair of siblings, whether it is expressed positively or negatively, the more energy they have to work with for a positive future. Some of my kids who kept a wary competitive eye on each other throughout childhood, insisting on intense engagement for better or worse (sometimes playing happily for hours, other times poking or provoking each other to get attention) are now intimate, committed best friends who choose to stay closely connected and turn to each other for comfort during hard times. I have known many, many children who bickered and competed as young people and who are now, in late adolescence or young adulthood, beloved best friends.

Still, the quality of life for me is diminished by having to listen to my children go at each other. Parents of only-children often feel the same way about their child and an intense playmate or cousin who serves a sibling-like role.

In St. Louis with my sister Miggie's family, I witnessed a classic sibling scene between her two amazing and delightful middle-school-aged children: Emma started loudly playing the piano right next to the construction project Hoben was meticulously completing. Hoben complained, "I'm in the middle of building something. You're making too much noise!"

Emma replied, "I can't play the piano anywhere else. I have to do it here."

Frustrated, Hoben started throwing his construction blocks at Emma, causing Emma to shriek, "Mom! Hoben is throwing things at me!"

For my own peace of mind, when this kind of interaction happened in my own family, I identified my options—not including murder, abandonment or insanity! Of course, when possible, I tried to have systems and plans to anticipate problems and minimize the likelihood of chaos. When these failed, strategies were needed.

Remove the Kids or Remove Yourself

Once I ascertain that no one is in physical or emotional danger, even though rough and mean things might happen, I tell my kids, "You have two choices: go away from each other, or else both of you go away from me if you need to keep doing this. Do it in another room. I am not interested." Or I will pick myself up and go into another room. If they find perverse pleasure in unpleasant mutual behavior, at least I don't have to be around it. The pleasure of going at each other is somewhat lessened when the Mama Witness is removed from the situation.

Both Emma the piano player and Hoben the constructor were justified in their positions, yet their needs conflicted. If they had the will to work out a mutually acceptable solution to their problem, such a solution would not have been beyond their abilities to devise. They didn't really need a grown-up to solve this problem for them, but they did need a grown-up to structure a way for them to solve the problem. A perpetual challenge for parents is having to discern when to intervene and when to leave kids alone to solve their own problems. I ask myself, "Can I add value to this situation? Can I intervene in a way that is developmentally helpful? Do I have energy and attention and willingness to be in that role at this moment?"

Institute the Family Meeting

Another option for conflict resolution is the family meeting.

When Rosi was 10 years old, Raffi eight and Zoe six, they had daily fights about which hook each one of them would use to hang their school backpacks. I had installed three hooks near the front door, intending one for each backpack. But it turned out that the third hook, which to me looked identical to the first and second hook, for some inexplicable reason had become unpopular. No one wanted to use it. This led to daily fights about who got the first and second hooks.

The tried and true institution of the family meeting is a great way to help kids actually solve problems. The parent starts out as a strong leader, gradually shifting leadership to the kids, who act as rotating facilitators. A Talking Object is any object that can be held in a hand and passed around. It starts in the hands of the facilitator and is passed to the next person who needs to speak and from that person to the next speaker, and so on. Only the person holding the Talking Object is allowed to speak. This sets up a visual cue for when it is time to be quiet and listen. A rhythm builds during the family meeting conversation that includes the pregnant pauses of silence as the object is handed from person to person. This simple ritual slows down the conversation and helps everyone remember to wait for their turn and respect others' turns, without needing much direction from a grown-up.

Anybody at the meeting can add an item to the agenda. Then issues are discussed and resolved one by one. There are many motivations in a family meeting. Some people just want the meeting to end so they can move on to something else they'd rather be doing, which is good motivation for being brief and quickly solving problems. Others want the glory of being the creative problem-solver who comes up with a solution that all can endorse. Others want to "win" on their issue. With this mix of motivations, meetings have intriguing potential for many people to shine. The bottom line is that every single person has a turn to express themselves constructively, every single person will be heard and considered, everyone has renewed hope that there are ways to solve annoying problems.

Kids have their own culture and don't necessarily care about the same issues that we as parents care about. Listening to their concerns and empowering them as problem-solvers can be enlightening.

When my kids discussed the problem of the backpack hooks at a family meeting, Rosi started by saying, "I think I should get the first hook because I'm the oldest." She passed the talking object to her sister Zoe.

Zoe said, "I don't think it's fair that you get to choose the hook you want, because I'm always going to be younger and I'll never get a turn to choose."

She passed the hook to her brother Raffi, who added his reason for why he should have one of the coveted "good" hooks. After a while, I started gently nudging the conversation along by saying, "Let's see if anyone can come up with an idea to work this out that feels right to everyone."

Usually their first attempts at problem solving are self-serving itera-tions of their own positions. Eventually they embraced the idea that a solution has to be acceptable to everyone. The kids resolved the Battle of the Hooks with an elegant solution that satisfied everyone. They asked me to install a fourth hook, and then they could continue to reject the third hook while each would have access to an acceptable hook for their backpack.

With open-ended family brainstorming sessions to solve a prob-lem you never know what humor and eventually what solutions will be generated. On considering how to feed the dear guinea pig while we were away for the weekend, a wild brainstorming session included ridiculous suggestions such as, "Set it free and let it forage," and "Put it in the refrigerator where the greens are." When people are giggling and relaxed, they are more likely to find workable resolutions.

That guinea pig got a lot of air time in our meetings over the years. I remember Mozi saying at a family meeting, "I don't like it when Joey says my guinea pig belongs to him because it really is mine."

"But it lives in my room and I feed it," explained Joey, taking the Talking Object. It's true that the guinea pig lives in his room, but that is because Zoe, who shares a room with Mozi, is allergic to pets with fur, so the guinea pig cannot live with its owner, Mozi.

The kids eventually arrived at an analysis, "The guinea pig belongs to Mozi. Joey, you're a caregiver, but Mozi owns it."

"Okay," Joey said solemnly. "I won't say I own it anymore."

If we expect kids to grow up to be problem-solvers in a democracy and competent partners in intimate relationships, isn't it a good idea for them to practice the skills they'll need? In a home with an only child, this kind of expression, listening and negotiating sometimes happens without a lot of planning. When it isn't happening organically, a family meeting can be useful even between a solo parent and one child. This format can provide spaciousness and structure to a dialogue. A structured format can also be especially helpful to family members who have social skills deficits that make it harder for them to participate in a spontaneous back-and-forth of constructive conversation. Family meetings can be called to order on the spur of the moment by anyone who feels the need for one, or they can be regularly scheduled events, or they can be randomly scheduled events. In my home, we have one about every six weeks, but not on a fixed schedule. Making space for each person's voice to be heard and engaging in collective problem-solving are ways to foster better family functioning.

One time, my sisters and I and our kids were all gathered during the winter holiday season at our mother's house in Washington, D.C. One of the young teenage cousins invited my young teen outside to the porch. I thought, "That's odd; it's freezing outside," and then I remembered that my sister had recently found marijuana detritus in her kid's bed. She had decided to handle it by acknowledging to him in a neutral way that she was aware of his activity, without making a big deal about it. She simply said, without judgment or much interest, "I saw marijuana seeds in your bed." I thought that was a wise approach.

Now I realized the reason for the cold-weather foray. Sure enough, it was soon apparent, through their whisperings and unusual comings and goings, that the young teen cousins were inducting each other into marijuana use and that within their cohort there was enormous tension. I suggested to my sister that we call them into a family meeting to address what was going on. Her teen had never taken part in such a meeting and declined the offer to speak first. "I don't want to talk," he said.

So, after I introduced the concept of the family meeting, the other cousins got to take turns explaining what was going for them, which involved the younger ones stealing the older one's marijuana stash and trying to destroy it because they were worried about him; the older one threatening to hurt the younger ones; the younger ones accusing each other of smoking also; and then each of them 'fessing up to their own occasional use. The parents learned a lot listening to them working through their conflict.

By mid-meeting my sister's teen was eagerly engaged in the discussion. No one wants to be left out once people have a chance to share their experience and views in a circle of respect. The attitude in a family meeting is not punitive. It's about curiously asking the question, "How can we make life together work well?" None of these kids ended up having a drug problem in their teenage years, and possibly the open opportunity to explore the temptations, pressures and anxieties helped them navigate these issues, which virtually every teen faces.

My sister Katie drives regularly from North Carolina, where she is a Ph.D. ecologist with the Forest Service, to D.C., where our parents live and where we often congregate. Her five kids—four boys and one girl— erupt into World War Three-like arguments in the minivan over who sits where and who chooses which DVD. The battles can last at top volume for the entire eight-hour journey. Katie often consults with me about what to do even while admitting that my advice is likely to go in one ear and out the other. I understand completely. When we walk in the woods together I love asking Katie the name of every leaf, tree, footprint, flower, even though I know I will retain the information for about two minutes tops.

If you can find a way to structure conflict so that people can express their needs and listen to one another, you are honoring your kids' strong feelings about what they care about. This is a good thing to do if you are trying to raise kids to have strong feelings about the issues important to them. You respect their passions and give them ways to engage respectfully about them. You create opportunities for all family members to express views, needs and desires with words rather than with annoying behavior. You also plant seeds of hope that real conflict can be constructively resolved. It does not have to be a festering, endless tax on family member's well-being. (The kind of conflict that actually makes them happy can be actualized far away from you.) Our job as parents, whether we have one child or many, is not to solve their problems but to guide them into a process for problem solving.

I say to sister Katie, "I wonder what would happen if the second you hear fighting, you pull the van over to the side of the highway and have a family meeting. No doubt real differences of need and opinion are at the root of these squabbles. The more that people are listened to respectfully, the less desperate they feel and the more every one's desires can be taken into account. Back in the car, when fighting erupts again within moments of pulling onto the highway, you pull the van over again to the side of the highway and call another family meeting. Every time the squabbling starts, the car stops and a meeting is called."

The message, loud and clear, is, "It is way more important that we find a way to get along, than that we get to D.C. quickly. We'll just keep doing this until we can ride peacefully in the car." Sooner or later the kids will get the message about your priorities. (Katie insists my idea would never work with her family and maybe she's right!)

Tactics for addressing kids' conflicts—removing myself or the kids or holding a family meeting—reduce the explosive, destructive aspects of conflict. They require an internal sense of yourself as leader and an external set of skills that you apply. Simply understanding that I did not need to be phobic of conflict, that I could cultivate my inner ability to stay calm and I could learn specific skills for addressing conflict were both reassuring and liberating to me. Once I had the consciousness that this was possible, finding the resources to grow as a parent in these ways was not hard.

The single most important message I can share with a parent who is struggling with conflict in the family is: You are the leader. Good leaders listen, deliberate and plan. Good leaders structure situations to work well. Good leaders also consult and collaborate. Rather than succumbing to the overwhelming experience of kids' conflicts, parents can learn to see the range of opportunities in conflict: a chance to address real issues in the family community; a chance for parents' to cultivate inner patience and thinking; a chance for children to gain worthwhile experience coping with disagreements. It is in my power to lead my children toward fair and satisfying relationships.

When I think of what the world needs most, I see the great value in being able to listen and respond constructively. There is no greater contribution that I could make to this world than giving it the gift of human beings who are capable of listening and responding constructively even in situations of great tension.

Conflict Between Partners

One regret I have is that so far I have never felt confident enough in a partnership to have open conflict in front of the kids. Sometimes it's because the subject matter feels inappropriate for kids. Sometimes I don't trust that our process would be something I'd be proud of modeling. Other times the conflict is about the kids and I don't want them caught in the middle. Therefore, like so many people, I engage in conflict with my partners privately, depriving my kids of any model for adult conflict and problem-solving. I wish I could model for the kids honest conflict and successful conflict resolution.

Since my partnering relationships have been organized in alternative ways and I've mostly been a single parent in my own home, much of my wisdom on conflicts between partners comes from helping hundreds of couples improve their family situations. Inevitably, two parents will at times have two different styles or beliefs about parenting. We aren't clones so naturally there will sometimes be difference.

Many partnering parents face a challenging dilemma about whether and how strongly to back up the other parent to the kids even when they don't agree with the other parent. In one home, the issue centered around one parent wanting homework to be done immediately after kids got home from school and the other parent feeling strongly that they'd do better if they had some free time first. Ideally, parents can set aside adult time to listen to each other, be curious about what each other thinks, feels and needs before trying to come up with solutions, and only after all that exploration and deep knowledge of each other make joint decisions for parenting. The same tools that are helpful with kids work well with partners: slowing things down, thinking well and taking a wise overview of the whole picture, structuring spacious time for listening and sharing, and having preventative plans in place. In partnering relationships there are also some useful fallback positions when working through an agreement doesn't seem possible because of relationship issues, time constraints or insurmountable differences. Sometimes, a Plan B is needed.

I think it is okay for kids to learn that Daddy does it this way and Mommy does it another way. When parents can agree to disagree, you might be able to work out creative solutions: every other day is Mama Jane's day to make the plan and the alternate days are for Mama Lorraine. Or, we take turns getting the right to resolve conflicts. I get to decide this one about whether or not to add another after school activity, but that means I am giving you the right to decide the next conflict without knowing exactly what will come up; therefore I have to think very carefully about how much I care about having my way on this issue.

In my family, the kids learned that Len allows sugary drinks; Mom doesn't. Mom will buy meat; Len won't. Mom lets you pick your own sneakers; Len does too, but not if they have skull and bones on them.

Even if you are the more primary, relevant parent in whatever sphere you are discussing, you show respect and good faith by consulting your partner. Including others in your decisions can reduce future conflict. When dealing with a partner, discussing a sensitive issue in advance, when possible, can set a respectful, inclusive tone. "Karey has been asking about her birth mother. Do you think it's time to show her the pictures? When and how do you think we should we do that?"

Developmental stages of relationships are an important factor. It is likely that new conflicts between partners will emerge in synch with the developmental stages of the child: new issues arise with the start of grade school, with the start of adolescence, with launching the child from the nest into the workplace or college. You might be surprised by a sudden eruption of unexpected conflict between you and your partner at those times, and when you take the wide-lens, big-picture perspective you realize that you are at a new developmental juncture. In my parenting partnership, conflict arose about dating norms and dress codes when we had a young teenager. Standing back a bit I was able to say to myself, "Oh, of course! We've never navigated this stage before!"

If you are in a conflictual relationship with frequent, obvious tensions, you are wise to protect kids from the fallout. Adults do well to monitor their own conflicts and exhibit self-control in acting out in front of the kids. If you are in a frequently conflicted relationship, ask yourself if this is the environment in which you want your kids to be raised. It always takes two to bicker. You have choices.

In reviewing our choices we have to weigh the value of kids seeing conflict and conflict resolution versus the value of peace and harmony at home. In Judaism, the concept of *shalom bayit*, peace in the home, trumps many other values. If you feel comfortable openly arguing or fighting with your partner in the presence of your child, it's also a good idea to check on how the child is processing it. One couple I know has fights that both Moms feel pretty comfortable with; they have a rhythm to their eruptions and recovery. However, their 12-year-old experiences the fights as devastating and brutal.

In conflict between partners, the same approaches that help with kids might be useful:

* Find your own solid, authoritative self that doesn't need to be bossy and that feels confident of having a worthwhile contribution to make.

* Slow Down and think instead of just reacting emotionally.

* Take a wise overview perspective and an up-close, engaged perspective on the conflict.

* Sometimes, move closer to conflict, connecting especially in positive ways with the person who is annoying or frustrating or enraging you. Be kind, draw close, ask questions.

* Prevent what is preventable by planning ahead and by consulting with a curious mind and listening ear. Do this both with the person in conflict with you and with your supportive resource people.

* Structure opportunities to have spacious, exploratory conversations before making decisions.

* If need be, move on to other problem-solving tactics such as making a plan about how to deal with disagreements even when they aren't resolvable.

Partnering is a complex, messy dance full of pitfalls and potential. If you are experiencing conflict with your partner, you're in good company with much of the rest of the partnering world. Yet, the rewards of partnering can be so great that it's worth putting up with some troubles to enrich your family with more caring, more ideas and more possibilities. Trying different approaches (which might even be contradictory, such as two of the options suggested here: radical inclusive consultation between you and your partner versus designing separate spheres for you and your partner) will give you useful information about what is possible in your situation. Look at your efforts as experiments that provide data. In addition, you might want to shift your attention to what does feel good and workable in your relationship and not dwell overmuch on the stuck places. Sometimes, we need to ride up over conflict and get on with life.

As you help your family deal with conflict constructively, you're preparing your kids for a world in which people do have different interests and needs, both on the political front and in intimate relations. On the macro scale, some of the most entrenched world problems—and on the micro scale, some of the most contentious relationship problems—are caused by our lack of experience and skill in being curious about one another, making space to really get to know what's going on with the other, and then growing in compassion and creativity in problem solving.

Families that can prevent destructive conflicts, manage inevitable conflicts and even celebrate their ability to create space for listening and problem solving are incubators for a world of justice and peace. At the end of a hard discussion, I tell my kids: "I'm so proud of this family for hanging in there and working through hard things."

Connection

One day, I looked at my first baby, Rosi Greenberg, 18 months old, toddling around with her socks on her hands like little mittens, chanting in her sing-song voice, "Mama, Mama, Mama, Mama." She was so thoroughly adorable and lovable. At that moment I had a flash of understanding about why adolescence was invented. If kids didn't go through a stage a lot less cute than this, we would never ever be able to let them grow up.

What I didn't know was how much I would passionately love parenting young people through their teenage years. Even at difficult moments when my frustration level is sky high, I can see that a mystery is unfolding. My child is rooted in what I know of her, but developing beyond what I created. What a fascinating privilege to be part of this unfolding. Still, I somehow have to survive the moments of struggle, self-doubt and stress that are part of this passage. Holding on to the big picture helps.

The big picture is that we're raising children to be part of human civilization and even, we hope, to advance human civilization. The qualities of civilization that we value need actually to be present in our lives. It's like the old adage: "To have a friend, be a friend." To raise humane beings, live like humane beings. Yet in the hectic crunch of family life some elements of civilization may seem elusive—elements such as reasonable discussion, peaceful problem solving and creative discovery.

In the following pages I reflect on some possibilities for sustaining a family culture that at least somewhat approximates a culture you'd choose to live in; that is, a culture that embodies qualities of civilization, respect, learning, kindness and tolerance. The focus here is on the teenage years because that is a time when parents and kids can lose their close positive connection to one another, either through conflict or through alienation and isolation.

Adolescence is a time during which young people can careen from feeling inappropriately, indestructibly empowered to feeling deeply hopeless and despicable. As teenagers become more independent and appear to need us parents less, we need to remember that these teenagers desperately need us as pillars that root them in a family where they belong, where there are expectations and allies. My mandate as a Mom is to realize how totally important I am in the lives of my children, while also realizing that there is an awful lot that is beyond my power.

Presence

My presence at home matters. One of the biggest gifts I can give my kids is just being around. Of course, as a single parent, I am a working Mom so I'm not home 24/7 and I wouldn't want to be. But I save all my housework to do in the presence of my children. I sit at my desk paying bills or stand at the kitchen sink washing dishes. I put laundry in and take laundry out. Having a parent visibly on duty is grounding and reassuring to young people. Driving carpool, the bane of so many suburban parents, counts as time being present.

Your kid or kids may not crave your presence. They may not be your friend during these adolescent years. But you matter enormously to them. Being available for teenagers, just hanging out, having a presence is a huge part of parenting a teenager. I often have to stay up past my bedtime in order to be around when they liven up. Around 11 p.m., my natural bedtime, the older teenagers emerge from their hours of homework and are ready for snacks and conversation.

We've had some funny scenes during those late-night hours. For years I've been a fan of the Tour de France which is shown on TV every evening of the three-week race. The dramatic culmination of the bike race occurs moments before midnight. This works out well, because I plunk myself down on the living room floor in front of the screen and the teenagers socialize around me. With one eye on the race, they chat with one another or with me about their days and their thoughts. The problem is, that late at night, I start falling asleep. One night, I was lying there on the rug moments before midnight, and I fell quite soundly asleep. Rosi, on the sofa next to me, not aware that I was asleep, started telling me her end-of-life wishes.

"Mom, if I'm ever a vegetable, I want to be disconnected from the machines."

Suddenly, I lifted my head to glance at the television, saw the main group of bicyclists huffing and puffing up the last stretch of the Alps, and muttered, "Those poor boys," before collapsing back into my own slumber. My teenagers never let me forget that one!

Although there is much that is hidden from any parent in the life of a teenager, being physically present can open important opportunities for parenting, as I discovered one night as Raffi lay on the floor beside my computer chair while I worked.

"Mom, it really sucks having to trespass on train tracks," he complained. "It's dangerous and you could also get arrested."

I knew he had been going on walks around the city documenting grafitti, but I didn't know he'd been walking along the train tracks. I was concerned, but I kept my tone light.

"Raffi, don't walk on train tracks."

He answered, "Oh, it's not that dangerous. Especially on a Sunday, when I know the train schedule. I've done it twice."

I saw how he himself was ambivalent about this activity and was downloading it, casually, but intentionally, perhaps to get a mature perspective on it. Not that he was directly expressing ambivalence or asking for my perspective. But why else would he bring it up?

"Teenagers think they are so invincible," I said. "It would be such a tragedy to the ones you love if you died at this age."

He squirmed uncomfortably. "Why is death such a tragedy?"

"I didn't say death is such a tragedy. I said it would be so tragic to the ones you love."

"Everything about life as we know it is wholly and completely attributable to the fact that things die. If billions and billions of genetic traits hadn't been killed off, we wouldn't be having this conversation now."

Zoe piped in from the other room: "It's natural selection!"

Raffi agreed. "It's natural selection. If I'm stupid enough to get myself killed on the train tracks, good for humanity."

"You are so philosophical!" I said.

Without bossing him around, I hope I injected a bit of guidance into the mix and allied with his own good sense. I'm so glad I stayed up past my bedtime to have these precious moments with my budding intellectual son.

Teenagers remind me of toddlers in their frequent and fierce desire to be independent and their simultaneous longing for dependence. The toddler who dashes off on new-found bipeds while looking back at Mama for reassurance every now and then mirrors the teenager who is charting a unique path while touching base with home. They can be 3-years-old and 33-years-old all in one 12-year-old self.

The summer before Rosi went to college, she was browsing on her computer while I read a book nearby. "Mom, when I go to college we're going to miss this kind of cozy time. I just can't imagine living without our daily Mama time." She and I joked that she was on a self-chosen six-foot leash. In the next sentence she said, "Wow, did you know there are foreign exchange programs where you can live abroad even in your first year of college? Wouldn't it be amazing if I could do one of those?" There seemed to be no disconnect in her mind between the longing for "cozy time" with her Mama and the desire to traipse around the world. She was expressing the full range of teenage and human longing, and I as her Mom had to rise to the challenge of embracing her simultaneous need for connection and independence.

Staying Engaged

Staying engaged with a child who is communicative, friendly, interactive, and who enjoys your company is not difficult. There are teenagers who are like this all through their adolescences. Then there are the ones who go through at least a stretch of much less pleasant and less rewarding behavior. It's just as important to stay engaged in the lives of the grumps.

As parents of teenagers we probably look overwhelmingly powerful to our kids. We know all too well that we have inadequacies, self-doubts, character flaws and all-too-human foibles. Our kids very likely, deep down, see us as omnipotent Gods who have power, money, mobility and morality on our side. The more disempowered they feel, the more they might act like we are beneath contempt.

People who feel good about themselves and have reason to expect that they can be efficacious are able to be calm and reasonable. Parents can help kids have a voice in a number of ways. One way of making room for them to have a voice is to draw out conversations when they are motivated to "get" something. Let them negotiate a bit, let there be a dialogue even when you know before the conversation even starts that you are willing to do it their way. Ponder their wishes. Let them convince you.

"Mom, I really think I should be able to see the new Harry Potter movie at midnight," Mozi lobbied me.

"You want to see Harry Potter at midnight? What is so special about seeing it in the middle of the night?"

"Mom, it's the first minute it's out. Everyone's gonna see it then."

"Won't you be tired the next day? It sounds exhausting."

"But Mom, it's once in a lifetime. I really want to see it with my friends."

"Well, I see what you're saying. Let me think about it."

Or, from Joey: "Mom, I would like to take the trash out tomorrow morning instead of tonight. I promise I'll do it."

"I'm afraid you'll forget in the morning."

"I did a good job last week, remember?"

"Yeah, that's true. But why can't you just do it now?"

"I'm tired. It's dark and cold. I'd rather do it first thing in the morning."

"I see your point. If that's how you think it will work best, I can go along with it."

It's easier to tune into some teenagers than others. I've had the range, from the child who hasn't fully experienced her day until she has funnelled her stories into my ears—chatting intimately about her thoughts, worries and reactions—to the child who, at his most communicative, let's me know about a major breakup in his romantic life by saying, "I changed my Facebook status today."

Zoe once described the range of communication in this way: "Mom, some of your kids greet you with a monosyllable and some with a novel." She's right. Needless to say, being in touch with the emotional life of a non-communicative child poses difficulties. There are no magic solutions, but I've worked on some strategies for enticing non-communicators into relationship.

Instead of letting the child retreat into her room, I insist on sitting together for a meal, stressing that I want my time with her and that it matters to me—I value it. She and I sit companionably, mostly in silence. I light a candle to make our Mom-and-daughter dinner special. Once a week, when all the others are out, she and I have a meal in front of the television and watch a show together. She never wants to discuss any aspect of it, but at least we have a shared experience and reference point.

Some non-communicators have an easier time sharing what's going on for them when there's a structured format. One easy model is to do "A Rose, a Thorn and a Bud." People take turns sharing something that is blossoming in their life, something that is a challenge, and maybe something that is emerging like a bud. This can be a dinner activity or be discussed at a family meeting or even in the car. Intimacy grows when we know what's going on in one another's lives and minds.

A simple way to connect with a non-communicator is to start tossing a ball or even a balloon back and forth, creating a rhythm of connection that might involve words or might not. Even without words, enjoyable interaction creates comfort and safety.

Even as you stay available to connect with your teenager, it's important for them to see that you have a life beyond your relationship with them. They need to know that you're okay so they can move on in their lives. This is a time, if you aren't already doing so, to be exploring some of your own interests, hobbies, friendships and dreams. One Mom who had neglected her friendship circle told me sheepishly, "My own children are just the most fascinating people on earth to me and I want to spend all my time with them while they are these ages." I can completely understand this and yet a healthy balance between family, work, community and self is good for all involved.

Transparency

One key to a happy life with teenagers is to help them register how much you care about them. Believe it or not, kids sometimes don't see the depth of your love and commitment to your family. At an age when people generally feel misunderstood—"Mom doesn't even care"—our teenagers may need to see our caring spelled out in giant, visible letters. We may feel that our whole lives are devoted to nurturing our families or providing for our families, yet much of our devotion is invisible to kids.

Like me, you probably work hard to earn a living to pay the bills for their entertainment, sports, transportation, education and wardrobe. You probably spend hours grocery shopping, cooking and cleaning. You may spend more hours arranging for doctors, dentists, tutors, school conferences and other activities. Most of this is behind-the-scenes work that doesn't necessarily tally up in a child's mind as a display of caring and commitment. The child literally might not see or notice your parenting activities.

Our support for our teenagers should be very visible and articulated so that it isn't taken for granted. If I commit to paying for a school cafeteria lunch 10 times a month, I'll dole the money out each week so that there is an interactive exchange. I point out now and then, "We do things to support each other in this family. I give you rides to tennis and you take out the trash. We all make contributions." I don't let rides or spending money become invisible. They are a gift to my child. When the child says, "Can I go to Sean's overnight. I need a ride anytime after 6:00?" I say "I can help you out in that way."

In the swoosh of family life, do I remember to say "I love you"? Do I remember to say, "You're a great kid. I'm so proud of you"? Do I make sure to comment on their efforts as well as their outcomes? "You're the best. You worked so hard on homework tonight." Letting them overhear you bragging about their excellent human qualities is a nice way to communicate your appreciation even when a head-on compliment might be warded off. On the phone, maybe you say to your sister, "I was just amazed at how patiently Joan finished her science fair project." If you said this to Joan's face, Joan might say, "Oh Mom, you're just saying that 'cause you're my mother." But I can wiggle my positive regard into her consciousness in ways that are not so direct and in a paradoxical way actually illuminate my feelings for her.

We can't assume that our kids are aware of how completely committed to them we are. Since so much of our love and worry and effort is invisible or can be taken for granted, I make a point of saying out loud, "I'm your champion. I'm here to support you." Then when my child tells me about his or her concerns, I nudge myself to listen really well even if my impulse is to leap in to explain the context or the other points of view in the situation.

One school week my 14-year-old had been getting out of bed three minutes before he had to catch his train, dashing out the door without the "collar shirt" he was required to wear for the school dress code, and without his homework. I got a few notes from various teachers and then a text from my own child. He had been held in for "working lunch," a detention-type response that the school gives to kids who aren't on top of their work. In his text he railed about how awful school was and how mean the teachers were. He added, "I wore my collar shirt today. I hope you love me."

I wanted to communicate both unconditional love and the expectation that he has to step up in taking responsibility for his life. With the onslaught of late homework and annoyed teachers, it took an effort for me to remember to comment, "I'm so glad you remembered your collar shirt today."

How do you communicate love and respect and eternal endorsement for the human being in front of you while addressing behavior that has to change? It's tricky!

"You're such a good kid. I know you don't want the teachers mad at you." Can you, the parent, become the ally who helps problem-solve about how to get the teachers not to be so annoyed? (How about the radical idea of doing your homework with excellence and turning it in on time?!) You are joining with the child to solve a problem he wants to solve. Seen from the child's perspective, the problem is that the teachers are on his back.

For kids to register that you are there for them, they really need to experience you as a supportive ally in their times of need. But to be a good parent you also need to have high expectations for your child. Transparency can help connect the two values. Say it all, not just the part about high expectations.

"I think so highly of you that I know you can work this out respectfully with the coach."

"I've been amazed at how you've found ways to solve this kind of problem in the past so I have confidence that you can find a way to make up the work."

"I know you want to be kind and also be in the cool group; I'll be championing you through every step of this hard situation."

Values

It would be hard to traverse our child's adolescence without ever having to probe, consider and reconsider some essential values. How much do you care about academic achievement? How much do you care about social proprieties such as language, appearance and manners? Teenagers have the daunting challenge of being true to their family's tradition while becoming uniquely themselves. Some teenagers are able to navigate this delicate dance gracefully while others have rougher rides. We, as parents, are inevitably hauled along for the adventure.

Teenagers appropriately look outward at this stage of life, away from the family and toward friends and activities. It's normal for them to self-define, separating from some of the family values. There has to be some elasticity while teenagers figure out how to be themselves and also be part of a family. But totally defying, denying and deposing the family's identity isn't going to help them or us in the long run. We as parents need to expand ourselves to accommodate new people, a new generation that will enrich who we are as a family even as new selves invariably change the flavor of the stew.

In my family we celebrate Shabbat every Friday night with candle lighting and a special dinner. When Rosi was in high school she asked if she could start going to the ice skating rink on Friday nights with her friends. That was when the open skating session happened to be. I had to clarify my values around this. Despite my feeling that our shared Jewish family times were precious I decided to accommodate to her wishes rather than setting up Judaism in opposition to her desire for fun. Taking into account the flow of our past, present and future, that decision made the most sense to me.

Another family might make a different decision that works best for them. One young teenager suddenly started refusing to attend church with his family. Because religion was very important to this family the mother was extremely perturbed. She wondered if her son was rejecting everything she valued. We discussed the situation at length. Finally, considering the child's developmental stage, the mother decided to compromise: the child had to drive with the family to church, but could sit in the car if he chose to.

I can picture some parents saying, "I couldn't get my teenager even to get in the car if he didn't want to." And in my head I am thinking a teenager is a dependent being living on your payroll in your house. Somehow, this child is feeling more entitled than is appropriate. Can you work out a cooperative arrangement whereby he is supported in his interests, which might include playing a sport, video games and having his own cell phone; and you are supported in your interests, which might include going to church, having family dinner and raking leaves in the yard together? Can you collaborate so that neither one is dictating to the other, but both are being respected and having needs and desires met?

The teenage years are a time when a family's religious practices, sexual mores, comfort zones, drug and alcohol policies, purpose in life and everything else under the sun might be challenged by a questioning, individuating young person. Often, just after emerging from the teenager's adolescence many parents go through a midlife crisis that has to do with defining self in the impending new era of the empty or emptier nest. I wonder if the teenager's struggles to self-define, to question, to be somebody, set the stage for the parent's own questing. Our development is deeply intertwined.

Patience

For many teenagers, at least temporarily, the crank on irritability and hysteria seems to be wound up to peak pitch. Every communication emanating from their mouths occurs at a frenzied level of emotion. "I can't find my homework! Someone stole it!" "Mom, I said I didn't want ketchup on my eggs!" "Get out of my room!"

"Re-wind," I say cheerfully. "Let's take that one over again." When my teenager is reasonable, I try to be exceptionally responsive and I comment on how reasonable dialogue is rewarding, "I like this reasonable conversation we're having. I'm really listening to what you want." Name what works.

I try to respond to the human being who is deep inside rather than to the unpleasant surface behavior. Sometimes, I need to require that behavior to change, but it doesn't tell me much about who my child is or what our relationship is. My child's momentary hostility or shunning doesn't mean he doesn't like me. And even when they don't like me, I need not to read much into that about the real nature of our relationship or about our future. Kids and parents know each other in very personal and vulnerable ways and there are things you like and don't like about each other. Teenagers can sometimes just be more tuned into the unlikeable or annoying things. Just as you forgive them, and see a bigger picture than the unlikeable brat, so, too, it is likely that the teenager will eventually grow into a bigger and more forgiving picture of you. In fact, the more you can model holding the big picture, not letting yourself get sunk in the difficult moments or stages, the more likely your child also will eventually hold a big picture that includes love, appreciation and gratitude in relation to you.

If you are parenting alone, finding friends or professionals who can help you hold the big picture will be helpful. If you are same-sex partnering and have an opposite-gender child—two Moms raising a son or two Dads raising a daughter—it will be helpful to have input and perspective from members of the opposite sex. Sometimes, during minute-by-minute life with a teenager, I feel myself sinking. "Please, God, is this child ever going to learn to do his own laundry?" That's when I know I need the big picture amplified for me. I pick up the phone to talk to my mother, Felice or Len. Outside support is so valuable for pondering the multitude of parenting issues that arise on a daily basis.

Families can be overly intense for teenagers who are desperate to be connected and also desperate to be free. A parent or two is not enough to hold a growing teenager. This is a great time to widen the circle of beloveds and friends both to dilute family intensity and to develop alternative resources. My family gets together once a month with a set of family friends for what we call "Dinner Coop." At our monthly dinner, I notice one of my kids discusses ideas and concerns with other adults, in my presence, saying things this child does not say directly to me. My child talks about how it feels to be a kid of color in all-white settings, about feeling inadequate in academic settings, and about wanting a romantic partner. This child uses this opportunity to confide in me without the vulnerability of actually revealing anything face to face to Mom.

Teenagers need you, but they also need smart, loving people to talk to who are not you. You can cultivate those relationships for them among your family and friends and even with professionals such as therapists, helping them widen their circle of support. This way they will have you and they will also have trustworthy people beyond you at a time when they need to move beyond family.

In the fast pace of family life, you'll be called on to make one parenting decision after the next. In this culture, for instance, a barrage of bad language is featured non-stop in mainstream entertainment so that every parent has to make decisions about curse words. Joey and I were leaving an evening Shabbat service, walking from my congregation, which is in an area of prime Philadelphia real estate filled with trendy cafes and bars, to the parking garage where our car was parked. Joey casually used a curse word to describe something we passed.

"Joey," I said, "I don't have a problem with you using the f-word when it's just you and me, but I don't consider being downtown to be private space. My congregants could overhear you and they would be very, very offended by that kind of talk." I realize that some families might have a totally different, equally legitimate position on curse words; this is my own personal comfort zone.

However, as we walked, we passed clusters of young adults out for Friday night entertainment. Emanating from every single cluster were phrases such as, "the fucking party last night," "fuck that, man!" "I told her, I am so fucked." We must have heard the f-word 20 times in those three blocks. The interface of family life and the bigger culture is complex. Luckily, Joey is developing his own good judgment about when and where to use these words. It would be hard for me to articulate for him every instance of when and how and where it is and isn't acceptable.

Hope

You, as the parent, are an important, steadfast source of optimism and encouragement for your child, even when things aren't going well. If you are frustrated with your child or in despair about your child, it is likely that your child is also feeling pretty low. Rather than reinforcing each other's worry, disappointment and pessimism, you can inject hope into the picture:

"I can't wait for the day when you'll have enough self-control to get to bed on time."

"I'm looking forward to the time when you'll remember to pack your lunch."

"I'm thinking about when we get through this hard time, we'll look back and say 'Phew!' "

Even in the middle of an upset, or right after it, you can put things in perspective in a way your teenager might not be able to do by saying, "I'm so glad I have a great kid even though I'm really annoyed about xyz."

"I'm frustrated about this situation but now that I've calmed down I'm remembering how many good choices you usually make and how hard you try."

Your teenager might think these upsets define your relationship and you, as the adult with the longer-term view, can situate the terribly annoying, frustrating, enraging moments in a longer-term context of growth, forgiveness and love, especially when you have your own support system.

Many families go through intense changes during these years, sometimes including divorce. No matter what changes the family is going through, the parent-child relationship has enormous potency for good. Re-creating civilization in our own little families is a big mission. I'm acutely aware of being accountable to the generations that came before me to continue raising up good human beings. I'm also accountable to the future roommates, spouses and children of my children to raise people whom someone would want to live with and love. And I'm accountable to myself and my child in this moment to be doing the best I can as a parent. My own parenting is nestled into this bigger vision of past, future and present interlinking with life on earth.

With so much accountability at stake I also need to hold the other end of reality, which is that we are just silly people who like to enjoy ourselves and one another. I don't want to feel like a walking-talking checklist: "Did you practice your instrument? Feed the pet? Gather sports gear? Take a shower? Do the homework? Clear the table? Stop pestering your sibling? Limit your screen time? Eat your vegetables?" Even though I am engaged in the serious act of reproducing civilization, my touch with my kids can be a light one.

Fun

Fun is an essential part of a well-balanced life with a teenager. A good working formula is to keep the ratio of fun to stress at a minimum of 5 parts fun to 1 part stress. This is the ratio determined by marriage specialist John Gottman, who researches optimal inputs for sustaining long-term marriage. In his studies he has found that a couple can fight a lot or have wildly emotional interactions without damaging their long-term union as long as certain conditions are met. One of those conditions is having a good balance of fun versus friction.

Intuitively, I think this same ratio applies to parent-teenage relationships. Finding such a balance between fun and stress during this stage of life can surely be a challenge. For one thing, our kids are likely to be busier than ever with homework, sports, friends and maybe a job. I have to force myself to ignore the messy room, let go of control over violent, sexist, racist, movies, songs and books at this stage and focus on being in an enjoyable relationship with my child.

Make sure to find places to overlap in joy with your teenager. Even with an uncommunicative, sullen child, you can share a TV series that you both enjoy, plan a meal of favorite foods, have weekly rituals such as a hoagie break or a late-night run to the convenience store. What are high-interest activities that you could share? Watching a team you both support? Buying clothes? (You can bond without spending a lot of money—several of my kids love thrift shops, where for ten dollars they can acquire a satisfying new wardrobe.)

To structure an interlude of family time together and to support the special learning needs of some of my kids, I've continued to read chapter books out loud all through the teenage years. We draw upon this resource as a shared reference point, a context for connection and humor. They groan when I call them to family reading time, but they often don't want to stop at the end of our session. To respect their declared opposition to family reading time, they hold veto rights that can be exercised once a week. Even with high-achieving teenagers, reading out loud together might be fun now and then. (See the section on Stories for more discussion of using stories in family life.)

Sharing music can be a bonding experience. Let your child educate you about what they like. Are you willing to endure a certain amount of unfamiliar and possibly even horrendous music in the name of parent-child bonding? Music is so meaningful to many teenagers—an identity claim, and an expression of feelings and ideas they aren't quite able to articulate themselves. In middle school, Raffi was passionate about a brand of punk music that sounded to me like one angry roar, no lyrics discernible. He plastered his walls with posters of these groups. The music seemed to express an emotional and political rage against injustice, helplessness and oppression that spoke to his experience as a powerless young person in a large public school. (This was the same year he stood up in class and announced to a nasty teacher who wanted to change his assigned seat, "I refuse to be subject to your tyranny.")

Sometimes doing something silly and unexpected adds delight to home life. Last night as my teenagers were doing homework I walked around with a can of whipped cream and squirted it into their mouths.

Other times, I put on music and dance, even as they hoot and holler at me, and sometimes we all end up bopping around together.

Humor is a blessing when it lightens up family life. There's nothing like a good belly laugh, especially when the joke is personal and truly funny. One time one of the kids accidentally opened the car door into another car, noticeably scraping the other car. We were in a supermarket parking lot, but no one was nearby.

"Quick, let's get out of here!" my child said, causing me to go into moral parent mode, modeling how we would write a note to leave on the other car's windshield with our insurance and contact info. That minor scrape cost me $1,000. As I wrote the check, Len made the whole episode worth it with a sardonic one-liner, "I'm not sure we can afford to raise an ethical child!"

Humor is a wonderful resource for parents, even if it is silly, ridiculous fun. Not only is humor fun, it has the lovely side effect of defusing tension. When you are laughing together you're not doing a lot of more unpleasant things with and to each other.

"Joey, have you put your nice clothes for the anniversary party into a pile for the cleaners?"

"No, Mom. I'm gonna."

"But you keep saying that and at this rate they'll still be at the cleaners when you need them for the anniversary."

"I'll wear whatever I want to the anniversary. I'll wear blue jeans." Irritated and defiant.

"You can wear your birthday suit." I giggle. He grins. "You can streak through the restaurant." We both laugh.

Another day, my family is hiking in the woods and the kids are getting hot and tired toward the end of the walk. We come to a small bridge over a creek. Joey blocks Mozi belligerently and she starts to holler. I approach, saying lightly "What, Joey, you're the Billy Goat Gruff?"

"No, I'm the Troll," he growls, moving aside.

Parenting is such a huge responsibility, it's important to add "Fun" to the checklist.

Slowing it Down, Speeding it Up

There's no reason every teenager has to follow rigidly a particular age-bound path into adult life. Some kids need more time to stand on their own two feet. Others are ready for dramatically more advanced learning and working opportunities even before they are ready to live entirely away from their families. Some kids are truly ready to launch at an early age. How can you tell what's right for your child? I expect my teenagers to be mastering independence in basic self management:

* Waking up and going to bed at reasonable hours without parental oversight.

* Managing personal hygiene without reminders to take a shower, do the laundry.

* Completing short and long-term homework assignments with a reasonable level of excellence and timeliness.

* Maintaining a relatively steady state mood without collapsing into unbearable despair or running wild with irresponsible elation. A full range of feelings is wonderful and managing one's self through all those feeling states is also important. Acting respectfully inside and outside the home, even when feeling irritable, is a sign of good self-management.

By junior year of high school if a child still hasn't achieved these developmental milestones, then either more time or more support or both are needed. Think creatively about options for your child. Would it be best for the child to repeat a grade to slow it down? Sometimes changing schools helps save face in these circumstances. Or perhaps the child could take a purposeful gap year after high school, or start at a college or job close to home—maybe even living at home and working up to a four-year, farther-away college or a more distant job.

It is possible to be completely transparent with your child about what needs to happen for your child's further independence. By these older teenage years children should be partners in their own developmental plan. "When you are able to get your own self up out of bed when the alarm clock rings, you'll be ready for more independence." Or, "If you want to succeed in college, you have to prove that you can turn your homework in on time every single week." Of course these truths should never be communicated during a fight or at a time of upset. Effective dialogue happens when both people are calm and connected.

Some kids are ready for way more sophisticated learning opportunities than typical high schools provide. I am not an admirer of high school education in this country. Even the best high schools, maybe especially the "best" high schools, rigorously grade, measure, compare and rate students multiple times a day. Imagine walking through nine periods a day of being tested in one way or another, mostly about what you know, and having numbers applied to you all day long: 76 on this test, 95 on that paper, 83, on the quiz. It's just not my idea of what is good for growing human beings. If a young person can create a plan to do something more meaningful than high school I would fully support it.

When I was in high school I attended a large, inner city public school that operated in a fashion somewhere between a prison and a holding ward for incompetents. I dropped out of high school when I was 16, worked as a waitress at Charlie Brown's Luncheonette to save money, and then travelled through Europe for four months with friends. In each country I read the literature of the land, visited art museums and historic sights and toured the schools while studying different education systems. When it was time to apply to college the only school that didn't want me was my "safety" school, which rejected me because I lacked Geometry and four years of Phys Ed.

Dropping out is not a good plan. But any plan that involves travel, volunteering, earning or studying could be great. Now that we know more about neuro-diversity, we know that some kids don't naturally produce high-initiative decisions. We all have different levels of "executive function." When you know your own child, you know whether you should respond to their self-programming or whether you need to take a more active role in structuring their program. In either case, the range of options for teenagers is so much greater than the normal institutions of adolescence might want us to think. High school and college are not for everyone!

Building on the Foundation

The foundation you've been creating all along of a family culture that supports good decision-making and conscious consumption will serve you well when your child becomes an adolescent. Rosi and her teenage friends found joy in running up and down the steps of the art museum, a la Sylvester Stallone in the movie *Rocky*. They also designed artistic tee shirts and made a club house in a spare room at school. Raffi immersed himself in serious competitive tennis and in documenting graffiti. Zoe took a passionate interest in drama. Joey started a collection of vaping supplies—vaping involves harmless electronic cigarettes that come in a multitude of flavors. Alcohol and drugs are available in their peer groups every step of the way and no doubt they each have tried these substances, but they have better and more fun things to do with the bulk of their time.

My teenagers learned how to be masters of their own lives rather than victims of an inane teenage culture that gives kids nothing meaningful to do, lots of stress, and unfortunate access to self-destructive options. I take only a piece of the credit for their wise choices in adolescence. I taught them that they had the freedom to create their own culture. But a parent can only add ingredients, stir, and then hope for the best. Kids get to make their own choices and kids have many influences other than parents. By the teenage years the balance of responsibility for life shifts from parent to child.

Open Mind

Keep an open mind when you consider how you will stay connected through turbulent teenage years.

* Be open to discovering and enjoying who your evolving teenager is becoming.

* Ask for lots of help from friends, family, clergy, teachers and therapists. It's a huge job to raise a young person—a way bigger job than any of us can do well alone. There is no shame in turning to your community for help again and again. In fact, you can be proud that you are open to other ideas and possibilities.

* Realize that parenting your child is not a test that you have to pass. Your parenting is a gift to society and you deserve every bit of support for making this project go well. You do not have to be on the defensive about what you need.

* Don't label too soon. Remember that teenagers are in a state of flux. I was surprised that my child who keeps his own room like a pigsty and resists my efforts to manage his slobbery was thrilled to go on an Outward Bound trip where the highlight was cleaning out a flamingo cage at the zoo. As he recounted his trip to person after person, he kept commenting on how great it had been to clean out the flamingo cage. I realized I was putting him in a box labelled Slob. Kids who seem lazy at home can be hard workers in a different setting. Give your kids many settings for success, especially where they can feel needed and relevant.

* Make time to reflect on your own experience as a teenager. Allow yourself to mourn for whatever did not work well in your teenage years or in your parents' parenting. Allow for the possibility that you will have a different take on your teenage years now that you are a parent.

* Think how much you've changed since you were a teenager. Your young person will grow up, too, and you will have made a solid contribution to humanity.

RACE

Waking Up To Race

❦

The Year 2000

In the morning, my brown-skinned baby boy, Joey, now four years old, runs from his bunk bed to find me in my bed. With passion and glee he yells, "Mommy! Mommy!" There is no one he is happier to see in the world than me. We wrap into each other's bodies under the blankets and snuggle for long, delicious moments before he gets "firsty" for a drink or wants to hear me read *Pocahontas* for the seven-millionth time. When I cuddle his precious little body, I am sometimes aware of my white skin ("the fairest of them all") and his beautiful tan skin side by side. This is the most intimate, definitely the closest physically and psychically, that I have ever been to a person of color. What a privilege; what a trust.

From choosing a neighborhood to choosing a nursery school, race has now become a major factor in my decision-making. Which is more important for my child: to have a choice of friends of all colors or to have the best education? These are questions that are relevant to all kids of any color and yet seemed particularly salient to me once I was parenting a child of color. He can go to an elite private school that is overwhelmingly white and wealthy where he will be surrounded by the best educational opportunities money can buy—reading and math specialists channeling the latest research from the Harvard School of

Education; gym four times a week; art, music, dance, wood shop, and science all with child-friendly specialists. Or he can go to the neighborhood public school, 90 percent black, 33 kids in a class where children sit in their seats or line up rigidly and get yelled at for much of the day, where the range of backgrounds and abilities is so great that no one gets their needs met, but where he will have friends of all colors.

As it turned out, at the neighborhood school he attended he became a target of bullying and was taunted by other kids who called him "Chinese Boy" even though he is from Guatemala. The teachers and administration were caring, but were so under-resourced and so pressured to focus on tests that there was no time for community building, teaching tolerance, or helping kids work through their issues.

On my small scale, I ask the same questions that institutions of higher education have been asking: How much educational value does diversity have in and of itself? What are the justifications for making decisions based on the color of skin in the name of a good cause (e.g. send my kid to the diverse but educationally inferior school so that he'll see his color reflected back)? What about making sure that I honor the other truths about my Latino son aside from his skin color: that he loves to run and climb and twirl and leap; that he's a very social child; that he's friendly and interested and eager to engage; that he's on the less-ready end of an academic spectrum of kindergarten readiness? I want to make decisions about the whole child, decisions that take into account the color of his skin, but are not limited to that issue.

My efforts have included living in this coop apartment where we have racial and economic diversity. In our building, built in the 1920s, we have spacious apartments with sunlight and hardwood floors; beautiful gardens in front and back tended by the neighbors of the co-op. But more important than the physical space, is the cooperative intention to work together across lines of difference. We share decision making about the budget, about cleaning the halls, about new tenants. When I first heard about this building years ago I was so excited that it existed, I raced to apply for residency, keeping it a secret from everyone I knew for fear they'd get in first and there wouldn't be room for me. Now I've been here for decades and this is my home. My neighbors and I have the context of joint residency to support interracial connection. Some neighbors are here because they are ideologically committed to that ideal; some are here because it's affordable; some are here because it's an attractive living situation. Even though we work on committees together and make decisions about our shared building together, there is still a social line dividing the races. It's evident in the way that we don't typically socialize in one another's homes, or attend one another's birthdays, graduations and weddings. But there's a friendly and respectful trans-racial collaboration, which is a hard thing to create in this society and especially across class lines.

Still, regardless of my living arrangement, I am a white Mom raising a child of color. There are places that I need guidance, for instance in presenting the police to my children. Until Joey became part of my life, I had always discussed the police with my little children as nice community helpers. "If you get lost you go to the nice police officer and he or she is there to help you get home." Once at a neighborhood fair, three-year-old Raffi did get lost. He wandered around in the crowd until he found a seven-foot-tall police officer in uniform.

The police officer asked him his name. Raffi gave it correctly. The police officer asked his address. Raffi gave it correctly. The phone number, too, the very little child recited competently. But when asked "Could you describe your mother?" he said, "No, dat's way too hard." Moments later, I retrieved him from the policeman's arms. This incident confirmed my children's confidence in the system.

My white consciousness was unfazed by the issue of racial profiling (when police stop people of color because they assume they are more likely to be engaged in criminal behavior), racist police violence and a racist criminal system, even though I had grown up during the Civil Rights Movement. I understood that apartheid was wrong long before

I understood the systemic nature of racism; that is, how many interlocking social systems cumulatively create second-class citizens. Then the O.J. Simpson trial gave me, along with much of the nation, a wake-up call. The fact that African Americans were so strongly aligned with this man, who in my opinion clearly and without a doubt murdered his ex-wife and her friend, made me realize that the experience of facing the American system was very, very different for people of different colors. The depth of pain and anger experienced by black Americans was proof to me that there must be racial inequality in the justice system. Through reading and paying more attention than I had before, it sunk in that there is a current of racism ever present and ever possible that goes way beyond interpersonal meanness.

I could imagine my gorgeous little boy becoming a lanky, tan-skinned teenager who would be stopped in a store on suspicion of shoplifting because a shopkeeper would see his skin color and not his gentle soul. How devastating it would be for him to have been raised to think that the police are nice helpers there to protect the good people, only for him to discover that only white people are considered good. Generations of black, Latino and Asian parents knew what needed to be done to prepare their children to face a racist world. I did not have my own wise generations informing me on this issue, but I soon understood that I needed to change the way I presented the police to my children.

The next time the occasion arose, chatting with my children, I interjected a story about police making mistakes. At the dinner table I told a short anecdote from the newspaper that day about how police had been caught purposefully framing poor black people in Philadelphia. Some of the people framed had spent long years in prison and were now being released as a result of this exposure.

Zoe looked at me with eight-year-old incredulity, "You mean the police did it on purpose?"

"Yes," I affirmed. "Sometimes police make mistakes, too." I could see her trying to compute this, struggling against the cognitive dissonance it caused with her prior education about the friendly police officer. I was doing this re-frame for Joey and I could see it was also shaking his notion of a solid, safe reality to think that the men in blue uniforms could do wrong.

"Everybody makes mistakes sometimes, but what's lucky is that the mistake got fixed and the police said they're sorry and they'll try not to do it again." (Let's not mention right now the 10 wasted years some innocent men spent behind bars because they were framed by cops.)

"Sorry is not enough." Joey shared his nursery school wisdom.

How do you teach children about the pain and injustice of the world while protecting them and giving them a sense of security, belonging and trust? I hate some of the things that my children need to know. It makes me so terribly sad that we live in a world where terrible things have happened and are still happening, and I have to somehow help my children face the truth. We have a set of family friends who avoided the issue by sheltering their little girls from all information about horrors. When their daughter Theresa spent the night with Zoe, she explained, "I'm not allowed to watch any TV shows with teenagers in them."

Zoe, who at age eight had read extensively about the Holocaust, said something about Hitler and Theresa responded, "Who's he?"

It may be possible to shelter the oldest child for a while, but in my family my little ones have heard things that are discussed by the older ones. And if I don't introduce these topics, their friends or the media or school will do it first. I'd rather it be me discussing these things so I can help them understand how to think about these terrible injustices.

In thinking about how to deal with racism with my kids, I turn to what I already know. The very first time I taught the- six-year-old Rosi about the Holocaust, tears streamed down my face. I didn't want her to have to know about such evil. I also didn't want her to feel that she was the target of such evil. It annoyed me that her Jewish nursery school kept teaching one story after another about bad kings trying to kill the Jews.

Later, as I mentioned in the section on Stories, I developed an appreciation for how these stories can become a template in a child's mind for the fact that bad things do happen in the world and that we can prevail. I began to see some of the value of communicating this mythic history to our children—not to teach the children to be victims, but as a way of dealing with the reality of evil in the world.

There's research that shows that young African-American teenage girls do better than white girls on self-esteem tests. One interpretation is that African-American girls are less affected by sexism than white girls because they have an analysis of racism that enables them to see that society is at fault, not them. An anti-racist education inoculates them, at least to some extent, against racism and sexism. Maybe good education that teaches about persecution and resistance can inoculate children against bigotry.

I struggled with how to teach my children about racism. Knowing the history of what white people did to the Native Americans or what white slave traders and slave owners did to Africans and their enslaved descendants, I wrestled with how to help kids understand this history. I didn't want to hate myself for being white like the oppressors or to wallow in guilt until I can't stand facing the issue anymore. I wanted to deal with these distressing issues of racism in history in a way that helps me and my kids develop into proud fighters for justice.

The language we use in our discussions of race matters a lot. I need to talk with the kids about issues of race in a way that does not polarize people along racial lines. Especially now that I am part of a multiracial family, I don't want an us-them consciousness within my own family. After struggling with how to talk to my kids about slavery or about the Civil Rights Movement, I eventually decided that talking about whites against blacks was counter-productive. Now I always refer to *"racist* whites" versus "African-Americans." It wasn't white against black. It was *racist* whites against blacks, which is an important distinction. This language leaves the door open for white people to be allies to people of color. I want my white kids to stand with the models of resistance, the Angelina Grimkes and Lucretia Motts of history, and I want my kids of color to be the Caesar Chevez, Martin Luther King, Jr. and Rosa Parks of the next generation.

The kids, like me, have had to grow into an understanding of racial issues. When Rosi was in kindergarten at the neighborhood, mostly black, public school, the school made a big deal of Black History Month. They studied black heroes and learned about Dr. King. Rosi came home with a work sheet one day on Dr. King, telling me, "We learned all about Dr. King today. He had to go to jail."

"Why did he have to go to jail?" I queried.

"Cause he killed someone," my five-year-old explained. When the kids were asked to draw pictures of Dr. King, they all made white men wearing crowns.

My own teachings weren't always much more understandable than whatever Rosi had learned in kindergarten. One day when my children were very young and didn't yet know that we live in a race-stratified society, one child asked me what was the Civil Rights Movement. I started talking about how racist white people didn't respect people with brown skin and didn't treat them fairly. Zoe, who must have been about five said, "You mean they wouldn't like Rosi because she has brown skin?" referring to her big sister Rosi's Mediterranean skin tone.

"Well, honey, Rosi has brown skin, but she's white." I said, making no sense at all.

How constructed the categories of race are! My first-born daughter has creamy, coffee-colored Mediterranean skin. She was a gorgeous baby with a head full of dark brown curls and sparkling dark brown eyes—an adorable child, and now a strikingly beautiful young woman.

I've always noticed and appreciated Rosi's beauty, but it used to be that when I'd see pictures of her and me or of Rosi and her grandmother, I would startle for a moment because our skin colors didn't match. Even though she was stunningly beautiful, a part of me expected her to match me. This was my reaction to a biological white daughter's difference from me.

Years later, along came Joey with his beautiful dark skin, sleek black hair and Asian-looking eyes, and all of a sudden brown skin in the family became normative. There were two brown-skin people in the family—Rosi and Joey—and I came to love the variety of skin colors. When I launched the next adoption, one intention was that there would be two children with similar features, both born in the same Central American country. I worried that Joey would feel isolated and different as the only adopted, Latino, ethnic-looking child in our family. I was motivated to increase the diversity at this point.

The Guatemalan baby home sent pictures of my daughter-to-be, Mozi, but I couldn't tell much from the low-quality pictures. They sent a video, but I could barely tell which child was mine in the film. When I finally went to meet my baby, I wandered through the baby home looking for her crib. There were dozens of beautiful brown-skinned babies with heads of black hair, room after room full of the cutest little babies with indigenous features. Finally, I came to the crib sporting a little note in Spanish: "They call me Mozi." I looked down at the infant. She had pale white skin, curly brown hair with dark eyes of the same color. I had imagined one of those brown-skin, black-hair beauties. I wanted someone to match Joey. Whereas a host of suburban white parents would have given a fortune to adopt a virtually white child, I had pictured a different kind of beauty.

The next day, during my second visit with my new baby, I had a mini revelation: this baby deserved to come into the family as her own person, not just as a little sister who should look like Joey. She had to be appreciated in her own glory. And glorious she was. Her pink skin was soft and rosy, her lush brown curls standing straight up in adorable absurdity above her perfect face, with deep, lively eyes. She couldn't have been more beautiful. She's Latina in her own way with her own skin color (which actually has become much more olive over the years). Once again a unique bundle of baby came into my life and I dedicated myself to raising this particular, precious individual.

So I have a white child with brown skin and a brown child with white skin. I speak honestly here about these sensitive issues because skin color matters. White skin privilege exists, expectations that families will have matching skin colors exist and our own discomfort with these topics exists. At first, my developing consciousness about race took place *on behalf* of my children of color. I wanted what was right for them. I wanted the language in the family and the stories we told to support their positive identity. The more I worked to make their lives congruent, especially on the racial issues, the more I felt they were being isolated and singled out in the family in a way that wasn't comfortable for them. After hearing his adoption story many times in a warm, accepting way, four-year-old Joey finally said," I don't wanna have a birth mother." I got that he didn't want to be different. He didn't want to be the celebrated example of diversity in our family.

My friend Abby Ruder, adoption specialist and family counselor, sat with me over lunch, listening, as she does so well, to where I felt stuck with my multiracial parenting. "I feel like in some ways I'm singling out my kids of color in the name of anti-racism in a way that just isolates them," I said.

Abby responded, "Your kids aren't alone in their experience of facing racism. You know, you are a Latino-Jewish family. This is a shared experience."

My consciousness expanded that day and I felt incredible relief that we were in this together; that my little children with brown skin didn't need to be the only ones in our family carrying concern about race and racism. My sense of stuckness melted away as Abby shared her insights about multiracial community. "You know, in my synagogue I tell people we are a multi-racial *synagogue* because we have some multiracial families. This is everyone's issue, not just the person of color's issue." All of a sudden I was thinking about racial issues for myself, not just for my children. A burden had been lifted from my Latino children as I, a white woman, began to share the need for racial justice.

This collective identity is where we need to go with the whole country. We need to get to a place where each of us, whatever our color, can say, "We in the United States are a diverse population. We need to make sure this country works for all of us."

I left the lunch with Abby feeling so grateful for her wisdom, so grateful that there are other families that have been through this multiracial parenting journey. There are even national organizations that address our realities. I'm now on the board of the Jewish Multiracial Network and there's also a terrific West Coast organization called B'chol Lashon. (It was young adults of color who grew up in the Jewish Multiracial Network who claimed the language "people of color." Others have commented negatively about that language so I name my source here.) I'm not alone, any more than Joey or Mozi is alone.

"Mommy, I luvoo," Joey says, nuzzling his soft brown face into my neck. We lie enwrapped on his little mattress in the corner of what is now the boys' room—his "area" as we call it. Miggie's colorful mural is on the wall and there is a shelf full of children's books and Joey's little treasures that include rocks we collected together in Oregon with my cousin Duvy, and marbles from his Aunt Liza's wedding. He's such a cuddle bunny.

My mind flashes, as it regularly does, to the fact that another woman gave birth to this little fellow. This little one, not my flesh and blood, not of my race or even fully my ethnicity, couldn't be more deeply bonded with me emotionally, now part of the ebb and flow of every minute's consciousness. I am his lifeline into the human race, his mother; he is my child.

He, so young, is mostly innocent of this, but I, who grew up in part in the racist, segregated south, can't help but be aware that still in this day and age, usually white people and brown people are not so intimate. My role models are all the domestics, people of color, who took care (I guess still take care) of white people's children. They have these kinds of intimate crossover relationships—the beloved housekeeper who nurtured the white people's kids. Even though we are probably at opposite ends of the spectrum of class privilege—the housekeeper who works in the privileged employer's home versus the privileged American who gets to adopt from a poor country—in respect to nurturing across color lines, I feel kinship.

When I conduct a wedding and there is one black woman's face in the sea of invited guests I'm curious about the background of the family's relationship with her. Is she the one who changed the bride or groom's diapers, rocked them to sleep, comforted fears and encouraged success, perhaps drove to the soccer games or to the drama practice? When else were people of color so regularly, intimately involved with the lives of white people? It's hard not to leap to assumptions. Maybe the lone black face is actually the CEO of the bride or groom's Fortune 500 company, or simply their neighbor. I notice that it's still rare for weddings to be racially mixed.

So here I am with my own strange mixture of privileges, a white woman with my little brown boy, feeling the connection with his beautiful, embodied self. Each one of my children is astoundingly beautiful to this mother's eyes. I could stare at them for hours, just admiring how completely gorgeous they each are. But even with that being true, I think his brown skin, black hair and Indian features are especially beautiful. When baby Joey first came into the family, Zoe kept exclaiming, "I just love his eyes! I want eyes like that. I want a husband to have eyes like that. He's so beautiful."

In the meantime, we are crossing a color line to be family. We are transgressing the subtle rules of separation that exist for people of different skin colors, transgressing them by being in the most intimate and central of relationships, family. And I am learning every day, with love and tears, how to make the passage.

The Year 2010

Being in a racially-mixed family and community opens a door and I am not surprised when my kids have racially diverse friends and partner with people from different races. Maybe Zoe will grow up to partner with someone who has beautiful, Asian-looking black eyes like her little brother Joey has. As we navigate issues of race and racism, President Obama, the nation's first African-American president, is elected at a fortuitous time for my multiracial family.

I put a big poster of Obama up in the living room, but Zoe says it's like Big Brother staring at us and maybe I will take it down. I tape newspaper photos of Obama and his white Mama on our kitchen walls, hoping my children will internalize the not-so-subtle point that Obama has a multiracial family. One picture shows five-year-old Obama dressed in a Halloween costume with his Mama standing close behind him. Another shows the two of them, shoulder to shoulder, at his high school graduation.

Maybe these kitchen decorations are infusing an important message, but in the meantime, Joey lets me know of his embarrassment at our different skin colors. As I drop him off at school he tells me, "Mom stay in the car. No one else has a mother with different color skin."

"Be proud of your multiracial family. It's like your president's family."

Race is a constant topic at our dinner table. We talk about Supreme Court desegregation decisions, quotas, the death penalty, poverty as racism, the prison system as racism. We have constant discussions of race and class. I can't shield my kids from living in a racist society, but we're sure not going to let the issues rest invisible. Race and racism are very lively concerns in the family. The kids see me challenging racism as an important strand of my life. They see my engagement enacted through what I read, what I watch, what organizations I belong to, where I live, what political work I do, which schools I choose. Listening to the big people share ideas and commentary about black and white, toddler Mozi pipes up, "Purple is a nice color, too."

In this city, most paid yard work and most low-level restaurant work is performed by Latinos. This is not the image I wish the kids were seeing. I try to give them context by explaining that immigrants start with the lowest jobs and work their way up toward a better life. Our Jewish ancestors came to this country with nothing, not even speaking the language, and made a good life even though there was terrible anti-Semitism. We hope that the Latino workers we see are in that generation of their families' journey.

Because most Latinos I meet in Philadelphia are from this very different class background, the obstacles to friendship are immense. The obstacles are cultural, geographic and also values-based. The swimming hole in our local woods is populated by Latino teenagers and young adults, and there are always smashed bottles and tons of trash left in the area. There's a machismo swagger among the young men and what I would call an objectification of women. Being culturally sensitive and being a feminist are two values that sometimes clash within me.

Luckily there is a growing community of progressive Latino men and our family is very fortunate to count our dear friend Jon, who has mentored Joey for years, among them. Joey, too, is proud to be a resource for younger kids coming up. He has a young friend named Eli, also born in Guatemala, whom he originally met at the Jewish Multiracial Network retreat years ago. Being a role model for this younger boy has been incredibly meaningful to Joey.

Raffi's lovely girlfriend is Japanese and African American. Both of them are students at Yale. When she comes to visit us, Joey asks how she explains her identity. "Sometimes I'm black, sometimes Japanese, sometimes a mix, sometimes a daughter or an athlete, sometimes a student," she tells him. I'm grateful whenever we can openly discuss these issues with other people who are living them.

A friend of mine has two teenagers who came into her family as babies from a South American country. My friend and I are in a discussion group where issues of race come up. I ask her how her children navigate having white parents and a fairly white suburban culture. "We've never discussed it," my friend says. I am astounded. How could this central reality in the kids' lives go unarticulated? How do children even process such silence?

At Joey's Bar Mitzvah, Len and I wove diversity into the ritual. Our theme, chosen by Joey, was that Jews come in many colors. He got the slogan from a poster created by the Jewish Multiracial Network showing dozens of people of all colors with the text, "Because Jews come in all colors." (The poster is available through the gift shop at Camp Isabella Freedman.)

Rosi volunteered to make Joey a multicolored prayer shawl (*tallis*) for the ritual. She decided to interview him about what symbols to put on this rainbow *tallis*. I watched as Rosi dialogued with Joey, asking him about each aspect of his identity and interests. "Do you want me to include a symbol about soccer? Do you want me to include a symbol about bike repair? Do you want me to include a symbol of Guatemala?" and he said "Naaaah," to anything representing Guatemala. There are other times when he proudly features Guatemala in his art or in his choice of wall decorations. I remember never to make assumptions about what is important to someone else at any given moment. I would have assumed, especially given his choice of Bar Mitzvah theme, that Joey wanted to emphasize his roots and his racial/ethnic identity, but he had other things at the front of his mind right then.

For the Bar Mitzvah, we had people read the Torah portion in several different languages. Cousin Lindsay read it in French, Rosi in Arabic, Zoe in Spanish and Joey in Hebrew. Joey wore the beautiful prayer shawl designed by Rosi and we had huge paper mache, pinata-style sculptures on each table that friends Susan and Moon and their three kids and my God kids, Nava and Yonah, made with us. I felt happy that we found a way to recognize and represent many strands of truth for Joey at his coming-of-age ceremony.

As a teenager, Joey does get followed in stores. When I take him shopping for a winter coat on a cold, blustery night, he happens to walk into the store without a winter coat. As he meanders through the racks looking at the coats, I notice a security worker tracking him carefully. Apparently, security workers are trained to be alert to people who walk in without a coat and walk out wearing one without paying. In my white-skin, female privilege I had never in my life known anything about this.

Joey has learned at a young age that he will be a "person of interest" no matter what he does. I see that when he walks down the street there are white people who cross to the other side or watch him go by before going into their homes. My sweet, tender boy is now in a category that is perceived by some as triply threatening: male, teenage, person of color.

Through many such experiences of being surveilled for no reason other than his skin color, now that he's a teenager he's super-conscious of race and racism. He's very aware of security cameras watching him and even has developed a bit of paranoia when out in public. I affirm for him, "It's true, you have to be extra responsible because there is racism in the world."

He thinks the conductor on his daily train ride to school is being racist.

"How is the conductor racist?" I ask, curious.

"Me and my friends were in the Quiet Car and he said we had to move 'cause we were making too much noise."

I don't want to dismiss his sense that there is racism in the world. I see that he is tuned into something very true and as a white person I probably underestimate how much racism there is. But in this case it seems to me that maybe Joey and his friends were making too much noise in the Quiet Car and anyone, whatever their skin color, making too much noise would be asked to move.

Yet, it's more important to me to be perceived by Joey as his ally than to reach a definitive analysis of this situation. Whatever the conductor intended, the context for Joey is that he's had many experiences of being unfairly considered suspect and I prioritize Joey's experience. I ask him sympathetic questions. I support him to advocate for himself by writing a letter to the transportation folks if he wants to.

I appreciate that Len and I are very much on the same page in taking racism seriously. I figure there are so many cases in which white people underestimate racism that even if we are overreacting about particular cases, it only helps right the balance sheet and raise the issues for inquiry. I hope I am encouraging Joey's empowerment, not his victimhood.

On the Board of the Jewish Multiracial Network, we are aiming to reach across the nation organizing support and advocacy for Jewish multiracial families. The centerpiece of the organization's efforts is a weekend retreat that has workshops for Jews of color, for families formed by interracial adoption, and for interracial couples and kids. The first time I walked into one of the JMN national gatherings, I saw a room full of people of all colors praying together in Hebrew. White people were in the minority that day, whereas in most of the U.S., Jewish communities have tended to be overwhelmingly white. I learned that historically Jews of color were actually the majority. Even in Israel, before the influx of Soviet Jews, the population was 60 percent Jewish people of color, from Middle East and North African countries. There was so much I didn't know about the diversity within my own heritage.

One of my tasks was to organize an event for teenage Jews of Color. Like I said earlier, the young adult Jews of Color, who grew up in this organization chose the terms; they were the ones who came up with the label "Jews of Color."

But I felt uneasy with the language. Are these kids Jewish Kids of Color or are they Jewish Kids? As a white woman I don't want to label kids who think of themselves as simply kids, not as Asian kids, or African-American kids. At some point the world, often at the college level, will tell them "You are Not White." But is it right for me to tell them that before it happens organically in their lives? How to identify without restricting? How to name without separating? The naming by definition is a form of separation. It's a "this" and not a "that." My hope has to be that the naming provides more connection and belonging than isolation and exclusion. It also seems important to give every kind of Jew a color adjective, for example White Jew, so that white Jews don't become the default norm.

Keeping an open dialogue about race requires me to accept that teenage Joey experiences the world in a fundamentally different way than his white mama and than his white brother and sisters.

I say, "We're going to a concert tonight at the Kimmel Center."

"There's just gonna be a lot of white people there," he says.

"Yeah," I agree. "Let's bet on how many people of color you'll see in that setting. Six?"

"None," he predicts.

We go to hip hop events and salsa festivals where people of color are in the majority and I experience the awkwardness of my whiteness in a sea of darker faces. When Joey started listening exclusively to hard-core rap music, I tried not to be defensive in the face of his strong identification with non-white culture. And I also don't cower at discussing the sexism and violence in this music while endorsing his attraction to it.

Meanwhile my college-student, white kids are embracing their multiracial family by doing fieldwork in Guatemala where their siblings were born; learning scholarly perspectives on varieties of family formation; researching the economics and history of international adoption. They've had to grapple with the recent tragic revelations about adoption fraud and with the sense that something sordid and unjust possibly (we'll never know) underlies their family's pure intention to be inclusive and diverse and to share love. The adoption experience, the multiracial experience, the complexity of the issues, has shaped us all.

The Year 2012

Seeing the world through anti-racist eyes, I frequently take a mental snapshot of scenes unfolding in front of me and do an internal color count: The Supreme Court; the teaching staff at my kids' school; my own circle of friends. Last month I gathered friends in my home for a Room of My Own blessing circle. I was moving into my own bedroom for the first time in 15 years, now that a few of my kids were out of the house. As I moved into this new physical space I was moving as well into new inner space and I wanted to fill the master bedroom with blessings to celebrate the move. At the blessing circle, my beloveds piled onto my big bed and crammed into the rest of the room to sing, bless and ready the room for me.

I looked around at the shining faces, taking the mental snapshot that I now take in most settings I'm in: how are we doing on racial diversity? Virtually all of my friends were white. These are the people I love, but how I wish that this was a more colorful picture. I understand that my family—myself included—would be nourished by a friendship circle that reflects our own family's diverse make-up, but making that happen in the innermost circles has been way easier said than done.

I wonder whether what I learned from bringing gender diversity into my life by having a son could help me with racial diversity. After taking my friend Jonathan's teaching to heart back then, I did accept the radical challenge of letting men into my inner circle so that Raffi would have good male influences in his life. My mother said at that time, "You don't have to marry a man or have a man live in the house. You just have to have men who you like be close to this little boy. He has to see that you approve of some men so that he can grow up to be one."

From then on Raffi spent a few hours a week with men who were family friends. The Jewish Renewal Life Center that I directed was a great resource; people without families either because they were young or they were in transition, were thrilled to spend time with families. It was win-win, mutually enriching for all of us. Little Raffi had wonderful adult male friends. We have pictures of Reuben, a bearded Israeli who came to spend a year in the Life Center and then stayed in the neighborhood, holding toddler Raffi on one hip with a baby bottle stuck in the pocket of his shirt. They had an outing every week for years and then Reuben would often stay for dinner. My friends Alon, Jonathan, David and Billy all spent time bonding regularly with Raffi when he was very young. As Raffi got older, he began to choose his own men. He was particularly close to Michael Cohen, another Life Center grad, who became a lifelong beloved. Len also became a constant man in Raffi's life. (I thought it was very important for my girls to have time with men too, and they did, but I have to admit that I prioritized that more for my sons.)

Could this experience of growing through difference in the area of gender diversity help me create a less lily-white intimacy constellation? One friend suggested: "Try making friends as political work. Cultivate friendships with people of diverse races because your vision includes racial diversity." I just can't see cultivating friendships primarily because the other person is a different color from me! Yet, I truly don't think it's possible to be fully aware of the issues that affect people of different races if you aren't in contact, in dialogue, in real connection with people who are most directly experiencing the impact of racism. Jonathan's guidance was to lead with love—to love my little boy so much that my life changed. Now I am being called on to make my life bigger again, once more starting exactly where I am and growing from there, giving this urgent priority.

Part of my commitment is to keep questing for racially diverse communities and for venues for effective work against racism. Just because it is hard to live in multiracial community in our stratified society, and just because it is hard to end racism, does not mean that I can walk away from the challenge. These are not excuses, just observations. "It's hard work—keep on working," I tell myself. As the ancient Rabbi Tarfon said, "It is not our job to complete the work, but neither are we free to desist from it."

I discovered that a place of positive interracial connection for me is in interfaith work. Joey and I—and sometimes my other kids—go regularly to community actions where religious leaders and congregants are advocating for jobs that pay a living wage and for better public education. I'm glad Joey can see me hugging my black minister colleagues and he can hear the eloquent imam inspire us. Class and race overlay one another, showing up in the decidedly less well-off economic status of so many of the black churches and the relative privilege of the Jews in our group.

On a day in January, Joey and I sat in a freezing-cold church in a poor Philadelphia neighborhood. We were there for an all-day strategy meeting to plan a campaign that would insist on fair and full funding from the state for the city's impoverished public schools. "Well," said the pastor apologetically as we huddled in the cold, "you know it's the end of the month." I knew she meant that they had a hard time paying their heating bill. This was what poverty was all about.

At another gathering, Joey proudly wore a shirt, along with dozens of other people, saying, "Put me to work and my city will work." We were organizing to have living wage jobs included in an upcoming expansion of the city's airport. Joey gave interviews with the local media. I have not perfectly diversified my inner circle, but I am trying to connect my family with people from diverse races who care about ending the systemic racism of poverty and ignorance.

The Year 2013

Zoe reads what I am writing about race. "Mom you can't say, 'Asian-looking eyes.' That is racist!"

"Why?" I ask. "Isn't it just a description?"

"No! It's racist."

"Okay," I accede, "I'll check it out with some other people."

I ask a number of people, including Joey, for their opinions on the use of the term "Asian-looking eyes."

Joey says, "I think it's racist. But I'm a teenage boy and I think everything is racist."

Everyone else I ask also agrees that there must be some other way to describe the kind of eyes I was trying to describe. Raffi points out that there's empiric diversity of bodies and then people's meanings get attached to bodies. He thinks what matters is how that translates into exploitation and violence. Raffi explains that "Asian eyes" aren't a stable thing in the world. The phrase is used for the way people with certain facial features get read and Raffi asks, "What's the purpose of reading it that way?" We each have our own language for talking about race. Raffi's language includes words like "empiric" and "exploitative," because those terms help him cut to the heart of the matter and clarify what needs to change.

I am still trying to understand why saying "Asian-looking eyes" is offensive because how should I describe the facial features that are being read a certain way? Or is the point that there is not even a "thing" that can be described separate from the naming? We have long conversations sorting out these questions. Even more important than the words we use is the active interrogation of these issues.

I left the phrase "Asian-looking eyes" standing in this section, simply to give context to the more important point, which is that being in dialogue about ending racism is what's crucial.

Aunt Miggie calls to say both her car and her husband's car are at the end of their working lives so she went out over the weekend and bought two white cars.

"That's racist," Joey jokes.

We can laugh together because our commitment to addressing racism in our lives and in our country is fierce.

LOSS

Change

"I'm in the hospital and they say there is this mass in my abdomen," my friend Felice said to me through the phone line. So much was still unclear about her situation that she was not paniced. But we moved into a heightened state of alert.

Those sudden moments in a lifetime lift a veil and reveal new aspects of reality. Change and loss and grief are elemental parts of life. Felice's illness called on me to confirm my commitment to this beloved friend and there was no question in my mind, no confusion or wondering about coming through for her. Felice was in need and I did not angst about what to do or how to do it. I knew I would just be with her through whatever she needed to go through, as much as I possibly could, and hold the truth with her that we didn't know if she would live or die.

In June 1978, I fell totally in love for the first time in my life. I was a 21-year-old feminist activist when I first met 24 year-old Felice. She was facilitating a tensely contested matter in the whole group meeting of the East Bay Coalition Against the Brigg's Initiative (the campaign that was featured in recent movies about Harvey Milk). She was in her full glory as a powerful activist, drawing on the mighty talent she used throughout her life to help each faction feel heard and move toward consensus.

During that summer of love we both considered her the wiser, older woman, much more experienced than me because of her being three years older. We worked passionately on the campaign, went camping and hiking all over the state and made glorious love, mostly in tents. At the end of the summer, Felice accompanied me back east where I had one more year of Swarthmore College to finish.

We were at a stage of our lives and in a culture such that we each eventually had other lovers and ended up in other cities for work and education. But we never broke up; we just morphed from being lovers to being close, life-long friends. My connection with Felice was so early and deep that for 33 years I felt that she could reach into my soul and take me to the next place I needed to go, and she claimed that I did the same thing for her mind.

She settled in Amherst, Massachusetts and I settled in Philadelphia. When Felice got sick, a five-hour car or train ride separated us, but it was somewhat on my beaten path as three of my kids were in college by then in that same northeast corridor. I spent at least four days a month with Felice while she battled her illness for two years. Sometimes I was there more often. Sometimes I'd take a kid or kids; sometimes I relied on the phenomenal support of Len and my mother to take care of the home front.

During the same period, I faced a crisis in my parenting partnership with Len that called for a decision: to separate or stay together. There was nothing simple or easy about making that decision or living with it. I realized that the dream I was holding, which included making a life with a best-beloved man friend, did not feel viable for my future even though I had been doing it for more than 10 years. A routine and expected event turned out to be the cataclysmic juncture that woke me up to this truth.

My third child, Zoe, was going to start college. This happy event—my middle child leaving home for college—was shockingly disruptive in my life. From single-parenting five small children, I was now co-parenting the two younger children still at home, who weren't even that young. When my first baby, Rosi, had moved on to college, her new stage felt huge and intense for me, but I still had four kids at home, very much filling my house and my life.

"Our hearts are going to grow to hold our far-away family members," I explained to the younger kids as Rosi went off to Brown in Providence, Rhode Island. Then Raffi went off to Yale in New Haven and I still had a high school senior at home who was a delight to live with and two younger ones with fairly high needs coming up.

I loved the joyful, demanding years of having a house full of kids. Now all of a sudden, at this tipping point, the question loomed, "What does the next era hold for me? What is my mission now? Who am I if I am not a full-time parent?" I know people who joyfully anticipate launching their kids into the world and opening up a new era for their own adult passions and pursuits. That was not me.

My nest was not going to be totally empty yet, but it was way way emptier than it had been. My experience of this emptying was of tectonic plates shifting within, releasing an overwhelming tsunami of emotion. In particular, flailing around, trying to find footing in my new chapter of life, I scrutinized my longings and unfulfilled needs.

Our little children weren't so little anymore and my own needs crept back up to the top of the priority list. The fault lines in my parenting partnership, its unsuitability for the next stage of my life, loomed. I felt like a snake outgrowing its skin. But the realization that our relationship was not working for me and that all doors for change within it seemed shut, was not welcome to me. As so often happens, insight does not arrive in a neat package, but shows up as upsetting, startling glimpses of reality.

There was no way to change the reality of Felice's diagnosis.

There was no way get past the obstacles in my partnership with Len.

When it comes to relationships, I have a questionable gift of not quite believing in the solidity of what looks on the surface to be true. Coursing underneath the surface of reality is potential and that's what I believe in: love, possibility, the invisible depths, the mystery that is not yet birthed, and I have lived my life taking the leap of faith.

"Mom, you are an eternal optimist," Zoe said to me once. Isn't it a good thing to look at a human being and not just see a static set of cells, but see the process of someone becoming? I look at people and see potential. I see them growing into themselves. Maybe there is an arrogance to falling in love with the person someone is becoming. But there is also nothing as transformative as love in creating the selves we are growing into.

When Len said he wanted to be a Dad in my family, I saw a person who had a lot of love to share, who was smart and funny and great with kids. I saw self-actualization in action in him and in me. I knew stuff would come up between us, but I felt optimistic that we could work our way through it, whatever it would turn out to be. Engaging this particular partner in discussions of what he wanted for his own "becoming" proved impossible. I noticed that we had no mutually acceptable process for co-creating a life and I minded greatly. But I plunged ahead anyway. I neglected my grandmother's key relationship advice: "Never marry (or partner with) someone hoping they will change." I hoped we would grow into making sense to each other, watching each other's backs as best friends in the world, championing and supporting each other and sharing a happy life. That did happen to some extent and for a stage of life.

Believing in development has served me well as a mother. Even as my child flings his socks on the floor and refuses to pick them up, I see him maturing into a respectful, responsible citizen. I guess in any relationship a balance of clear reality perception coupled with strong belief in potential will serve us well. The roles of mother and partner are different though. I have no expectation of being peers with a young child in the development of our relationship. I expect way more of myself than of my child and have unconditional patience in rising up over bumps in our path. With a partner I want to consciously co-create our lives with mutual responsiveness and respect. I had different expectations for peer-ness in my relationship with Len than I had with my kids.

There we were, my parenting partner and me, with a whole life together that basically worked well, except that it did not feel emotionally satisfying to me and there was no recourse or path toward resolving that. I had made all the unilateral changes I could think of and I could not find an effective way to talk with him about our relationship. With great effort and great reward, we had learned in therapy to talk cooperatively about the kids but he maintained that talking about our relationship was off limits.

The problem with moving away from my relationship with him was that we were parents. If we separated, the difficulties we experienced in understanding, communicating, and problem-solving together were likely to be exacerbated. That's why for years I focused on what did work, what could grow, and coped with the utter frustration of all the walls and limitations by cultivating my own patience, awareness and love. During those years, I thought to myself, "If it's a pain to communicate now, just imagine what a worse pain it is going to be to communicate if we aren't connected in the loving ways we have now." Many times, feeling disappointed in aspects of our partnership, I asked myself if I should continue in this relationship or leave it. I stayed for many reasons. Being in relationship with Len was like making my way through a salt marsh, wending my way through reeds towering over my head that obscured what was ahead; avoiding the swamp on one side, the rotting logs on the other, delighting in a beautiful view when it was there to be seen. I held each of my children securely in sacred trust. Each time I wondered if I should end my efforts with Len, I decided the best choice was persistence.

Now, at this new juncture in our lives with Zoe leaving home and Felice fighting for her life, the question was louder and more persistent. Len and my relationship took up the emotional space and time commitment of so much more than co-parents. I considered us life partners, although our relationship had not been acknowledged as such, or named as such. Now I felt ready to explore new, non-mothering sides of myself. I wanted to share a less kid-focused future with my life partner who was my good friend and co-parent. I wanted to share a future that was about Us and our desires, not just about raising children well. Sex was not the issue. I did not need our relationship to be sexual. I did need it to be about me as a partner in life, as I grew beyond parenting, not simply about me as a partner in parenting. Over a two-year period I had tried without success to have conversations about this with him

Finally, I sent him an e-mail asking whether all the questions I was raising about my future were questions we faced together or not? I wanted to make sure I was reading the situation correctly so I asked one more time, "Is this something we face together?"

He wrote me back: "I am completely happy. I do not want to engage more. We are not a couple."

There was my answer. We are parents. Not life partners.

The reality now was that, with the oldest three kids away at college, Len and I existed in a new and different family. The home front was now a small nuclear-style family with Dad and I living three blocks apart. Ironically, our relationship was as good as it had ever been, and we had mastered the art of quick repair of our connection when we had problems, but I had reached the end of my tolerance for our stuck places and the end of my willingness to spend hundreds of dollars on one-hour therapy sessions every few weeks, or sometimes every few months, so that he and I could have a real conversation. The limits of our intimacy felt unacceptable to me.

The human spirit yearns for both stability and growth and only I, as the agent of my own life, could decide what combination of the two I could live with. The choice seemed to be to wither into myself denying a life force or to burst forward without Len, horrendously disrupting the delicate, beautiful, functional web we had woven.

On the eve of the Jewish New Year I was in internal uproar facing my own future. Each moment was agonizing as I asked myself if leaving was the right decision. Was the right decision to stay and continue to thwart my longing for more connection? Was it right to emotionally suicide myself in order to stay? How could I be a woman who doesn't only surrender self to an Other, who insists on having a voice, who loves and respects her own wishes, desires, intelligence, sense? Of course, I also am a woman who, like most women in this society—thank God—tunes into relationship, who responds to the other, who steps aside, accommodates, compromises and makes peace. How should I hold both of those forces in myself? Len and I were like oil and vinegar, and with hard work, we had figured out how to make a salad dressing that was pleasing to both of us for a period of time. But it wasn't enough for me now in a new era of my life.

Meanwhile, my Zoe was trepidatiously launching into her own independent college life, following her brother to Yale, and I wanted to be a rock for her, so solid and safe, so that she could unfold her new wings to fly. My steadfast mothering and painful partnering coexisted, each authentic and deep. Every day I texted and spoke with my new college child, encouraging and supporting her. Every day I cried with my mother, my friends, my journal. Felice cried to me and I cried to Felice.

With my own life cracked wide open, light illuminated new truths and I saw clearly, past my hopes and dreams and desires, that the primary partnership of Len and I was suited to a certain limited stage of life and we were not going to grow beyond that as primary partners in any way. I simply could not flow past, around, over or through that truth. I felt like a plant; I needed to grow or die.

A friend quoted a Woody Allen film to me: "Relationships are like a shark—they have to move forward or they die," says one character to his partner.

"Honey, I think we have a dead shark on our hands."

I'm a snake, I'm a plant, I'm a dead shark, I'm thrashingly trying to figure all this out.

Finally, the murky waters of uncertainty parted and I saw my way clearly. I gave up my willingness to be his partner. I had no desire to challenge his nature or push him into territory that was anathema to him. And with new-found clarity, I knew it did not work in my new stage of life, in our new family format, for me to continue within the boundaries that he required. I made a decision. Later he invited me to "drag me kicking and screaming into the next stage of our lives." But it doesn't work to drag someone kicking and screaming into growing as life partners.

We stopped partnering. He stopped making financial contributions to family life. I pushed the re-set button and returned to solo decision making. We undid the legal papers that had made us heirs to each other's estates (such as they were). Predictably, our communication, empathy and cooperation deteriorated. Breaking up is such a blunt, clumsy way to change a relationship, but sometimes there isn't enough skill on the planet to do it differently.

Felice's aggressive cancer was spreading and she was getting sicker. Felice and her wife of many years, my dear friend Felicia, were pondering how to support their daughter, Shira, in facing the illness and ever-more-likely death of Felice. I was hoping to support my children in facing the changes in our family life. None of us wanted to deny grief and also we did not want to impose our own grieving on the kids.

Eleven-year-old Shira, Felice and Felicia's beautiful, brilliant daughter, conceived with the same donor with whom I had had a miscarriage, went to overnight camp for the summer. On visiting weekend she wept gigantic sobs of grief for hours, clinging to her mothers. She had been to camp for several years and had never been homesick. She knew from the beginning that her mother had cancer; the news was not new. Felice was alarmed by her daughter's pain.

"Are all these tears helpful?" Felice asked as she and I drove to her weekly healing session. As usual, she urged me to pass all cars in sight, drive in the fast lane, speed. "How much should I let Shira get her feelings out and how much should I help her get her attention back to having fun?"

"I don't know. I think being aware of your feelings and naming them and feeling them are all so important, but so is building the capacity to handle them. Capacity gets built by helping the child step out of the feelings and have some perspective. They learn that this too shall pass, it won't always feel this bad, things are really gonna be okay."

"Well what kind of balance should there be between listening to the feelings and helping someone handle the feelings?"

"Maybe you have to be aware of which position has more of a call for you—do you gravitate toward *expressing* feelings or do you gravitate toward *coping* with feelings? And then, once you're aware, you can correct to pay attention also to the other place."

"Where do you gravitate?" she asked me.

I pondered her question. "I would be more likely to emphasize coping and handling feelings rather than feeling them. So I need to adjust in the direction of listening to feelings more, don't you think? How about you?"

"I think I err on the side of focusing too much on the feelings," she said.

"So maybe the parenting correction you make is to focus more on building resilience?"

"Yeah, okay pass that car, you're going under 70. How do you build resilience?"

"You bolster the part of the child that is strong enough to handle the big feelings. You communicate reassurance and optimism and help her get her attention on what's fun and what she's looking forward to."

"Could you speed up a bit? You have to be more aggressive."

"Okay," I said, "A dilemma I have is that the time my kids are most likely to express feelings is when they are overly exhausted and it's way past bedtime. So I'm torn between listening to the feelings and just thinking 'Get this kid to bed.' "

"How about putting them to bed half an hour early?"

"When they aren't over-tired they don't go to that place of pouring out the feelings. They cope better. But it's probably good for them to just lose it some of the time."

"Speed up, please. It's hard to know the right balance between making space for the feelings and doing the other family management things that keep the kids functioning, like putting them to bed."

We went to Felice's appointment and then spontaneously had the idea to continue down the highway to visit Zoe, whom Felice adored, at her summer job in New Haven. Everything went wrong with the plan. There were closed entrance ramps, traffic jams, we almost ran out of gas, we got back on the highway in the wrong direction and finally made it home way past midnight. I didn't care about any of that. I just relished being with my beloved Felice, soaking up every minute of her presence, processing life and love, learning together as we had always done. I never wanted to parent with Felice, which was my main reason for not making a long-term partnership with her in the same home. We had found the perfect form for our love.

Even while I was with Felice that day, my mind kept darting back to lick the wounds of disruption between Len and myself. How do you know how much perseverating is helpful? Like a tongue returning to a canker sore, feeling the pain, assessing its extent, testing for healing, my mind went back again and again interrogating reality, interrogating my decisions.

I wondered whether my endless thinking crossed the line into obsession. Cuddled in Felice's king-size bed, I asked Felice what she thought when she was between naps.

Felice offered, "Your mind is trolling for insight and understanding. What have you learned? What will you take with you into future relationships?"

"Be more aware of my own motivations in choosing someone. Pay attention to whether I feel good partnering with that person."

"Do you regret the years with Len?"

"No. I'm proud of the choices I made. I'm proud that I took that leap of faith and gave it my best. We both poured our hearts and souls into making it work and we really did make it work for that stage of life. It feels like a huge loss that I don't have his friendship, at least not now, but I'm actually glad the kids have a beloved who is totally committed to them."

My dreams die hard. Maybe everyone's do. Mourning the lost dream, the lost partner, while parenting full-force ahead, was very very hard. What an ironic situation: to be divorced without ever having been married! Len is emotionally a full parent in the hearts of the younger kids, who have known him as Daddy most of their lives. He is as important a parent emotionally to them as I am and he's significant as well to the other family members. Those relationships are good for everyone and I support them, even when it's hard to share the kids now that he and I are not primary family to each other. It feels right that after all we've been through together, our destinies will be connected for the rest of our lives at least through our children's lives. I have to be willing to deal with my own upsets about separation without spewing them into the kids' lives. It's always good for kids to have more, rather than fewer, adults committed to them.

So I held my screaming inner life private while ministering competently to my children. I made space to listen to them, feed them, chauffeur them, provide for them. There's no perfect way to make family transitions like this. You want your inner and external life to have congruence, but kids know when you're sad or shaky and as they are older teenagers and young adults you shift toward more to sharing with them as peers and friends. On the other hand, I didn't want to overwhelm the kids with my inner turmoil. I made my way through it knowing there would be a better day, reminding myself that families go through hard times and come out the other end. I reassured myself that the huge ratio of solid ground in these kids' lives will compensate or at least balance the cracks. I had faith this would be true for me as well.

Grief

In my free moments, I tried to conjure helpful images of disruption, breakage—all part of life's momentous force. So much of my life had been oriented toward growing, building, creating, joining. I am a master of sustainable relationships—long-term relationships at each of my workplaces, long-term friendships with my beloveds. Now I needed new images. What are images of positive disruption? What are images of things falling apart for the best? The connection between Len and me, in its current form, had reached its limit and my sad choice was to move forward without him. But freedom can be heart-wrenching.

I gathered images from far-flung sources that would nourish my soul, keeping me strong as I continued daily parenting and work in the world. At hard times a parent needs to draw on every source of sustenance for meaning making and nourishment. This is one part of the work we need to do to be available to others in our families and beyond. Without my own attention to re-gaining a steady state in the aftermath of disruption, I wouldn't have much to give to others. Self care is an integral part of a world that works. Here are some items from my collection in case they can be of help to others:

The hymen breaks so that seeds of life can grow. I was a hymen.

The sac of birth water ruptures so that new life can emerge. I was the birth membrane.

The ancient, holy Temple is destroyed, the walls breached and tumbling. I was the crumbling Temple.

Living human bone decays, signaling new bone to emerge. I was disintegrating bone waiting for renewal.

Limbs pulled from living flesh, raw sinew and vessels dangling, blood hemorrhaging and the ferocious white blood cells gathering to activate the mending. I was a mangled human body on the mend.

I knew deep down that I could get through this separation because I had survived earlier separations, including the one from Rebecca. I knew that each separation can re-traumatize old sores, but also has the potential to reignite the resiliency of survival. I felt wiser for having been through my own grief before and for having accompanied hundreds of other people, as rabbi or therapist, through their times of mourning. Reassuring self- talk was a part of my salvation.

* This too is holy.

* Embrace the mess.

* The solution starts with this body, this breath, this brain.

* *Ring the bells that still can ring*
Forget your perfect offering
There is a crack in everything
That's how the light gets in
–Leonard Cohen

* "Mourning a relationship isn't the same thing as wanting it back." Zoe Greenberg's commentary on breaking up with her first boyfriend.

* Transition is fluid, the outcome is not certain, you never know what is around the corner.

* Sad is part of life too.

* This too shall pass.

* You're exactly where you need to be. Rosi Greenberg's commentary on going through a hard passage in her own life.

* Be right here, right now.

* There is a time for every season, turn turn turn.
A time to build, a time to break down....
Ecclesiastes

* You are stretching your capacity to hold hard things. You emotional insides will be deeper and wider after this. You'll have greater empathy for others, more understanding of literature, more humanity.

* Be incredibly compassionate to yourself. You're going through a really hard time.

* You have the full range of emotions. This grief is part of being human.

* It's a big world. There's enough for everyone. It will be okay.

I found that my experiences with loss deepened my own wisdom and ability to be present for the ups and downs of my kids' lives. I trusted that the kids could handle the upsetting reality that relationships go through changes. We were all learning to tolerate and integrate sad as well as happy feelings. I believed in all of us. I hoped that Len would turn to the many resources he had available to him for similar messages of resilience and nurturance. He had never wanted those messages from me anyway.

Members of a whole cohort of my friends who were approaching, or were already in, this less-child-focused stage of life were also questioning their primary relationships. Partners who couldn't traverse the transition away from full-time parenting were separating or considering separating. I noticed a gender dynamic, too, in that women were expecting men to be responsive to them and making decisions not to stay with men who could not be responsive to their desires. This seems to be a new variation for a generation of Baby Boomer women who, thanks to feminism among other things, have more economic independence and more rights to define what they like in relationship than women in past generations. In the past, midlife men had a tendency to be done with first wives, to perhaps trade them in for so-called trophy wives, but I was seeing midlife women now making choices about the relationships they wanted. I hadn't been aware that this transition beyond parenting was a danger zone for intimate relationships of all kinds. I didn't know I was entering this particular sea, until I was swirling around in its muddy waters.

I decided this traumatic passage must be my midlife crisis. It culminated with me taking all five kids to Guatemala for a month, and spontaneously, crazily, rescuing a furry white puppy from a shelter, flying it home, fostering it until we found another home for it since Zoe is allergic to mammal fur—the whole plan ridiculously pointless, costly, impractical, deeply symbolic of something in some mysterious way....

Felice was a maker of family beyond biological and legal family. She chose her family. She gathered family members into the Circle of Felice, life-long relationships from every decade of her life. In her last two years of life she was surrounded by magnificent support from the amazing community of beloveds she had gathered over a lifetime. We were there with one another constantly during those last two years, accompanying her to doctor appointments, operations, hospital stays or just cooking, cleaning and hanging out in the king-sized bed. There was tremendous communal support for and among the loved ones of Felice, Felicia and Shira. I felt honored and privileged to be on call for Felice and also deeply affirmed in my understanding that there are many ways to create families that work.

Felice's funeral took place in the midst of a major blizzard that shut down New England for three days. I led a powerful service and buried my best friend. One of the most moving moments of my life was when my five children walked into the synagogue, delivered with Len's help moments before the pending blizzard. I was intent on separating from him and did not want him to stay for the funeral, but I will be forever grateful for his assistance in bringing our kids to that funeral.

During that intense and sad time, I made love with Jerry, a close friend of Felice's, whom she had known since college and I had known since I was 21. Jerry was a divorced Dad and the ex of another friend of ours. There was solace and connection in his little co-housing bedroom, the size of a closet, and in his arms. But I didn't want my younger kids, who were just getting language for Len and me separating to have this new relationship tangled up with that. The timing was really not right and after some months I let the Jerry lovering taper off because it did not work for me in my family context. Still, in the moment of Felice's death, loss and renewal were intertwined.

I returned to Philly from the funeral, at 11 p.m., in the dark night, with sleepy Joey and Mozi in tow. We found bags of delicious food waiting outside the door, friends gathered later for a memorial feast.

I felt loved and cared for even in the great loss of saying goodbye to my oldest, closest friend. There was something pure, simple and clear about the tragedy of losing Felice.

By contrast, changing my relationship with Len involved questioning myself every single step of the way. What was the best way to do this? How could I inflict the least harm? How could I maintain my own integrity? How could I make it work for each child?

Because we had never publicly celebrated or named our relationship, there was no community of support surrounding me with understanding or comfort. People said things like, "Oh, I never knew exactly what your relationship was." Our relationship had been so vague to the public that its change did not register. Also, people are threatened by divorce because it challenges their hope for bedrock stability with their own mates. Society at large does not know how to handle separation. Whereas Judaism offers a brilliant structure of support to many people (not all) who mourn the death of a loved one, there is no framework of separation equivalent to a funeral, *shiva*, *shloshim* (thirty day mourning period), unveiling or the daily practice of saying the *kaddish* prayer for 11 months after the death and then at periodic memorial moments for the rest of your life. Whether there is public support or not, relationships go through changes.

I grieved in isolation, my joy diminished just as drops are taken from the Passover wine when we recite the plagues that rained down on the Egyptians because freedom is complicated and Egyptian people had to suffer for the Israelites' liberation.

Gleanings

One day, my Rosi, now a conscientious young adult who sparkles with warmth and humor, bought tickets for me and her to visit Longwood Gardens, a botanical marvel. What a grown-up thing to do. She drove up from Baltimore where she was teaching at an inner-city public school, her first real job. I drove down from Philadelphia and we met at the Gardens, at the end of a long winter, to celebrate the explosion of gorgeous orchid blooms.

Rosi regaled me with hilarious stories of life with her boyfriend: "We both finish a grueling day of teaching and say to each other, 'Is this what we want to do for the next 40 years? Maybe we'd rather do urban homesteading.' We fantasize about living closer to nature, but then reality hits: we can't even manage to plant our four-foot-by-four-foot garden box in the back yard. The compost sits next to the sink for six months 'cause neither of us wants to go out in the cold to dump it. And what we really enjoy is turning on our high-tech movie projector and vegging out on the sofa. I've even convinced Rich that using the dishwasher saves water." Arm in arm, we laughed raucously and enjoyed the flowers.

Then over a picnic lunch ("lesbian lunch" my strapping son Raffi calls these light, delicious spreads of a few crackers, a little humus, and some olives, that my girls and I relish), the talk turned tender and deep.

Rosi's college roommate's parents are separating after launching four of their five kids into college. Rosi's friend, a recent college graduate like Rosi, is distressed. With the segue of this update on her friend, I asked, "How is it for you that Len and I are separated?"

"Truthfully, it's kind of awkward," she admitted. "It also shakes me because I'm at a stage of life where I'm thinking about long-term relationship choices."

"Yeah, I can really see what you mean."

"I mean, it makes me wonder if I'm going to break up with Rich after 20 years. I don't want that!"

"You look at these models of people separating after a lot of years and it makes you wonder?"

"Yes. It's pretty discouraging. Because it feels so right with Rich now, but what if it doesn't in 20 years?"

I wish I could protect her. I wish I could give her the Treasure Cup that would prevent all future relational pain and suffering and make every life transition and stage of life happy for her. But I know I can't. I know that as life unfolds, partners can't always traverse transitions together and people have different needs and desires at different stages of life. It's impossible to predict whether her relationship will still work for her and for Rich in 20 years.

"Well you can't guarantee that you'll be together forever, but the one thing you know is that you can trust yourself to know what's best at each step along the way."

"That's true."

"Sometimes I wish I could show you a different relationship path, but it isn't all in my control. I hope I at least am showing you that human beings make the best choices they can under real life circumstances."

Connecting around being human beings living a life to the best of our abilities felt profound. This mother-daughter friendship means so much to me.

Wisdom does accrue by living and then reflecting upon life. Life is ragged and messy and an amazing teacher when we pay attention. I've made plenty of mistakes but I will share here the best of what I know about helping kids through change.

* **Help kids know what to expect**. They can then brace themselves for experiencing and mastering difficult feelings. Parents have the power to orient kids in ways that strengthen their resilience. Knowing the plan, knowing the schedule, being able to trust the parent's word, adds reliability to a frightening situation. Kids worry about the ways their own lives might change when parents go through changes. Mozi knows that on Tuesdays and Fridays after school she will spend a few hours with Len. This is stabilizing and orienting for her.

* **Give permission for kids to have their own feelings and perceptions.** Give names for feelings. Work on being able to just be with the feelings without interpretation or problem solving. One of my kids says, "Len buys all my clothes for me," and I think of all the hundreds of dollars I've spent on shoes and athletic gear and clothes (and yes, Len does buy the kids clothes, too) and shut my mouth. Each child is allowed to have their own experience, their own interpretation. I'm sometimes tempted to correct my child's perception or try to negotiate about a feeling and I have to remind myself just to let it be.

* **Structure a holding place for feelings through ritual.** For years I had three car seats in the back seat, one for Rosi, one for Raffi and one for Zoe. Rosi grew out of her car seat, and then Raffi grew out of his car seat, but even as a five -year-old, Zoe loved being in her car seat.

(Now kids stay in car seats till the age of 8, but back then they were designed for younger children.) Maybe she resisted the change because the hefty car seat raised her petite little self to a height of equivalence with the bigger sibs and to one where she could see comfortably out of the window, or maybe it was because she did not see herself as equal to the big kids and felt how presumptuous it would be to join them on the level seat. Finally when she was five plus some months and barely fit into the contraption anymore, it was time for her to give up her baby seat. She was not on board with the decision. She grieved, complained, negotiated and mourned.

We made a plan. (Really, I made a plan and presented it collegially to her.) "In one week it will be time to stop using the car seat. You will sit like Rosi and Raffi in the car. Every day for a month at bedtime we'll take time to say goodbye to the car seat. What do you want to remember about your wonderful car seat?"

During those years, Zoe slept on the top bunk of a bunk bed. Each night I leaned in and asked her to picture her car seat and say "Good-bye car seat, good-bye car seat, good-bye car seat." It became a fun and somewhat silly ritual that we both enjoyed. By the end of the month she had adjusted to sitting in the car like a big kid.

One nice thing about creating a simple ritual is that you can save "dealing with" an issue until ritual time. With Zoe's car seat separation I did not want to have a big fuss and discussion about it every single time we got into the car. I could say, "Remember, at bedtime we're going to say good-bye? Right now let's listen to Raffi-the-Singer."

* **Attend to the small losses; they prepare kids for bigger losses.** Leaving a car seat behind seemed like a small thing, but each time Zoe and my other kids rallied their strength and faced such challenges in a nourishing context of support, they were stronger for the next one. They were like seedlings that need to be hardened in the elements

before being transplanted to the garden. Moving up to the second floor of the school with the bigger grades, moving to a new school with a completely different culture, eventually leaving home to start college—challenges that seemed close to insurmountable were integrated. And when bigger losses happen, they especially need time and attention.

* **Open spaces for discussion and feelings around loss.** This helps integrate those themes into life. At the dinner table, when I occasionally say, "I wonder what our birth Moms did today?" I'm holding open space for that topic to be part of our family life. (I also sometimes talk about penises and vaginas because I want those words in our vocabulary.) The kids roll their eyes at me. But a day after one such comment, one of my kids who came into the family by adoption, woke me up at night, fell into my arms and sobbed, "I miss my Mom, I miss my Mom."

* **Don't assume you know what's going on for your child.** Remember to listen. Kids interpret new experiences within the thematic frameworks of their own emotional life. For instance, big themes in one of my kid's life are adoption and competition with a big, imposing brother. When this child learned that Daddy and Mommy were separating, her grief was about how first the big brother has more connection to his early life in Guatemala than this child does (because we know his foster family) and now this loss has been added to that. My child went right to the adoption wound, and the not-as-good-as-brother place.

* **Attend to your own earlier experiences of loss.** These shadow whatever current loss you're enduring. Make special space for your own inner life and inner nourishment at hard times. I spent time reflecting on how my own parents' separation was the same and different from this one. I am not my mother and Len is not my father and

I get to choose my part in this without necessarily repeating patterns from the past.

* **Ally with your child's ability to handle the losses of life.** Raffi went through a stage around the age of seven of missing his donor at bedtime. He would come out of his bed for heart-to-heart talks and special attention from me for many nights. Naturally, I wanted to be there for him with this issue in his life. In fact, I was probably super-primed to pay attention to this exact issue for him. Eventually, I sensed that he had learned this topic could be used as an excuse for staying up late, and I started to respond to the midnight mourning by saying warmly and encouragingly, "Let's talk about that more in the morning."

On the first anniversary of Felice's death, Felicia, a wise mother, took 12-year-old Shira to a breakfast house that Felice loved, in her memory. On the anniversary of Len's mother's death, we served the kind of lollipops that this Grandma used to like. Try to remember the good times, not just the loss. Take to heart the wisdom behind celebrating a birthday rather than a death day.

I tell my kids sometimes, kindly, "You can handle that. You're bigger than that."

* **At a time when you have huge need, enormously bolster your sources of sustenance:** be extremely kind to yourself; indulge in what is comforting or distracting to you in the least harmful ways, e.g. T.V. shows rather than alcohol; let your friends and family know how much you need them—it is a gift to your people to let them care for you; if you belong to a spiritual community, show up because prayer and song and light can replenish you; know that the more you take care of yourself the better it is for your child.

* **Include the other parent's name and make mention of happy times together.** I often tuck Mozi in by saying, "Mommy loves you, Daddy loves you." Even when Len and I are disconnected, I want to give the child the privilege of integrating herself through entwining the two people she loves most in the world. The challenge when you have an ex is to uphold unifying engagement with both parents for your child even as you work to separate and disentangle from your ex. For a lost loved one who wasn't an ex, it's also important to weave memories and mention into the life of the living. I made a point of keeping pictures of Len in different family groupings on our mantle.

* **In the face of tumult and change, keep whatever you can stable and reassuring for you and your child.** Try to minimize changes to the child's schedule; feed the child comfort food that they enjoy; spend time relaxing, being silly, doing fun things together. You may feel stunned inside, but your physical calm presence is reassuring to your child.

* **Let some of the demand go.** While actively integrating big loss, do fewer chores, less pet care, less nagging and more just being together. Psychic space is required for you and your child to assimilate change. Other pressures can be shelved for a while. Don't shame and blame yourself to move faster with whatever aftermath needs to be handled such as sorting through things or updating paperwork, or even progressing with emotional healing. Healing takes lots of energy and time and you need exactly as much time as you need.

* **Accept that life isn't always going to feel good.** Sometimes life hurts. It will hurt at times for our kids too. Your child will have an easier time bearing their pain if you can manage to tolerate your own pain and also their pain. A lot of suffering comes because we wish pain

didn't exist. Sometimes we wish it so much that we can't even see the pain our kids are feeling. You can assume, no matter how much you wish otherwise, that the separation of parents or the loss of a parent is deeply painful for any child. Kids will have times of unhappiness and they'll be better off if we can acknowledge and bear that truth. Rabbi Ruth Sohn offers a beautiful image for the pain that is a part of life. She imagines a Lake of Pain that we all take turns lapping from. We might as well accept that each one of us, including our children, will have a turn to lap from that lake.

Love doesn't die. Love transforms. Love can transform into hate or into many other things such as old fond friendship. I get a say in the alchemy of this transformation through my wishes and actions, although the whole recipe isn't in my hands alone. Looking back over the years of being in close relationship with Len, I'm proud and I'm sad. I wish I had the skill and wisdom to do the impossible, to somehow walk with my friend into a future I imagined together. We are walking into a future of some kind or other, our destinies inextricably interwoven, and I hope to make active choices about doing that as best as possible. I live with the understanding that things begin, that things end, that things change and I don't have the ability to shape everything the way I wish it to be, that I *do* have the power to make choices every step of the way.

I believe in building sustainable relationships. You love someone because they are lovable and because you have enormous capacity for love. Changing the nature of a relationship can be incredibly wrenching but can the relationship continue eventually in some way? I am close friends with most of my ex's and certainly not enemies with any of them. I have hope that this transition with Len will evolve into a friendship some day. Not the intense, interdependent friendship of primary partners, but something connected and sweet. Rebecca and I are dear, dear friends now and we surely went through a substantial period of separateness. I don't know what the future will look like for Len and me, and it will be beyond my power to author it on my own.

Helping our kids face loss and transition is an important part of raising them for the world they will live in. They will face the personal losses inherent in any life and also at this particular moment in history, they will also face the loss of the planet as we have known it. They will live on a planet that is coping with drastic losses of biodiversity and climate stability. Their abilities to face the reality of change, even sad and difficult change, will strengthen them for forging ahead in creating lives worth living on an earth worth saving.

Because loss is an inevitable strand of life, it calls on parents to integrate the challenge of change and grief and resilience into our parenting. Parents have inner lives and sufferings and joys, and we need to persist through our trials and tribulations with steady, good parenting whether it is just the parent holding loss or the parent and child holding it together. The great spiritual teacher Reb Zalman says that we cannot control the current of the river, but we may be able to steady and steer the canoe.

As parents, we help our children by doing the best we can through turbulent times knowing there will also be calm, clear waters ahead. We have some degree of power to prevent trauma from pouring heedlessly from one generation to the next. We can commit to at least trying to do our own work of healing, growing and being good people; to protecting our young children from the full force of adult troubles. Attending well to our own mourning is a part of this work. When we accept loss as an inevitable component of life, we become freer to re-engage with life and love, with projects and people, and with whatever our future holds. And we show our kids that all this is possible.

SHARING

Good Deeds

❧

A Jewish teaching explains that reality consists of both harshness and kindness. Since the world already contains enough harshness —sickness, death, financial factors beyond our control, war, and other terrible curses—people were put into the world to add the element of kindness. Our main job is to add kindness to the universe.

Families can play a crucial role as incubators of connectedness and caring. While American culture has been championing the self-actualized, autonomous individual, many of us know that people feel calmer, happier and kinder when they are embedded in caring networks of mutuality. People isolated in privilege suffer high rates of anxiety, depression and existential angst.

Parents, especially in upper-middle-class families, need moral support to link our child's well-being to the well-being of the rest of the world. When you know you are your little person's primary advocate and champion in life, no wonder you are drawn to focus intensely on maximizing your child's potential, to focus fiercely on your child's schedule, fine-tuned to enhance all talents, interests and correctives. Your child does need you and it is right for you to think well about helping your child develop.

Part of what will serve your child well is the opportunity to develop a sense of being part of an ecology of family and community life, attuned to the needs and desires of others. High-achieving parents whose anxious rat-race to maximize their child, with all the attendant research, paperwork and logistics for all the child's activities, may diminish the joy experienced by the child and themselves, joy that is inherent in being, belonging and contributing. A life overly focused on the individual may actually deprive your child of being part of something bigger than herself.

Generosity, if it is on the "To Do" list at all, can become one more item to check off, rather than a theme to be deeply integrated into family life. Many social commentators are concerned about the cultural time bombs inherent in high-pressure production of the self-actualized individual so here we ask what we can do in families to prepare kids for a life of generous interrelationship. How can we parent from a deep place of understanding that life will be more meaningful to children who act generously, understand their interconnectedness and feel compassionate? Acting, thinking and feeling are all interconnected and we need to move forward on all fronts to help kids grow into lives of caring and sharing.

There is no one "right" way to be an incubator of connectedness and caring. This mandate does not need to be added to the high-pressure list of things we must accomplish for our families! It can be a value that informs day-to-day living, with a bit of reflection to raise its salience in our consciousness. Generosity starts at home in very small ways, with people we know well, and grows from there. Finding routines that work for you where you can check in with each other, plan together, consult one another, is important. Also being part of something bigger than your family unit has high value, whether it is a congregation, a civic group, a neighborhood council or a cause.

In American society, because of the relentless cultural emphasis on individual pleasure, satisfaction, achievement and comfort, parents have to be equally relentless in creating community within the family and beyond. To be a champion of community will go against your natural grain if you grew up in this culture. You will try out a congregation and you'll think, "There aren't enough kids, the other people are too conservative or too hippy-ish or too something, the leader isn't very good, it's too expensive, the drive is too far, it's not my kind of religion."

Felice was always dissatisfied with her Jewish community options. One synagogue was "too straight" and didn't have a lesbian presence; another synagogue had plenty of lesbians, but not enough children; and finally the place that had her brand of spirituality and included lesbians and children, had no politics. We joked that she could sit on a rock, alone, and have the perfect combination of sexual orientation, kids, spirituality and politics. But she wouldn't really be in community.

Any one concern might be something worth weighing in choosing places to belong, but beware negating any possibility of connection by insisting on perfect satisfaction, perfect individual fulfillment with every aspect of the experience. Generosity builds community and being part of a community requires generosity. We have to realize that each aspect of a shared experience might not be exactly suited to oneself, but might address the needs of someone else. Can I find a good enough match for my self and my family with some group that is bigger than us? Can I open my heart enough to belong? Belonging is really good for kids. From a base of belonging arises the capacity to care for others.

I sit at the family dinner table, cheerfully set with mismatched ceramic plates. Four of my kids are arrayed around the table, ages three to twelve. Raffi is seated at the end because he's a leftie and he won't bump into anyone down there. Every now and then I keep things lively by tossing broccoli down the length of the table and into his mouth, to the delight of the young ones. We hold hands to say grace before eating and then serve up the victuals.

When every plate is full, I broach an important question, one that I wish I would remember to ask more frequently. "Who did a good deed today?"

This question is important to me because so much of the kids' worlds are focused on achievement—grades, goals, money. Be a fly on the wall sometime and observe just how much time is spent discussing how much things cost, purchases, plans to purchase, among adults and among children. We live in a very money-oriented world that promotes greed and selfishness. If we truly want to raise kind kids we will have to redirect some of our devotion toward the inculcation and appreciation of kindness.

"Did anyone do a good deed for you today?"

"Did anyone notice someone else doing something really kind or helpful today?"

My interest in the subject elevates the value of kindness with my kids.

Children need to be givers as well as getters. I have to work hard to pay attention to my children as givers because so much else distracts me and demands my attention. There is always one more thing to want, to buy, to own. In the culture of Too Much, it's easy for kids to feel powerless to make a generous difference in the world. When they see the things their parents want—a new grill, an iPad, a Wii—things that are beyond kid-reach, financially, kids can get discouraged into abandoning the effort to be generous. Kids also see huge world problems that seem impossible to fix. Finding ways for kids to make a genuine contribution to people they love and to problems that they care about is essential. This has to be a high, high priority of parents because it is not easy for them to do alone.

In families with two partnering parents, one role spouses can play is to help kids plan gifts for the other spouse. In families with one parent, grandparents or friends can be enlisted to do this. I'm sometimes amazed at how many kids are not expected to give gifts to their parents or siblings. Gifts from the heart are so much more meaningful than some pricey object that the parents could have bought for themselves. For example, a piece of hand-made art; an original card listing some things the child enjoys doing with the parent; a purchased card with a particularly relevant message. A cute bumper sticker or refrigerator magnet are good gifts for parents—fun to choose, easy to order and affordable for kids.

I always appreciated receiving coupons for services, such as one coupon for sweeping the floor, one coupon for carrying in grocery bags, one coupon for taking out recycling, one coupon for tech support when needed. Children give the gift of a performance of theatre, music or dance, or a back or foot massage. They can cook a special surprise item or meal for the parent, which can be as simple as making pudding or as elaborate as a five-course dinner. Kids learn that giving feels good. Once Mozi memorably gifted me with unlimited use of a special, big mug that belonged to her.

Spending quality time together should be treasured as a gift. Kids can give the promise to accompany the parent on an outing of the parent's choosing, such as a walk in the woods, a trip to the grocery store—even a night at family friends' that the child doesn't typically enjoy.

Helping a child give to a parent is nice for the parent and it's terrific for the child's development. The night of Hanukkah that we dubbed "Kids' Night" unexpectedly became the annual highlight of the holiday. Each child gives the other siblings a small gift. Sometimes the gift is a coveted hand-me-down object that moves from an older to a younger child. Sometimes, I subsidize the ideas of the youngest kids. Tremendous thoughtfulness and humor have gone into these gifts. For single parents and solo kids, making a tradition of joining with one or more other families, annually, to do this kind of exchange enhances the generosity potential.

To emphasize the giving aspect of the tradition, we sit in a circle, focusing our attention on the giver, not the receiver, of each gift. If it is Rosi's turn, she gives each sibling a gift. Then we move on to Raffi as the giver. To focus our attention on the giver rather than the receiver, is a subtle shift with a large significance.

Helping kids make note of generosity (with the goal of encouraging it) can happen throughout daily life. When I share with my kids a bite of delicious food that I'm eating, or a portion of the quilt on the sofa, now and then I say, "I'm being generous with you because I want to fill you so full of generosity that it overflows into you being generous with others."

When playing board games or card games with your kids, offer generous moves "I'll give you $400 extra dollars to buy that property," or "You can have my turn because you're so close to getting to that space." I'll say: "Oh, take another card! It's more fun that way!" Your kids will let you know when they want to play more competitively. In the meantime, they learn from you to practice generosity.

There have been times when I was in the midst of scrubbing mashed potatoes off the floor or wiping wads of dust from behind the playpen and a flash of self-reflection dazed me. "My children constantly see me cleaning. Is this what they think I care most about?" Cleanliness and order are not really my highest values, yet conversations about cleanliness and order constitute a huge percentage of my interactions with my kids.

"Your shoes are in the living room. Someone left their hair products on the sink. It's time to clear the dinner dishes. Whose backpack is this? When the juice spills, please wipe it up."

So I'll leap up, dust mop or rag in hand and shout to whoever is listening, "Let's buy some food for the hungry people."

"Are you hungry, Mommy?"

"No, but some people don't have enough to eat and we can buy them some food."

"Why don't they go to the store themselves?"

Hand in hand, off we go to the food co-op, pockets stuffed with coins from the *tzedakah* (charity) box we fill with coins every week. I explain along the way to my puzzled children why this is a good deed to do.

Better yet are opportunities for kids to engage in generosity on a consistent, routine basis: volunteering weekly in a retirement home; cooking for the homeless shelter; playing with cats and dogs at a rescue league; helping younger children at an after-school program. I know it is definitely a problem that so often intensive adult participation is needed in order for kids to have the opportunity to be of service. Don't we already have enough to do? Yet the value of helping kids practice giving back is immense.

For years, Len took Mozi most Friday afternoons to lead a prayer service in the assisted-living facility where his aunt lived. He was extending his personal, family visit to be of service to her whole community. When the aunt died, the two of them continued to go frequently to the facility. My bouncy little girl delighted the community, and for her it was a special time with her Dad. In fact, he kept doing the service for way longer than he would have because she didn't want to stop the tradition.

Keeping your eyes open for ways that kids can help might identify some possibilities. Does a neighbor's dog need walking? Could a house-bound elder use some help? All around us people are in need. The closer to home and the more connected to a child's real self the better when you are trying to help children find generous motivation. Eventually, they can grow to analyze complex needs even in far away places but for starters small needs that stare your family in the face will help kids connect awareness of need and impulse to help. For a child interested in sports, helping with Special Olympics or even informally with a special needs participant on a local team would be super. Issues that are close to home and close to the heart are a good place to start.

Try to connect your child's genuine caring to good deeds they can do. Mozi enjoyed a special outing with her Dad to the nursing home so she was always glad to go, and the elders loved seeing her there. The plan was a win-win plan for all involved which is the most fun kind of plan. But there will be times when your child is not highly motivated to be generous. For example, she might not want to spend an afternoon helping an elderly neighbor pull weeds. When your child grows bored or frustrated or tired of persisting with the generous behavior, you can coach the child to stick with the good deed even after it stops being exciting and new. The reward is in the giving itself, even if the process is not as entertaining as they might want.

"I see you're bored with this and you have other stuff you want to do, but just because you're tired of helping Gramma learn how to use her scanner doesn't mean the job is done. She needs you until she feels confident that she can do it herself."

"I see you're tired of helping out, but this isn't about you right now; it's about the people who need the food we're packing." Aligning yourself with the importance of generous behavior uplifts the value of giving.

Perhaps you are in a position to open up these opportunities to other people's kids. Do you work in a nursing home or after school program or in a social service setting or with disabled people? Creating multigenerational opportunities for being of service is a much needed mitzvah (the Jewish word for good deed.)

I will be forever grateful to a single Mom with three kids of her own who moved into my apartment complex when I was juggling my newborn third child, a rambunctious toddler and a sophisticated four-year-old. This Mom offered to do our weekly grocery shopping. I didn't even know this woman when she first made the offer. For a full year her family helped my family. She was no doubt looking for ways to involve her own elementary-school-aged children in meaningful service.

Now, a few times a year I volunteer with my kids in a program for homeless families. Just about every time my shift comes up, I feel "too busy" and consider cancelling it just this one time. I've learned that if I want this activity to be part of our family's life, I have to be consistent or it won't happen. My kids play with the homeless kids, which gives the parents in the shelter a break and gives the "guests"—as the residents are called—some fun. Our experience there has led to complex conversations.

"Mom, how come those kids were wearing really expensive designer shoes and they don't even have a place to live?" "How come almost all the people in the shelter are brown-skinned people?" "Why can't they get a tent and live in it?"

The great Rabbi Abraham Joshua Heschel taught that we are not guilty of creating the world as it is with all its problems, but all of us are responsible for making it better. I want to raise kids who feel responsible for contributing to the well-being of the planet, and I sometimes feel that I'm working against a corporate advertising onslaught that would rather young people think only about buying the next product.

Pets can be a way to foster the relational responsibility of caring and sharing. In the old days, when the cows mooed, the milking chore needed to be done; when the hens clucked, the eggs could be gathered. Now, when the puppy is hungry, feed it; the guinea pig cage is damp, clean it. People and animals evolved in a close symbiosis that is no longer reflected in modern society. Many kids are exempt from the real work that goes into caring for animals, but those kind of caring responsibilities are wonderful opportunities. I said this to a friend, who laughed dismissively, "My kid was interested in the fish for about five minutes." But there is value in teaching the child to follow through with care even when interest wanes.

"Honey, let's imagine how the fish feels when it's really hungry and no one feeds it."

"But Mom, how about if you feed it?"

"I have my jobs. I feed this family. It's your job to take care of the fish."

You can help structure the care giving so that the child can succeed. "Mozi, remember, first thing you do when you get home from school is fill the dog's water bowl." Attaching pet care to other things that happen routinely, such as walking in the door or brushing teeth, can help a child remember to do the tasks.

My sister and her three daughters foster newborn kittens who need to be socialized before being offered for adoption. My sister engages her kids in this demanding project that can't be abandoned midstream. She is truly modeling and involving her family in a good deed. Lizie and her girls also host a huge, gluten-free bake sale every year and split the proceeds between the animal shelter and a gluten-free advocacy group.

World Connections

In addition to the hands-on service we do, it's important—especially for older kids—to understand the political context for social issues. In my family, we watch the news together, go to rallies, plan protests and participate in elections. Even if these aren't your main interests, you can open the world for your kids when you share these experiences with them. Most local governments have open sessions where the public can witness and sometimes influence decision making. When we look at huge social problems only from the platform of life in one family, it's too easy to feel hopeless and even despairing, and it's too easy to think our small contribution won't make a difference. The more children are taught to see that each person's efforts add up to make a tremendous difference the more likely they will become human beings who care about the world around them and work to make it a better place for everyone.

Many parents simply can't figure out a way to make a difference and therefore avoid or ignore major issues that threaten the futures of our own kids—environmental concerns, political and economic issues, social problems. Venturing out into the public sphere with our kids and volunteering for a neighborhood organization, a political campaign, a nonprofit organization, an advocacy group can make the whole family feel hopeful and energized. It's hugely empowering for kids to see people joining together to improve the world. Standing on a bigger stage with our kids lets them know that they belong to the world and the world belongs to them.

To help kids think in a big way, try asking open-ended questions that help them go deeper into complex social problems. Open-ended questions have no one right answer.

"That person is sleeping on the street because he doesn't have a home," I say when Raffi asks me why the man is lying on the sidewalk.

"Why?"

"What do you need to have in order to have a home?"

Raffi, at that time a three-year-old concrete thinker, answers, "He needs a hammer and some wood."

Rosi, a few years older, can already think more abstractly. "He needs money to pay for the house."

"And how do grown-ups get money?" I ask them.

"They have jobs. Why doesn't that man have a job?"

We talk about education, the profit motive and the global economy. As we drive through our city, the kids can see abandoned factories and devastated neighborhoods. We discuss the links between good education, good jobs and good lives. As the kids grow, these conversations become more and more sophisticated, helping them think deeply about social issues. If you don't think of yourself as a think tank on issues of the day, you can always use resources such as op-ed pages and blogs to offer multiple perspectives on important issues.

One question that arises for parents is how to shield their children from feeling scared, overwhelmed and helpless in the face of realities like racism, violence, poverty and abuse. We have to keep in mind stages of child development and have age-appropriate conversations. Young children under age eight are still developing the basic inner scaffolding of a secure self, so telling them about children who are kidnapped and forced to be soldiers or about tsunamis that devastate dozens of villages will be too traumatic. One day I was listening to NPR in the kitchen while washing dishes when Rosi, around age five, entered the room. The news reporter kept referring to an escaped serial killer. Rosi said, "I didn't know cereal could get killed." I quickly switched stations.

One of the ways we build strong human beings who can withstand the hardships of life and work for social justice is, ironically, by protecting them until they are ready for the "real world." A sheltered childhood isn't a bad thing. When 9/11 happened, no one knew what awful thing would happen next—we waited to see what airplanes would next fall out of the sky and what buildings would be destroyed. But many parents decided not to talk about it too much with our kids because worrying our children about it would only cause them nightmares and fears. The principal of Zoe's school sent a letter home to the parents that spoke about "preserving the childhoods of our children" by continuing the happy rituals of childhood in a calm setting. (That school really knew how to do ritual. They invented lovely ceremonies of passage such as involving each middle-school grade in decorating chairs and creating wands and flower garlands to initiate children moving into a higher grade.) I was deeply appreciative of this woman for taking leadership to reassure her community and remind us that our young children would not have the skills to process the terrible things that were happening in New York, Washington and Pennsylvania.

I wish we could preserve the childhoods of every single child on the planet, including the inner-city child who has seen dead bodies by age 5; the Syrian child who watches bombs falls on her town and the refugee child who has no home. Safe childhoods are good for all children. While we work actively for that day, it's also important to remember that a huge part of what makes the world safe for your own kids is *you*, their primary person. Even in the midst of instability, disaster and trauma, your safe relationship is a harbor that holds your child. The security of your child's relationship with you will mediate and mitigate every dangerous situation they encounter. Even in dangerous times, you have huge power to make the world safer for your child.

Since we care passionately about our kids, we also have to find ways to actually make the world better for them. The emotional security you provide is not a substitute for making a world that actually is a safe and healthy place. In her powerful book *Raising Elijah*, Sandra Steingraber tells the story of a classroom during the Cold War. Students at that time were learning to use bomb shelters in case of nuclear war. The teacher asked her students to raise their hands if they were worried about the Cold War. All the kids raised their hands except for one. "Why aren't you worried?" the teacher asked this student.

"Because my parents are working to stop it." The student said. I hope that our deep desire as parents to have a good world for our children, will push us to engage beyond our own families in fixing the problems that hurt people and the planet. By giving our kids a reasonably protected early childhood *and* by letting them see us engage to make a difference, we strengthen them for the work of building a livable world.

As kids get older they will be more and more aware of the news around them. Not only is it impossible for you to prevent school-age kids from knowing about things like a big earthquake, nuclear disaster or bombing, you wouldn't want to keep them ignorant forever. This is their world with all of its beauty and all of its horror. Instead, you can help find ways they can help: donate a winter coat, a can of food, money, a note of condolence. You ingrain the idea that our plenty and our good fortune and privilege obligate us to respond to others in more difficult situations. I take my cues from the kids: if they seem disturbed or ask questions about a world event, I try to find a way to help them take action to help. We all have to accept that bad things happen, but we do not have to be docile in the face of injustice, disaster or cruelty.

Even if you know that donating a can of food will not affect world hunger in any significant way, your young child does not yet understand the complexity of intractable problems. Concrete think-ers make concrete links: there is a flood so you donate a blanket. By the time your child can do more systemic thinking, they will also have opportunities to engage in helping actions on policy and advocacy lev-els. These actions are more distant from direct service and are designed to intervene in the system that keeps causing the need for more and more direct services. When kids are ready to understand more sys-temic interventions there are many ways they can get involved. They can join a letter-writing campaign or a lobbying group; they can work for a candidate or be part of street theatre to educate passers-by about an issue.

When Occupy Philly set up an encampment at City Hall, I took my kids with me to deliver food and participate in the Open Mic gather-ings. My younger kids were not thrilled at having to abandon their free time to participate in this. They squirmed when I lectured to them on the way to the occupation about how Martin Luther King, Jr., in his time, did what needed to be done to end segregation and now in this time it is our turn to do what needs to be done.

"Mom, do we have to talk about it?" complained Mozi.

"Yes, my dear, for a few minutes we do have to talk about it."

We were in the season of the Jewish harvest festival, *Sukkot*, so I led a prayer service for all people at the Occupy camp in the fragile harvest booth called the *sukkah*. The simple shelter, at the heart of the holiday, is open to all people. Then my family joined with friends to set up our own tent at the Occupy encampment, but the Occupy policy of radical inclusion for people with all types of mental health or lack thereof and all types of behavior, proved difficult. Mentally ill people kept peering into our tent and swearing at us. As the night darkened and traffic noises soared, my kids were scared. We ended up evacuat-ing in the middle of the night. Being involved in real social issues isn't always pretty or easy. For future forays to the Occupy encampment, we delivered food instead of camping out.

In my family, we connect the giving of financial charity to three holidays in the year: Rosh HaShana, Hanukkah and Passover which occur at seasonal intervals in the fall, winter and spring. Other families give at birthdays, or before Shabbat. I give each of my very young children $18, a number that is equivalent to "Life" in Jewish tradition. They can designate their money to go to good causes. (They supported a lot of animal shelters.) As they get older, I agree to match the amount of their own earnings that they decide to donate. Recently, we've pooled our money to support a family in Guatemala.

Some kids are giving, while others have a much harder time sharing, seem greedy and tight-fisted, even with good parenting and material abundance. There's no need to judge your child. Instead, gently encourage, reward and laud the behavior you'd like to see. You can also discuss instances of sharing that you observed, comment to friends about it in the child's hearing, and even reward the behavior. "Because Raffi let Zoe have the front seat an extra time, I'm going to give Raffi first choice about what story to read tonight."

Compassion

❦

Parenting towards compassion means helping your child know herself *and* helping your child see the world through the eyes of others. When you "see" your child and communicate your seeing through validation of her experience, you help your child know herself. You reflect back an affirmation of her own experience and she internalizes a solid sense of self.

"Mommy, it's so unfair, Liliana just wants to get included in everything me and Grace do. She just bugs me and she's so irritating," Mozi complains to me.

I make sure to take a minute to listen to her experience and to share with her that it makes sense to me.

"I can really see how you'd be annoyed if someone always wants to join what you're doing. That must be irritating."

And then I also want to stretch my child to see the world from the other person's perspective because "taking the role of the other" drives moral development.

"Why do you think Liliana wants to do what you're doing so much?"

If Mozi can't figure that out, I lead with compassionate possibilities.

"Does she feel sad when she's not included?

It is important to me to help my kids develop behavior patterns of generosity so that their impulse will be to respond in helpful ways. I also hope to help them connect the dots to see systemic causes of social and personal problems. I want them to be able to address the underlying causes of the troubles they see. When they see a homeless person I want them to think about mental health services, good schools and availability of jobs and to think through even small ways that they can have positive impact on the underlying stressors that result in homelessness. I hope that nurturing compassion is a way to develop generosity on personal and policy levels.

One way we can instill generosity is through the ways we speak about other families. Every family has its own dynamics and challenging personalities, values, behaviors and situations. Some kids are just harder than others to raise. Even the best parents can be swamped by a particular child's difficulties. But parents can end up feeling isolated and flailing on their own even when they are in partnerships or marriages. Families with troubling kids get way fewer invitations, less respect and support. I used to judge other parents, especially the ones who had less confidence than I did about their roles as parents, or who made parenting decisions that I could see were likely to lead to negative outcomes down the road. I thought badly of close friends who were floundering as parents, as if it we were in a race and they were falling behind. I look back on my younger self and regret that I didn't yet have the compassion to see that we were all doing the best we could. If I had been able to acknowledge my own insecurity and my need for perfection in my parenting, I would have been a kinder friend.

Generosity of heart allows us to see that each one of us has a unique journey. There was no reason for me to compare myself or anyone else to anything or anyone. Early in Zoe's experience at Yale, Dean Hicks offered advice that I find enormously helpful, too. He suggested we imagine we are each riding a bicycle and we see someone pass our bicycle. We might start worrying that they are ahead of us, surpassing us. But really we have no idea where their race started or where they want to go or what obstacles they've faced. The truth is, we're all on our own bicycles, taking our own, unique, incomparable journeys. Sometimes, when we're feeling insecure or envious, Zoe and I remind each other, "You're on your own bicycle." My job as a friend in the parenting community is to stay on my own bicycle and offer support, not judgment, to fellow travelers. I didn't always know that.

As I succeed in parenting and feel my confidence blossom, I grow in compassion. And as I fail in parenting and learn the vital lessons of humility, my compassion also grows. I watch my kids become lovely, whole, independent people with a good sense of themselves, and I see my kids struggle with problems and issues, just as all of us do in our lifetimes. My passion to be their Mom, and my commitment and even skills will never be enough to make their lives free of pain. Knowing this—accepting this—I have become kinder to myself and to other parents.

Each of us can play a role in shifting the climate of parenting in this country, a climate that is already moving in the direction of less parent-blame and deeper understanding of neurobiology and neuro-diversity and other factors that affect family well-being. Still, we can help move the culture in a positive direction by opening our hearts with empathy for other parents.

One of my congregants had a schizophrenic son in his early adulthood who lived on her living room sofa. She had never told her friends about his mental health problems. It may be she couldn't even admit the painful truth to herself. Other congregants regularly said to me, "What is the matter with her, letting her grown son live at home like that?" Without violating confidentiality I would try to engender empathy by saying things like, "Yes, it's really a hardship when a family member has a psychiatric disability." Each time this happened it was like a light bulb went off in the critic's mind and they became less judgmental.

Money is another place where judgment, criticism and lack of compassion affect families. People rarely understand one another's financial backgrounds, situations and choices. Walls of silence prevent us from sharing honestly our shame, fears and anxieties about these issues and our critical judgments go unchallenged. If we really knew the story behind the social masks, our hearts would more easily find compassion instead of criticism.

Changing the boundaries around money can liberate families from social isolation. In middle-class, Western culture, each family is supposed to figure out how to fund its own individual shelter, food, education, medical care, transportation, etc. In reality, individuals do not have absolute control over ability to work, availability of jobs, living standard of a job, availability of good schools and healthy food. These factors are socially determined issues, yet families are held fully accountable for thriving despite the lack of adequate resources and lack of access to what they need.

As a young adult in a social change group called Movement for a New Society, I was interested in exploring new ways of interacting around money. Felice and I learned a process for sharing money called cost sharing. She went on to develop and teach this process all over the country. In cost sharing, people engage in honest, structured discussion about financial resources, decisions and needs and then share certain costs. For instance, if a group is attending a weekend retreat, each person does not pay a standard fee, but rather pays an amount that they determine is fair based on their resources and background. In a safe setting people have the opportunity to support or challenge one another about their stated pledges and each person can choose whether to adjust the pledge up or down. If all the funding necessary to cover costs is not forthcoming in a first round of pledges, further rounds take place until the costs are collectively met.

I've been at gatherings where some people paid thousands of dollars and other people were paid to attend because they were missing opportunities to earn while they were away. This process worked because we had real relationships with one another and we allocated plenty of time to have the necessary conversations to reach agreement.

A small group of my friends and I decided to share costs for "extras" that would not be possible for all of us unless we collectively paid for them, nonessentials such as pool membership and summer vacations. We had organized ourselves into a women's group that we called our Covenant Group. Every week or so we'd meet in one of our living rooms. This group came together before any of us had kids and stayed together for years, until our lives with older kids eventually grew too hectic and society's individualistic thrust prevailed. Basically each family was responsible for supporting itself and for making decisions to live within its means. In this closest circle of friends the means varied wildly as some people had inherited wealth, had higher or lower paying jobs, had different numbers of dependents and different family structures that determined how many adults were contributing to the family funding. Usually, in our society people don't form cross-class relationships, but we had plenty of other things in common and made a conscious point of dealing with money issues. We mostly did not share costs for basic living expenses, but for optional expenses. Our ethic was if you have more, you pay more. It wasn't charity; it was our sense of what was fair.

In addition to that group's efforts, money has been a topic of open discussion in some quarters of my Jewish feminist world. One friend paid for much of my children's early child care expenses and has helped now and then with other tuition bills. One of Felice's last acts was to organize a scholarship for Mozi, who needed to be in an expensive special school that could support the way she learned best. Felice sent letters out to a long list of people she knew or I knew. Some of them were close friends; others had reason to care about education or about community responsiveness. Ninety percent or more said yes and pledged to make contributions for the four years of middle school.

Each year as I collect that scholarship, I receive the nicest notes saying things like, "So glad to help," and "Good luck to you and Mozi."

If you are interested in exploring cross-class relationships, you might be able to create or find a support group focused on this. One way to do that is to start with people who share other values or frameworks, such as a group from the same church or school or political group. These groups can be powerful for all involved, connecting people in new ways. We live in a class segregated society and I have seen the mutual benefits, many times, for people breaking through the barriers of class. One of the reasons I originally supported the homeless program that has met for decades in local churches and synagogues around here was because of its potential for cross-class relationships. People with less privilege end up linked to someone who has an extra refrigerator sitting in the garage or who needs a new employee to do photocopying.

Cross-class relationships can start small, without any expectations of where they will lead. Get to know each other and be curious. Find ways to create an atmosphere of safety for everyone. Whatever emerges will grow from real relationships and real understanding.

There is a Jewish teaching that even the poorest beggar is expected to give money for justice, called *tzedakah*. No one is too poor to give. Wherever you are on the class spectrum, you can be a giver. As a rabbi, I work with my congregation to make sure that we have open doors for our services and holy days. All are welcome, regardless of financial means. People are asked to make contributions from the heart, giving whatever they are able to contribute. The donations flow in with great generosity. Some would say this isn't actually generosity, but rather it's each person's sense of what their fair share is. In my Bar and Bat Mitzvah classes there are often kids benefitting from full or partial financial aid.

Sharing across class lines challenges the prevailing reality of each family, financially isolated from others, trying to make a go on their own. Often, religious communities understand how to care for one another better than typical American citizens. Orthodox Jewish communities ensure that everyone has clothing, food and tuition, with no shame attached to receiving help. There is a communal ethic of caring and sharing. In modern, liberal society we struggle with finding a balance that honors autonomy rather than forced conformity, but also upholds generosity and accountability. There are challenges, of course, and there isn't one formula that works for modern society. Money-sharing might sound like an unrealistic utopia, but I have seen it start small and happen in many, many situations.

Fundamentally, giving is good for the giver. Not in a tit-for-tat way, but in a more cosmic way. Opening to your own generosity also opens you to the abundance of the world. There have been stretches of times when I have been so caught up in my own family and work life that I haven't been able to think beyond that. That happens to all of us—it's okay to have different levels of availability at different stages of life. When you've just brought a new baby home you may not have time or attention to march on Washington. Maybe someday you and your five-year-old will show up.

Even when family life is too demanding for you to spend hours on activism, it's easy to choose a few organizations that you respect and let them organize you into doing very simple things such as letter-writing or calling a politician. When I'm not sure who to vote for in an election, I gratefully turn to a chosen organization's recommended list. We each can't take on every single issue and be fully informed and activated, but we can be part of an interconnected web of action for a better world.

Like many of us, I like to "pay my dues" when I'm able to, such as helping other parents with transportation when I'm driving anyway, or making extra soup for someone in need when I'm cooking anyway, or advocating at the public school for all kids who share my child's need. I'm grateful to others who think beyond their own small families and give to community and civic life. I'm also grateful to all of us who scoop each other up into bigger political actions to make the world a better place. Our kids are watching what we care about and how we commit to what we care about. We nurture their ability to be socially conscious every time they see us behaving with social conscience.

Through face-to-face generosity to advocating for systemic social change that aims at global systems of equity, the lessons of being engaged start at home. On both the micro and the macro levels, we help kids realize that they are part of a web of planetary interconnection. We connect our kids, in developmentally attuned ways, to caring acts that make the world better in small and in big ways.

A spiritual chant teaches, "From you I receive, to you I give, Together we share and from this we live." Parents who uplift the value of generosity give a priceless gift to their children and to the world.

Endnote

❧

With whatever dreams and whatever baggage we bring to the task of parenting, we are the artisans who build the world one family at a time. To meet the unpredictable highs and lows of the journey, we bring our best resources to the task: our love and our commitment and an enormous amount of hard work and we do the best we can with whatever we encounter. What we encounter as parents is so much bigger than anything we could have predicted. The love is bigger, the challenge is bigger, the depths of ourselves that are called on are bigger—there are peaks and pits we could not have imagined.

Through it all, each one of us becomes a specialist in bridging the gap between profound ideals and mundane matters. We care about peace and justice, race and class, the earth. Some of us were activists before we were parents, or we were involved citizens, and now we are burping a baby and managing squabbles at the dinner table. Let us attend to the practices that link our big values with day-to-day life in a family. How to make that linkage is an enduring topic for reflection within ourselves, with partners and throughout our communities. Questions about how to contribute human beings to the civilization we want to live in are essential questions for every parent.

In this work, I have looked at how one of the most personal and precious endeavors of our lifetime, parenting, can help transform society into a place where human beings get along with respect, justice and peace. I've shared my views on some ways in which we can organize family life to nurture and support children, and to ready them to participate in and contribute to a good world. I hope and pray that we use our freedom, intelligence and passion as parents and as friends of families to help the human species progress towards compassion, wisdom and justice.

Thanksgiving is approaching now. Later in the year Mozi will graduate from eighth grade, Joey from highschool and Zoe from college. I picture the interconnected circles of celebration for each of these milestones with our intimacy constellation: my beloved Rebecca and her life partner Barbary who is my new friend too, my God Kids Nava and Yonah, Len who is the cherished Daddy of some of my kids, Felice's family (may her memory be for a blessing) Felicia and Shira, my children's aunts and uncles and cousins and grandparents, new friends and partners and my children themselves Rosi, Raffi, Zoe, Joey and Mozi, the next generation rising up to carry on the human mission, facing what they will need to face with all that I and our circle of loved ones have been able to give them. Building the world we want to live in starts with our own labors of love, right here in our families.

About The Author

Julie Greenberg is a mother, author, rabbi, family therapist and activist in Philadelphia.

She would love to receive your feedback, questions and comments at JustParentingBook@gmail.com